THE LADY OF MERCIA'S DAUGHTER

MJ PORTER

MJ PUBLISHING

Porter, M J

The Lady of Mercia's Daughter

Cover design by Shaun @Flintlock Covers

Map design by Shaun @Flintlock Covers

Ebook ISBN 9781914332388 (MJ Publishing)

Paperback ISBN 9781522079743

❀ Created with Vellum

For a woman of courage, strength, tenacity, skill and unswerving faith.
I miss you.
M.L.F. 1920-2017

BRITAIN IN THE 10TH CENTURY

N

W E

S

ORKNEYS

CAIT

SCOTTISH
WESTERN
ISLANDS

Atlantic
Ocean

FORTRIU

KINGDOM
OF THE
SCOTS

DAL
RIATA

ATHOLL

ST ANDREWS

North
Sea

KINGDOM OF
STRATHCLYDE

BAMBURGH

Tyne CHESTER
LE STREET

EAMONT

KINGDOM
OF YORK

YORK

Irish
Sea

Ribble

Mersey

Don

DUBLIN

IRELAND

GWYNEDD

POWYS

OFFA'S
DYKE

Severn

Trent

Welland

TAMWORTH

EAST
ANGLIA

HEREFORD

DEHEUBARTH

GWENT

Wye

MERCIA

WESSEX

Thames

KING'S
WORTHY

KINGSTON
UPON THAMES

WINCHESTER

KENT

EXETER

Tamar

English Channel

0   50   100   MILES

CAST OF CHARACTERS

Mercian Court

Lady Æthelflæd (c.AD870-918), sister to King Edward of Wessex
m. **Lord Æthelred** of Mercia who dies in AD911
Lady Ælfwynn, their daughter and only surviving child born c.AD888
Archbishop Plegmund, Archbishop of Canterbury from AD890
Ealdorman Æthelfrith of part of Mercia,
His sons – Lord Athelstan, Ælfstan, Eadric and Æthelwald
Thurstan, one of Cousin Athelstan's warriors

Wessex Royal Family

King Edward, official title is king of the Anglo-Saxons in all but 2 of the surviving charters
m. 1 **Lady Ecgwynn** – (little is known about her and she was quickly replaced when Edward became king after his father's death)
Athelstan
Ecgwynn
m. 2 **Lady Ælfflæd** – (she was 'divorced' in the late AD910's and spent the remainder of her life in Wilton Abbey, where she was later joined by two of her daughters)

Ælfweard
Edwin
Æthelhild
Eadgifu
Eadflæd
Eadhild
Eadgyth
Ælfgifu

m. 3 **Lady Eadgifu** – (the daughter of Ealdorman Sigehelm who died in AD902/3 fighting for King Edward against his cousin, Lord Æthelwold, she would substantially outlive her husband)
Eadburh
Edmund
Eadred

Rǫgnvaldr Sigfrodrsson of Dublin/York/grandson of Ivarr of Dublin/Ivarr Ragnarsson

Lady Ælfwynn's warriors
Eoforhild
Ymma
Lioba
Firamodor
Leofgyth
Erna (her squire)
Mildryth

Sigehelm, Reeve of Derby
Osbert, Lady Ælfwynn's scribe
Eadig, Lady Ælfwynn's young squire from Nottingham
Lodeward, Archbishop of York

CHAPTER 1

JUNE AD918

The men of the witan stand before me in my hall at Tamworth, the ancient capital of the kingdom of Mercia. The aged oak beams bear the brunt of centuries of smoking fires. Some are hard men, glaring at me as though this predicament is of my making. They are the beleaguered Mercians, the men from the disputed borders to the north, the east, and the west, if not the south. They're the men who know the cost of my mother's unexpected death. And strangely, for all their hard stares and uncompromising attitudes, their crossed arms and tight shoulders, they're the men I trust the most in this vast hall. It's filled with people I know by name and reputation, if not by sight.

Those with sympathy etched onto their faces are my uncle's allies. These men might once have understood the dangers that Mercia faces, but they've grown too comfortable hidden away in Wessex and Kent. Mercia has suffered the brunt of the continual encroachments while they've been safe from Viking attack for nearly twenty years. Some are too young to have been born when Wessex was almost extinguished under the onslaught of the northern warriors.

Even the clothes of the sympathetic are different from those with hard stares. Not for them, the warriors' garb. There are no gaping spaces on warrior belts where seaxs and swords should hang, but don't, as weapons must not be worn in my presence.

No, they wear the luxurious clothing of royalty, even if they're not members of the House of Wessex. They have the time, and the wealth, to ensure their attire is as opulent as it can be. They don't fear a middle-of-the-night call to arms. They don't need to maintain vigilance or continuously be battle-ready. They don't have to fight for their kingdom and their family at a moment's notice or be ready to lose a loved one or face a fight to the death.

Amongst the number of those not overtly hostile to me with their fake compassion, I count some of my cousins. Not all of them. Never that. But my uncle has an abundance of children. Of them all, I only know the oldest two well, Athelstan and his sister, Ecgwynn.

Cousin Athelstan's young face is one of those that I trust. He carries his worry as lightly as possible, but his heavily shadowed eyes attest to grief and disquiet. He wears the apparel of a warrior, his warrior's sword still sheathed on his back as a mark of his position as a king's son. As such, he's more honoured than I, a mere niece who must wear the clothes of a woman. At the same time, he's also less respected. The politics of our positions are always complicated by far more than our friendship. The fact that cousin Athelstan stands for Mercia, not Wessex, is the most telling.

We've been raised as almost brother and sister. His father abandoned him and his sister to the care of my mother. No sooner had uncle Edward inherited the title of king of Wessex than my two cousins were deemed surfeit to requirements. My grandfather, Alfred, called 'the Great' by those who didn't know him, wouldn't have approved.

Uncle Edward found a more suitable wife to birth new sons for him. Lady Ælfflæd wasn't the misdirected object of his young lust that Lady Ecgwynn was. Lady Ælfflæd was a woman with the right connections and a regal aspect to make his sons throne-worthy, as our ridiculous conventions dictate. Lady Ecgwynn is only a faint memory for cousin Athelstan and his sister. I remember little more than that she had long auburn hair and smiled a great deal.

I've never met Lady Ælfflaed, mother to Ælfweard, Edward's oldest son by his more 'regal' wife. And neither, it seems, am I ever likely to. After seventeen years of marriage, and almost as many children, eight surviving early childhood, Edward has repaid her with divorce and banishment to the royal nunnery at Wilton. For all her strict adherence to providing the kingdom with multiple potential heirs, æthelings one and all, throne-worthy provided they're male, she's been set aside.

Now Edward has a new wife, more than half his age, in fact, younger than I am, and already he has a new child growing in her belly and a new kingdom to add to Wessex. Lady Eadgifu brought my uncle the kingdom of Kent with their union.

My uncle keeps his throne-worthy children far from the reaches of Mercia and far from me. I imagine he worries I'll infect his female children with the 'independent' spirit he so resented in his sister, my mother.

But I've no more met his third wife than I have his second. I hear she's beautiful, but then, men will say anything to please their king. To be honest, a woman who's even remotely good-looking will hear the word beautiful on the lips of the warrior men of Mercia. They little understand the concept of beauty in Mercia, only blades and blood, honour and disloyalty. Our world is channelled into a few concepts. The assumptions of men and women are made on little more.

Cousin Ælfweard, the king's chosen heir, resembles my uncle. The likeness can't be denied, from the mane of straw hair that sheets his face to the overly inquisitive nose and eyes that are sharp and too narrow to be deemed beautiful. Not that the word beautiful should ever be used for a man who's supposed to be a warrior. But cousin Ælweard lacks the muscle tone and physique to actually swing a sword and hold a shield at the same time. He's not the sort of warrior that I've ever encountered before.

I've met Cousin Ælfweard a handful of times. He was a spiteful child. He was too aware of his future role as the king of Wessex. Since before he could toddle, he's been nothing but imperious. I've always been wary of him on cousin Athelstan's behalf. Cousin Ælfweard had no respect for me as his elder and has even less now that my mother is turning cold in her elaborate grave.

Cousin Ælfweard observes me as I do him, his hands folded over his crossed legs as he leans back on the high-backed chair he's insisted upon. It befits his rank as the king of Wessex's acknowledged heir, even though he sits amongst the general people who respectfully stand.

Some of his closest followers surround him. And some of my uncle's most loyal men, tasked with ensuring he doesn't embarrass in this public arena. This is a real test for cousin Ælfweard. One, I hope he fails magnificently. And one I hope my uncle witnesses forcing him to consider the suitability of Cousin Ælfweard to rule after his death.

Cousin Ælfweard's voice is too high when he speaks, a reminder that he's yet to become a man in all meanings of the word. Only that fact saves my anger on cousin Athelstan's behalf. Men might yet see the true nature of the king's chosen heir. While uncle Edward lives, there's time aplenty for cousin Athelstan to prove he should rule after his father and for cousin Ælfweard to prove that he shouldn't.

Cousin Athelstan is a man grown; tried in battle with a scar slicing his bearded chin to prove it. It's he who should be his father's heir. No matter how many times Athelstan and I have discussed this issue, my outrage has never dimmed. Cousin Athelstan hides his frustration keenly, locked away under his façade as the dutiful if overlooked son of the king.

I would be unable to do the same. My mother never asked me to pretend I was something I wasn't, and she shared my anger on Athelstan's part. We both knew he was more honourable in accepting his father's wishes than we would ever have managed. Far more admirable than his father should have expected or could have hoped for.

The step-brothers were raised in different kingdoms but share their parentage too closely for any to doubt that cousin Athelstan is his father's son. Yet I imagine that uncle Edward would welcome the opportunity to discard his eldest son and daughter, should he ever have the chance to do so.

Aside from my male cousins, one welcome and the other ... less welcome, the massive hall is filled with men and women who are influential within Mercia. Some of them hold power within Wessex as well, although the number is few and far between.

Mercia and Wessex stand together and yet always separate. A strange alliance extends between us, resented by every man, woman, child and beast within Mercia, whereas Wessex revels in the agreement. Wessex uses Mercia as a buffer zone, a war zone between their settled life and the elongated and protracted war of attrition that stretches between Mercia and the Viking raiders. The Viking raiders demand war and tribute, shed blood and death as payment.

Some of these people were my mother's staunchest allies, and it's they who look worried. Some are my uncle's cronies. They look smug and self-assured, when not feigning empathy. They believe they have a right to be here. I disagree, but I'm not yet assured enough in my role to act against them. Neither do I wish to incur the wrath of Uncle Edward when my mother is newly interred in her grave in Gloucester.

She understood her insecure brother well and endured many humiliations at his hands, but also inflicted far more back in his direction. She knew how to fight, with all the guile of a woman, and the swordsmanship of a man.

Even the choice of my mother's burial place has thwarted uncle Edward. Not for her a family internment in the heart of Wessex, the kingdom of her birth. No, she chose to be forever placed next to my father, a man she might never have loved, but who was a Mercian, just as she became, and just as I have always been.

Gloucester has always been part of Mercia, and she's been buried with the saints she most revered, albeit, the saints of another kingdom, Northumbria. Saint Oswald died fighting a Mercian king. I think she admired Saint Oswald's warlike nature just as much as his strict faith.

I will miss her. Deeply.

It falls to the archbishop, as he and I discussed beforehand and in-depth, to open the proceedings of the first Mercian witan since my mother's death, only seven days ago.

Archbishop Plegmund is a Mercian, as I am, but more than that, he's respected at my uncle's Wessex witan as well. He's my ally and friend: a rarity to be treasured even when he annoys the hell out of me. He was an ally of my mother's and I'm keen to retain his services.

He's an old man, but his vigour and booming voice would dare anyone to think him too aged for his tasks. His hair is a wispy grey, his chin devoid of all growth, more closely shaven than anyone I know.

He says he's blessed to lack exuberant facial hair growth, but I think the archbishop would prefer a long and flowing beard to match his hair, which cascades to his waist in tidy braids. Each is christened with small wooden and silver crosses of his Lord's crucifixion, a very Norse dress style worn on the holiest man within Mercia and Wessex. I never fail to be amazed by his brazenness.

He's come wearing the costume of his holy position. As he raises his hands to bless the assembly, the rustle of his expensive and expansive sleeves and skirts is audible in the suddenly hushed room. When Archbishop Plegmund speaks, all listen, be they sinners or transgressors, frequent allies or calculating politicians, enemies in all but name.

His voice, although strong, is also soft as a whisper, his grief for my mother evident to hear in every single word he speaks. He never stumbles or pauses to collect his thoughts. He knows the effect his presence can have on the assembly. He intends to use it to its full extent, be those listening Mercian or from Wessex.

'Lady Ælfwynn,' he intones, his introductions done, and now it's my turn to speak before these people, friends and enemies alike. I've dressed carefully, as my mother always did before me. Everyone knows I'm her choice to succeed her: everyone. But that doesn't mean it's universally acclaimed. So. I wear her jewellery, a gift from my father on becoming his bride.

Their marriage may have contained little love, but they knew their strength lay in who they were and what they represented as a combined force. What did that have to do with love? Love was an irrelevance in the face of opposition from the Mercians and the Viking raiders. It had nothing at all to do with the politics of their union.

The gold around my neck is ancient and symbolic. My father wanted to believe it stemmed from the ancient Mercian tribes, the Hwicce and the Magonsæte. And that it had been clawed from some pagan grave by the rapacious and lucky. My mother allowed him his folly but knew the piece to be far less aged.

Yet the gold is ancient and burnished with the sheen of time as opposed to the polish of youth. Such things are essential in conveying the correct impression. The longevity implied by my pagan golden torque is intentional in Christian Mercia, with the pagan Viking raiders on our doorstep.

The cross, which also falls heavily against my chest, is far too elaborate, a statement not of wealth but of conspicuous devotion to the Church that Archbishop Plegmund represents.

I don't like it. I find its decoration garish and overdone – its rubies, sapphires, jades, and ambers clashing in a riot of summer promise and winter bloodshed.

Yet, it was my mother's all the same, and I wear it with the pride that she wore it and also the irony.

My dress is far plainer, not a virginal white; that would be ridiculous for a woman of my age. Neither is it the imperial purple that uncle Edward and his heir prefer to fashion into every item of clothing they wear. The gaudiness of their purple offends my eyes.

Instead, I wear sombre blue, with a hint of the Wessex dragon pricked out on the skirt in small stitches and even smaller jewels. I'm not an extravagant woman, but I understand the importance of display. I need to wear my wealth and affluence but in an as understated way as possible while still alluding to it.

Around my waist, I wear the symbolic keys of my hall in Tamworth, as befits a good woman of noble birth and rank, even if she's unmarried. They're huge, clunking things that bounce painfully against my hip when I walk. Typically, I prefer to leave them in my bedside chest, for I use them so rarely. Today they're as important a feature as my cross and golden torque.

And there is also more. Archbishop Plegmund averts his eyes, so he doesn't have to see the sword that hangs from my reinforced waistband. It doesn't make it disappear. This is another badge of my office that I wear with great pride. Others would rather forget that I'm a warrior as well as a woman. They try to forget that I'm everything a woman should be, with the advantages of being a warrior.

I stand, my dress falling to the ground so that all who actually look can see my illusion to the royal House of Wessex in its standard that adorns my hems. I am, apart from my living uncles, King Edward and Lord Æthelweard, the oldest embodiment of it. I'm the oldest woman of our clan who yet lives within Mercia and Wessex, and I'll be heard, just as my mother always intended.

'Good people of Mercia and honoured guests of Wessex.' Cousin Athelstan was adamant about these words. He said I must use them. I must be conciliatory toward Wessex without giving them more rights than is their due. I must refrain from implying that their presence here is a given in light of my mother's death.

My uncle might be my cousin's father, but this is our Mercia and will remain as such. My mother and father always intended Mercia to stay independent. They beat the Viking marauders back, securing each newly won settlement with renewed walls or new walls, depending on the age and current arrangements in place. They didn't do so for the benefit of Wessex.

I see cousin Athelstan's shoulders relax as I voice the introduction cleanly and with just the right amount of arrogance and guile. My chin is raised at precisely the correct angle so that the Mercians see my mother's shadow in my posture, and the West Saxons see my uncle and my grandfather, should any be old enough to remember him. Amusingly, at the same moment, cousin Ælfweard's posture tenses. That's more telling than if he'd simply stormed from the hall, returning to his father, outraged at my assumptions of a continuing independent Mercia.

'My thanks for attending so promptly and for your kind words and actions following the loss of my mother, Æthelflæd, Lady of the Mercians, wife of my father, Lord Æthelred of the Mercians, daughter of King Alfred and scion of the House of Wessex. She'll be greatly missed by all of Mercia and by her enemies on the quarrelsome borders.' I speak slowly and measuringly so that my eyes can travel over the faces of those assembled.

While King Edward can lay claim to all those same pretensions, I must remind them all that my lineage is just as good as ætheling Ælfweard's and even my jilted cousin, Athelstan's. My mother, Archbishop Plegmund, and even cousin Athelstan were unyielding on these points whenever they were raised in the past. During the last seven days, the heat of the argument has intensified even further. I'm a woman that can't be denied. My ancestry is impeccable, my previous actions as my mother's daughter speak for themselves, and my sword articulates everything else.

There's a rumble of agreement as I pause, and grief sheets the faces of those who served my mother for almost thirty years. Her death has come as a shock to many, including myself, but her long-standing achievements can't be denied. Neither will they ever be, not by any Mercian within this room nor by any Viking raider who wears their wounds with pride and speaks of the Mercian woman's prowess in battle.

My grandfather might claim to have halted the Viking raider attacks, but that's all he did. He stopped them when there was almost nothing left of Wessex to hold onto. My mother and my father pushed and prodded until the Viking raiders gave back what they'd taken. My grandfather might have saved Wessex, but my mother and father regained Mercia.

I allow a moment for the gentle conversation that's sprung up to die away: a moment of remembrance, a sacred thing when politics and kingdoms are at stake. It's a significant mark of respect that the Mercians feel she should be honoured and remembered in such a way.

'Mercia finds itself in need of a ruler; a military commander, a voice for the people and a proponent of the church and more, a ruler who is 'of' Mercia, who understands how Mercia breathes and grows.

Who's been raised amongst its forests and its hills. Who's fought to keep it whole against our enemies.'

My voice is rising. Saying the words is stiffening my resolve. The resonance of their 'rightness' makes me stand taller, and allows me to understand, finally, what it is my mother, and my father before her, expected of me. My words, penned by Archbishop Plegmund, so closely mirror how I feel, standing alone and proud on the raised dais, that I'm wondering why I so strongly objected to them before. Why did I fight for a more conciliatory approach to Wessex?

As my hand wavers to grab my sword from my waistband, hovering over the inlaid handle unconsciously, cousin Athelstan is already applauding, saluting my words. And he's not alone. Only the Wessex men stay sullen as cousin Ælfweard barely contains his fury. He sits stiffly, his face frozen in a rictus of indifference, the lie given by the tightness of his bearing. I take the time to think that his father would, at least, be proud of him for containing his fury before I continue.

'With the support of the Mercian witan and my uncle, King Edward of Wessex, I'll replace my mother as the Second Lady of the Mercians. I'll continue her policies of fortifying Mercia and growing Mercia until all that once belonged to our country has been returned and the Viking raiders banished.'

I raise my fist as I speak, unheedingly but righteously. This is a cry, not for war, not yet, but for solidarity and continuing alertness. My words are all that's needed. I wish I could wave my sword in the air, my Mercian forged sword, but even I mustn't bear arms during the witan.

Every Mercian in the hall follows cousin Athelstan and Archbishop Plegmund's resolve to show their support. Feet stomp on the wooden floor, hands clap, and voices ring with assent, fists pumping the air in agreement. I note with amusement those who reach for a sword before realising they've been surrendered at the doorway.

The Mercians are a martial breed.

I meet the eyes of those I pick out in the sea of rapturous acclaim –

reasserting personal bonds that have been stretched in the traumatic week since my mother's death.

And slowly, so slowly as to make me doubt what I'm seeing, first cousin Ælfweard and then the other men of Wessex unwillingly join the acclaim. After all, it's what my mother and my uncle agreed on long ago. Much as my grandfather designated Edward his successor in his lifetime, so too did my mother brand me as hers.

I'll be as my mother before me, a woman with a kingdom to command. I'll honour her name and her legacy, for I'm Ælfwynn, Lady of the Mercians, and the Viking raiders and their allies will learn to fear my name just as they once did my mother's.

CHAPTER 2

I barely have time to enjoy my triumph, the blackness of my grief turned to the lightness of having succeeded where my mother demanded I should, before news from the north turns the minds of all to York and the plague of Viking raiders who sometimes inhabit the shadowy regions of the ancient kingdom of Northumbria.

'Warriors, my lady,' the dusty messenger informs me, his summer face as dirty as a pig wallowing in its muddy hollow all day long. 'Their ships wear the masks of the pagans.' That's hardly a helpful description, but I allow the man to show his fear. I've seen the ship-heads of the Viking raiders and the Danes before, snaking along Mercian rivers. I know they're designed only to cause terror and are very effective both to those so used to living in fear and those unaccustomed to warrior men leaping from the boughs of such sleek vessels.

'Where?' my cousin Athelstan barks, summoned along with me to hear this unwelcome, though not unexpected, news. He's attired in the clothes of a warrior in training, and he's almost as dirty as the road-stained messenger. I hold that thought to myself. Cousin Athelstan is a proud man. He wouldn't wish to know he looks little better than a dusty messenger.

'Beyond York, my lord,' in the face of Athelstan's implacable calm, the messenger recovers his poise. I bite back my frustration that he would dare to show me his fear, thinking me a weak woman, and would then find his resolve when faced with my warrior cousin.

'How many?' I interject, my annoyed eyes arresting Athelstan from his questioning, with a wry smile of apology on his face and a slight bow to his head as he appreciates that I must speak for myself, just as I fight for myself when I train.

He's used to supporting my mother but understands that I need to be seen, for the time being, as the only leader of Mercia. Once my position is assured, I'll be able to consult him more publicly, as I would want to in matters of battles and Viking raiders. He's not spent his years training and riding with the Mercian men of war to have his substantial talents disregarded now.

He could, I have no doubt, have claimed Mercia for himself in the wake of my mother's death, but we're closer than the bonds of a shared parentage, and a deeper respect is the result. We've long known who's destined to command where in future years, and Athelstan accepts that Mercia is mine, just as I push him to take Wessex for himself.

For now, cousin Athelstan denies his inheritance and right to Wessex, determined to allow my weak cousin Ælfweard his chance to rule. In time, I hope that Athelstan will understand the folly of his decision, although I can't help but respect him for it. He is, and I'll never tire of saying this, far more honourable in his actions than his errant father deserves.

The messenger, perhaps more astute than I initially gave him credit for, turns his gaze to me and his eyes stay fastened on mine without wavering to either side and the men who inhabit the extremities of my great hall, who draw nearer to hear his words. The man wears the filth of a hurried journey along roads awash with summer's rain and summer's dusty drought combined, but beneath his cloak, his weapons gleam brightly, always alert and ready to face any danger. I reconsider my original thoughts of the man. It seems he's an asset to my service, after all.

'Twenty ships, my lady. I stayed to ensure I counted them all and quickly spread the word to the Archbishop of York, Lodeward. He bid me hasten to you with all speed.'

'He was fearful?' I ask, surprised and annoyed that my astonishment shows in my slightly squealed reply. The men and women of York are almost immured to attack and skirmishes. I would count Lodeward as one of the staunchest proponents of York's independence and longevity. The thought of twenty longships so far north shouldn't concern him unless he knows something that I don't.

'No, my lady. Well?' and he reconsiders. 'He may have been, but he believes that the focus of the attack lies further north. Perhaps more the concern of Constantin of the Scots and the Lord of Bamburgh than York, let alone Mercia.'

I smirk at his cocky reply, pleased to hear it. I can imagine the archbishop uttering those words. He fears nothing except his God and perhaps his mistress and the children she's birthed for him: vicious little bastards, the lot of them, with no fear for either the Christian or the Pagan Gods. I met them when my mother arranged meetings with the archbishop as the representative of York. Unlike my cousin Ælfweard they were vicious in a bloody way, never far from a physical attack.

I preferred their savagery to cousin Ælfweard's haughtiness and superiority. I can cope far better with a bit of spilt blood than with arrogance and conceit.

'Mercia has little to fear or worry about, then?' I ask the question, but it's more of a statement and not a new one, either. Neither is it only for my assurance, but for those who stand in the hall, listening while pretending not to, only their unintentional stillness giving away their awareness of our discussion.

'We should send a scouting party north,' cousin Athelstan comments under his breath, his lips barely moving. 'Watch this enemy.' He is, of course, right, but for the time being, I had been more concerned with a disdainful retort. There are too many fearful eyes in the hall, already questioning my right to rule at this first minor obstacle so very far from Mercian borders.

I suppress a sigh. I am my mother's daughter, but I don't yet have the military reputation to go with the title. I must command well to get that, which means making hard decisions and showing no fear of Viking raiders

'We'll send two forces north. Small scouting parties, one directly to York to ensure it still stands, and one further north, to press into the wild lands of Bamburgh and determine if Constantin of the Scots will counter the threat alone. We must also send word to Wessex.'

The collective sigh of relief at my words is too loud to be comforting in the large hall. I gaze at my people, my expression as neutral as possible, although quietly, I seethe with anger and annoyance.

I'm not some spring-born lamb come to the slaughter. My mother may have been the face of Mercia since my father's death, but I'm a woman grown and was, even at his death. I've ruled with my mother, and yet few realise how much she allowed me to command. That was an error of judgment on both our parts and one I think she under-stood as her death stole her from me, denying her the time to correct it.

'My lady,' cousin Athelstan bows before me, and I know better than to argue with him. He'll only be content when he sees any threat with his own eyes. I assume he'll take the far northern mission and will appoint one of his warriors to lead the expedition to York, perhaps one of Ealdorman Æthelfrith's sons.

I'd rather send someone with more familial affinity, but cousin Ælfweard has skulked back to Wessex as though burnt by the Mercian witan and its desire to support me. I can hardly send Athelstan's sister, Ecgwynn. She's a woman in every sense of the word with neither the training nor the desire to be seen as a warrior in a world inhabited by strong men who understand only actions and never thought; only blood and never peace.

As this is being decided, cousin Athelstan moving with purposeful-ness but not fear to ready his men, Archbishop Plegmund seeks my attention. No doubt some weak-willed follower has scampered to him as soon as the words of the messenger were first spoken.

His countenance is serene as he offers me a quirked smile of apology and keeps his eyes on my face, purposefully ignoring the clothing I wear.

We all have our parts to play here. Plegmund's my ally, and he's trusted by King Edward, a heady mix that even cousin Athelstan can't claim. Cousin Athelstan is also a Mercian, too much my mother's creature, aggravating my uncle.

'Good day, my lady,' the archbishop greets me cordially, but my eyes are arrested by the slim shape sliding back into my hall behind him. I must endeavour to find out who runs to him without hearing the full story, sending the archbishop scurrying to me, his Christian work forgotten about in the face of news of this new Viking raider incursion.

'Archbishop Plegmund,' my tone is neutral. I have a spy within his household too. We must all do what needs to be done to keep our alliance honest.

'There is a messenger?' he inquires, his eyes turning to watch cousin Athelstan and his men leaving my hall. Cousin Athelstan takes with him some young men I know quite well, sons of old Ealdorman Æthelfrith, a stalwart of Mercia since my father's marriage to my mother.

'Warriors of the north. Twenty ships. But York doesn't worry.' If my words are as clipped as debased Wessex coinage, I don't mean them to be, and I hope that cousin Athelstan's actions now speak to that.

'Very good, my lady,' he mollifies about to bow out of my presence, any previous haste forgotten about when I remember I need him.

'Archbishop, would you be kind enough to dispatch one of your men to King Edward's court with the news?' It's an order, not a request, but couched in the way that makes politics work. I've no doubt that the archbishop will know my uncle's whereabouts. He'll have men scattered all around the Wessex and Mercian kingdoms, keeping the king abreast of events, rumours and strange happenstances, as well as the archbishop's demands, whatever they might be. I imagine that in recent weeks, he'll have grown his group of messengers and spies both, the sudden change in the political climate catching even him unprepared for the eventuality of my mother's death.

I have the same number of men, women, and children at my beck and call, inherited from my mother, but I must give the archbishop a token of my trust and esteem. Great supporters need to know their worth, or that patronage is likely to evaporate as summer rain when the sun once more burns the land.

'Of course, my lady. I'll see to it with all haste. In the meantime, will you alert the witan?'

If I sent messengers out now, I would no doubt catch most of those who attended the witan that proclaimed me as Lady of the Mercians before they completed their journeys home. They might interpret it as a misstep of an untried ruler and yet to not do so will highlight my insecurities more, and my inexperience, trying to conceal any perceived failings by hiding the truth.

I consider. Cousin Athelstan and I didn't discuss this before he left. Then I remember who I am. I'm my mother's daughter, and I rule Mercia, not cousin Athelstan. What then would my mother do?

'I think that would be advisable. Twenty Viking raider ships is no small army, even if they land far to the north.'

I don't miss the quirk of agreement and respect in the archbishop's eyes, and I reconsider my earlier, perhaps less than charitable thoughts. He doesn't wish me to fail, no matter what others might think. His very presence here is maybe not endemic of my uncle's fears but to the archbishop's desire that I should be allowed my first baby steps and not be castigated for any initial failures. Not that I'll allow myself to fail. Mercia is strong, and York is as far away as Winchester, the capital of Wessex, is to Tamworth, the capital of Mercia. It would be a very long way for Viking raiders to progress without some counterattack or misfortune befalling them. Yes, they could use the rivers to infiltrate inland, but we would know they were coming long before they made it to Tamworth.

Mercia is stronger than it was at the time of the Viking raider invasion over fifty years ago and, more importantly, far better prepared. Mercia will, and can, protect itself and its people. Intermittent warfare has raged for years on the periphery, and yet, and I smirk at my illusion to progress, baby steps have become the assured stance of a nation proud to reclaim itself and honour me with leading it.

The archbishop leaves me, a flurry of his skirts, and I can return to my interrupted task. A woman must prove herself in battle, as well as in the arena of politics. Stepping once more into the bright daylight of a summer's day, I walk to where my warriors are practising on the grassy ground behind my hall, the double rivers sparkling in the sun's glare behind them as they glide serenely onwards. Some of the warriors have discarded their training byrnies in the heat of the day; some are almost naked as sweat trickles over their exposed, muscle-bound flesh. I leave my household warriors to their tasks in the dusty field and instead seek my opponents.

Ten women are training in a distant corner of the enclosure. They're all flushed with exertion; their long hair pulled back to keep it off their faces and elaborately plaited to keep it out of their eyes as they swing their heavy swords and shields with great skill, perhaps more than the men I've just watched. We women may not have the muscles and strength of men, using both lighter shields and swords, but we also use our greater manoeuvrability, making us just as efficient. If not more so, in my humble opinion.

I rush to join them, exhilarated as my sword is pressed back into my hand, and my shield is given to me by my waiting squire: a young girl, Erna, who strains under its weight, no matter how much lighter it might be. I thank her, noticing that she's cleaned it while I was away from practice. She's both diligent and belligerent, and I would wish her my daughter.

So encumbered, I step into the dust and sweat of the training yard. The clothes that archbishop Plegmund strove to ignore, my grass-stained trews and dusty byrnie, are ready to resume my interrupted practice. After all, I'm the Lady of the Mercians. I must be able to protect this land with my intelligence and my body.

CHAPTER 3

I t's cousin Athelstan's warrior who returns to me first. Barely three weeks have passed since our initial news of problems in the north. His bored expression is all I need to see to know that the northern borderlands of Mercia with York are safe.

He and his band of nine warriors arrive hot and bothered at the end of a particularly humid day. I'm still at Tamworth, the doors on the great hall held wide open by huge wooden props to allow the hoped-for chill of the night to creep inside, cooling us in a way that drinking and removing layers of ceremonial clothes simply won't. Those from the northern kingdom tell me that Mercia lacks a decent wind to drive the heat from the land, but I say better to swelter in the summer than brave the dagger-sharp tips of a northern wind in winter.

'My lady, Ælfwynn,' Thurstan bows low before me, a flourish to his tired demeanour, ignoring the filth of the road that litters his body. 'There's little to report. York is unmolested. We rode another two days north, and still, there was nothing to be seen. Lord Athelstan will ride further, I don't doubt it, but there's no sign of stress in the general populace or fearful lines of men, women, and children from the outer settlements streaming toward the dubious safety of York and its decaying walls.'

He uses the tone disparagingly. Much has been made of the weakness of York's walls compared to those of the burhs my mother and father built and the building of which continues apace even now. First, Mercia must win back a settlement from the Viking raiders, but then it must hold it. That is done with the wood of Mercia's forests and the iron of her warriors. York's walls are riddled with holes and gates, almost as though they were made to keep people in once they entered, not stop people from actually getting inside.

'My thanks for your hasty journey and actions. Mercia is grateful to know she's not currently open to attack.' While I'm pleased not to be tested yet, I know it'll come in time. Mercia's geographical extent is a full half of its previous self before the Viking raiders came. It'll only grow now through assimilation and war.

I imagine that one day a generation will be born who don't reach for their swords, seaxs or humble knives at the out-of-place sound of a horse hoof or clutter of footsteps, the sharp tang of iron, but it will not be my generation; or even the children of my generation. It'll be a future I can't yet imagine or see clearly. I only know that it will come and that everyone in Mercia dreams of it. We fight for our independence now with the belief that, given time, Mercia will rise from the ashes to be as magnificent as she once was.

I call for food and drink for the men, a wrinkle of my nose at the smell of sweat and horse not going unnoticed by Thurstan. He offers a shrug of his massive shoulders as if to say, 'what do you expect?' and I dismiss him. In the shadows at the recesses of the hall, I see a flash of black detach itself and rush out of the open door.

I sigh with annoyance once more but accept that I now don't need to send for the archbishop and inform him of Thurstan's report. No doubt he'll send to King Edward and the ealdormen of my witan before I have the opportunity.

I owe my ealdormen my thanks for the trust that they've granted me. My initial message regarding the sighted Viking raider ships didn't, as I'd feared, result in them rushing back to Tamworth to demand more action than a few scouting parties. Not so the reaction of my uncle. Even now, I know that three hundred of his best warriors are threading their way to Mercia. Edward was never as protective of my mother, and I suppose I should be grateful for his care for Mercia, but I resent his assumption that Mercia has suddenly grown weak with the death of his sister. After his death, does he expect Wessex to falter? Does he think cousin Ælfweard will look to another older and wiser king for guidance and support, or does he accord his son far more respect than he does his niece?

Perhaps, as arrogant as everyone is of their mortality, he doesn't think of the future at all.

I stretch my arm before me – tweaking an injury sustained during practice two days ago. A sharp jab of pain reverberates up my sword arm, but the pain is good. It reminds me of what I can achieve and what my body can do. It was caused by no small blade but rather a whack of a shield boss hammering against me. It was the male warrior I battled who fell, not myself, and he who still bears the bruising from my shield across the bridge of his nose, swollen to the size of a pig's snout. He, too, must hear the ridicule from the other men. They won't be quite as derisive when I manage to win the upper hand in a skirmish against them as well.

My uncle might believe that I need others to fight my battles for me, but he's mistaken. I know my strengths and weaknesses as intimately as I'm aware of Mercia's assets and failings.

I might have Wessex blood in my body, but my father was a Mercian, and my mother became almost more Mercian than he was. I know Mercia more intimately than I've ever known the touch of a man, and this is what gives me the will to believe in myself and to trust my instincts and my warrior's arm.

My uncle is a politician. My cousin Ælfweard will be one after him, but I'll keep my kingdom safe with my iron and my warriors. The ealdormen of Mercia trust me to do so, for now. It's more than I can say my uncle does.

CHAPTER 4

Cousin Athelstan arrives with the beginning of the harvest, not that he hasn't sent me news beforehand. He has. Almost so much news of nothing important that I'm surprised when he greets me with no worry in his eyes but something else. He holds almost a whiff of conspiracy about him, and that intrigues me rather than concerns me.

In the moment before he speaks, I take in his appearance as a whole. He's rugged, his hair grown long and shaggy, his beard and moustache bushy and fairer than usual. His skin, too, bears the cast of a summer's month living out of doors with no means to ensure he maintains his façade of elegant if discarded prince.

I almost envy him for his freedom. Almost.

'My lady, Ælfwynn,' he greets me formally. Only in private do we use our childhood names of Elf and Stan; shortened because we grew tired of the formality of our friendship and the necessity of contorting our mouths to make the 'Ælf' or 'Æthel' sound. He was so small when I first met him that I was almost incredulous that he would ever grow to be a man. As unused to babies and small children as I was, even I knew that Athelstan was a fragile, tiny creature to be treasured and dotted on. No more, however.

'Ætheling Athelstan,' I intone. There are spies from uncle Edward in my court, and so I strive to use his official title in public. Athelstan berates me for it frequently, but today he nods serenely, perhaps thankful for the reminder to himself and others of his official title. There's nothing like living rough for a month to make a man forget he has any occasion to amount to more than his fellow warriors. He will have been brash and foul-mouthed while he was away. In my hall, he'll need to temper his speech a little.

'I bring news of a battle, a retreat and the rumblings of unease within Northumbria.' His eyes still flash with some hidden purpose. I wonder what he thinks he's seen.

'Then come, recount the tale, ensuring you leave nothing out. But first, I would assure you of Mercia's integrity and resilience in facing my mother's death.'

The faint shadow that crosses his face is perhaps only witnessed by myself. I don't know if it's the reminder that my mother is dead that causes it or the feeling that he should have asked about Mercia first. I try and draw his eye and encourage him onward, but he allows himself to be distracted by mead and food first as he recovers his poise. I didn't mean to discomfort him, but I always remember that my mother insisted on speaking of Mercia's strengths before any could report the whispers of a battle to come that would involve the iron of Mercian men.

I wait patiently for him to speak, and into his silence, more and more people pour, as though his return is the most excitement we've had for weeks. I suppose it is. It's been a lazy summer as I struggled with my grief and my new duties, content to know that no sudden summer storm destroyed the crops and no blight killed our animals where they drowsed on crisping grass.

'We travelled three days passed York until we saw any sight of the rumoured. The River Tyne, not the Humber Estuary, must have been its destination all along. And what a fleet it was – even as we watched from the high ground, we could appreciate its size and provisioning. I knew then that the leader was not to be dismissed easily. It takes a strong man to have so many men and women swear their oaths to them and an even richer one to have so many ships to hand to be filled by those men and women.'

He pauses for a moment, and there's not one sound within the hall above the slightly flushed breaths being taken. I allow a small smile. Cousin Athelstan has always loved to tell tales, each telling becoming more elaborate and detailed. I prefer my stories with much more action than description, but then, my mother always told me I was impatient and likely to miss some important detail in my haste.

'Each ship had the same sail, of blood red with a wolf's head emblazoned on it, and each ship was crowned with a wooden wolf's head.' I want to ask him how he could see such detail from his vantage point, as he's just described it, but I know I'm being perverse. He's been much closer to the fleet during his time away than his story so far implies.

'We watched them scout the area, but I could tell that the man who led them was no stranger to the lands he surveyed. I sent two men to the kingdom of Bamburgh to advise the lord of the House of Bamburgh, but my men returned to me almost immediately, for we weren't alone at the River Tyne.'

'King Constantin?' I allow myself to breathe, and he nods just a little, his eyes cautioning me for my impatience. It so vividly reminds me of our childhood together that, for a moment, I forget he speaks about the genuine possibility of war.

'My men told me of warriors racing from the north with a large force of men on horseback led by two banners. I grasped it would be King Constantin of the Scots and the Lord of Bamburgh. All that remained to discover was the identity of their enemy. I thought long and hard about my options. The lands so far north are inhabited by Saxon and Dane in near equal numbers, and none of them recognises the authority of Lady Ælfwynn of Mercia or King Edward of Wessex. I knew I could be a valuable prize in the hands of the wrong Viking raider.' This is as much of an admission of Athelstan's status that I've ever heard him give voice to before. It seems that his heritage does pray on his mind almost as much as mine.

'In the end, I decided it was best if I stayed undetected and saw what happened. I was sure there would be a battle, but there was also the possibility, slim as it might be, that these men were already allies and not enemies. Could it be that this massive force planned to combine and attack York instead of arguing about the lawless land we found ourselves within?'

'That night, my men and I were nervous, hidden away from the prying eyes of all but unwilling to expose ourselves further. We kept no fire. It was difficult and followed by a tough day. The men in the ships struck out, exploring the land once more for its richness in wild animals, and yet the force from the north didn't appear. It was then I realised they weren't allies and that I had, unintentionally, taken my warriors to the middle of a coming battle.'

For a moment, I think cousin Athelstan condemns me for sending him north. Only when he resumes speaking do I realise his voice is filled with excitement, not fear.

'It was on the third morning that my men and I travelled half a day inland toward Cumberland before striking out north again. King Constantin has been only an occasional supporter of Mercia, but he's more an ally than the leader of this new Viking raider attack. By now, I had this man's name, Rǫgnvaldr, grandson of Ivarr Ragnarsson.'

The name of Ivarr is heard with some sharp intakes of breath. His legend is well-known in Mercia, and he's a nastier bastard than it's hard to describe. One of the leaders of the attack on Mercia fifty years ago, he'd been encamped in Dublin for many years, kept regally entertained and fruitfully employed by the men and women he tried to subjugate to his will, sometimes with great success, and sometimes not. After his death, his sons, and now it seems, grandsons, have continued his legacy.

'We were met by a scouting party close to where my warriors had initially seen Constantin's force. It seems that King Constantin was playing the same game as me. I didn't give my actual name but introduced myself as a warrior and offered all the information we'd gathered from watching the force disembark. The leader of the scouting party was keen to take me to see King Constantin and Lord Ealdred of Bamburgh, but I refused to journey into the heart of their army. King

Constantin has met my father, and I didn't wish to be discovered with such a small force to ensure our freedom. The scouts also assumed I was from York. I didn't want to be caught in a lie.'

'The men were filled with battle-lust, saying they'd be a battle no matter what, but they were guarded as well. They didn't give away their plans, in case we'd lied about who we were – which we had – but for different reasons than the ones they assumed.' Athelstan's voice is lighthearted at the thought of so much intrigue.

'I return to the site of the ship-landing after our meeting but instead waited to see where Constantin's men had chosen to make their stand.' Here he pauses and allows a smile to steal over his serious face. 'King Constantin is a wily warrior. He chose an excellent site, just this side of the Old Wall, but near an old Roman settlement. His men could hold the hill site and gaze southwards and see the enemy when they were still far distant. But that wasn't the place where the battle took place. Constantin moved his force down the slope, near a river in spate, and it was there that Lord Rǫgnvaldr brought his men.'

'Was there no talk of truce?' I interject, and Athelstan shakes his head.

'I didn't see it. It happened while we were inland. They wouldn't agree to it. I wasn't surprised. Lord Rǫgnvaldr's force was huge. I imagine all the men and women wanted to fight and that King Constantin and Lord Ealdred didn't favour an uneasy alliance with such a vast number of enemy warriors. They might have made peace one day and reneged on it the next.' I nod in understanding. The Viking raiders aren't always the most trustworthy of allies. Cousin Athelstan and I have learned this throughout our lives.

'The forces finally clashed around midday. A strange time for battle when it was so warm, but I assume the men took the time to ready themselves. When the days are so long, it seems foolish to rush into battle and death.' Athelstan shrugs as he speaks, having given the idea much thought.

'The two sides were equally matched concerning numbers, if not experience. King Constantin's men were well-trained and well-equipped. So were some of Lord Rǫgnvaldr's warriors, but it was also filled with men and women with barely any warriors' equipment to their name. It was evident to me that Rǫgnvaldr must have convinced many of them to come with him, promising land and riches. Some had little more than the clothes on their backs and their rusty old war axe passed down through the generations from their great grandfathers and grandfathers who attacked Northumbria and Mercia two generations ago. But these were no warriors.'

'It was apparent from the beginning that the battle would be over quickly and that it would be indecisive. King Constantin's choice of the battle site made it difficult for all of his warriors to attack at once, whereas Rǫgnvaldr threw all of his warriors at his enemy in great waves, one after another. It wasn't the most inspired of battle tactics from either leader nor were they successful.' Cousin Athelstan speaks with disdain in his voice. He's spent many years studying battles and determining the best way to break through enemy lines and win the day. He's an expert tafl player. Whether he's the attacker or the defender, few can beat him with his carefully considered battle tactics.

'Neither King Constantin nor Lord Rǫgnvaldr engaged in the battle themselves, relying on their commanders and their warriors. It was a poor decision. Men will only fight for their kings and leaders when those leaders and rulers are heading the attack, and they have something to fight for.'

I smile at his words. Even my mother always tried to fight with her warriors. They rarely let her, but just having her near the battlefield was all that was needed. It seems that cousin Athelstan has his own opinion on the matter as well. I agree with him.

'Even so, the battle raged for much of the afternoon, although I saw few men fall to their death. Some unfortunates drowned in the swollen river, and yet others were wounded, but the battle began as a stalemate and ended as one.'

'What happened afterwards?' I almost whisper but somehow manage to keep my voice steady. I have a terrible feeling that the next words will cause great consternation.

'King Constantin and Lord Ealdred sent men to treat with Lord Rǫgnvaldr. I don't know the actual outcome of their talks, but I know this, the men didn't part as enemies, even if they were hardly allies either. There was no exchange of treasure, only a handful of hostages. I doubt either side was content. This skirmish won't be the only one this year.'

'We witnessed the men feasting each other, and messengers were sent to proclaim their agreement. But King Constantin didn't alert Lord Rǫgnvaldr to my presence, and I think he half suspected who I was. On the way home, I sent a small force into York to determine the nature of the message, but York was sullen and unhelpful. None of the traders, churchmen or women that were approached wanted to speak of Lord Rǫgnvaldr and King Constantin. Even now, I don't know if they've signed an accord to work together to defeat Mercia or whether it was just an agreement not to fight.'

Athelstan's words fall into the silent hall with unease. It seems this is what his cautioning eyes were trying to tell me when he first arrived.

CHAPTER 5

The arrival of Archbishop Plegmund, all anxious eyes and flapping hands, is no surprise to me, as cousin Athelstan pauses to gulp ale and gobble food as though he's been starved for the entire time he's been away. I watch loaf after loaf of bread being consumed by him and his men. Bread can't be baked over a campfire, and it seems it's been greatly missed.

I consider what he's told me. Cousin Athelstan has watched a large but indecisive battle between two forces – only one of which has even remotely benign intentions toward Mercia and Wessex. Lord Rǫgnvaldr may not have won and claimed the land between the kingdom of York and the House of Bamburgh for himself, but neither has he been defeated. Clearly, he remains in the hinterlands of Northumbria, not threatening the kingdom of the Scots or the House of Bamburgh, but there all the same.

This worries me, and likewise, it should worry everyone who understands Mercia's ever-shifting borders. Those of my immediate supporters fete the news that cousin Athelstan brings, he among them, although even he must realise it's not the good news that others imply.

While I'd never rely on another kingdom to keep mine secure, I would have appreciated it if King Constantin had chased Lord Rǫgn-valdr all the way back to his ships or, better yet, killed all the Viking raider men and women and burnt their ships to deter others from the same game.

Archbishop Plegmund's worried face matches my thoughts, although my face is serene, as my mother's would have been in the same situation. In this matter of Lord Rǫgnvaldr, I must make right and just decisions or I fear my uncle's ambitions will override the will of Mercia if I don't.

'My Lady, Ælfwynn,' Plegmund grabs my attention, unsettling me from my thoughts only to drag me into darker ones.

'I fear this is no great saving grace for Mercia,' he begins, his voice hushed, standing almost obscenely close to me at the front of the great hall, as ever filled with men and women eager to hear news carried from the disputed north. 'Lord Rǫgnvaldr unconfined in Northumbria, King Constantin of the Scots and Lord Ealdred of Bamburgh unable to defeat him. These are not the events I wish to hear about.'

'You think we should launch an attack?' I whisper back, seduced by his tone, into speaking as confidentially as he does. The words fill me with dread for those who will die and also unease. I've not yet commanded men and women to their death. I swallow uneasily at the thought, my sour mouth alerting me to my inner unease.

'Not yet, my lady, but perhaps soon. We must consider how vital the lawless lands north of York are to Lord Rǫgnvaldr's ambitions. If it's all he wants, can Mercia stand between him and his desires? We only hold Mercia. York is much further north, deep in the uncontrol-lable land that's fallen under the spell of the Viking raiders, with only the Archbishop of York as our unsteady ally. If Lord Rǫgnvaldr takes York, Mercia will be threatened once more. It can't not be.'

'But if we let him take York and allow him to stand with the power of his ancestors and extended family behind him, the House of Ivarr, can we hold Mercia against an onslaught, if it should come? East Anglia is not yet fully reunited as a kingdom and probably never will. Neither is it reconciled to Mercian rule, and the Five Boroughs stand mostly aloft, only Derby and Nottingham acquiescent to Mercia. There'll be supporters there keen to have a Viking chieftain as their ally instead of a Mercian. They have an idea of Daneland, not England.' I speak out loud the thoughts running through my head in response to Archbishop Plegmund's words.

'We need to look at the burhs we already command. Ensure they're in an excellent state of repair before we do anything. If Lord Rǫgn-valdr seizes York, or if he's also thwarted there, he might simply pursue an objective further south.' The archbishop's words aren't the comfort I expected from him but reflect my thoughts exactly. And neither is he finished yet. 'If Lord Rǫgnvaldr can't take York, he'll have no chance against the burhs. But you're correct; it would be advisable to have their defences checked. And perhaps more.'

'More?' I ask, but I hazard a guess that I know what he's about to suggest.

'You and Lord Athelstan should progress north, visit all the burhs, show people you have no fear. You should also go to Colchester or command King Edward to do so. It's much closer to Winchester than to Tamworth.'

There's wisdom in Archbishop Plegmund's words, even if it makes me uneasy to involve my uncle in such a way. I'm in Tamworth, from there, it's not far to Derby, Nottingham and Stamford, and even Hunt-ingdon, but Colchester is a long way south and far to the east. I could work my way steadily south, visiting the burhs of Warwick, Towces-ter, Bedford, and Hertford, but Colchester would still be some days' travel. During those precious days, I should be near the northern borders, not appearing weak by skulking close to the Wessex border-lands as though seeking the shelter of my uncle. I'd rather spend my time at Chester, Runcorn, and Eddisbury to the west and cut off any possibility of Lord Rǫgnvaldr getting reinforcements from his allies in Dublin, the Isle of the Manx or any of the northern islands he claims to rule.

'I agree with you,' I finally sigh.

Archbishop Plegmund offers me a wry smirk.

'You're as wise as your mother,' he offers, an assurance I wish I could dismiss as just massaging my fears away, but I find I suddenly need the reassurance.

'Yes, she would have done the same,' I agree, and by then, cousin Athelstan has returned so that the three of us can discuss my intentions along with those of my only ealdorman in attendance, Æthelfrith.

Ealdorman Æthelfrith was once an ally of my grandfather and then my father, and then my mother, and now he's my ally as well. He's always been dominant in the area of Mercia that most closely borders the smaller kingdoms of the Welsh to the west. But he's not quite the aged and infirm man that I portray him to be. And he has sons who are not much younger than cousin Athelstan and me, quite a few sons, and two of them have been in the north with Athelstan already.

'We'll need to ensure that Tamworth is protected in our absence and that riding away with our armed warriors causes as little fear as it's possible to arouse in people so used to violence and bloodshed.' My voice is stern as I consider what needs to be done very shortly. I meet the eyes of Ealdorman Æthelfrith to see he's nodding at my words. That bolsters my confidence for my next sentence.

'I'll send a messenger to King Edward of Wessex,' I caution the archbishop with my eyes. I'm grateful for his friendship and support, but I also know that with the threat of an attack, his absolute loyalty is to my uncle and not me. I want to ensure that my uncle appreciates who leads Mercia and who's making the decisions.

'Very well, my lady,' he concedes, bowing his head to acknowledge my authority. 'As I planned, I'll ride to Lichfield today. I've been summoned to deal with a church matter. Something a little trivial in light of this news, but it will be better handled as soon as possible.'

The archbishop strides from my presence with those words, not so much unhappily but rather with recognition of our relative positions with regard to this new threat. I sigh deeply, dragging cousin Athelstan and Ealdorman Æthelfrith from their surveillance of the maps of the burhs before them.

'You're right to fear my father,' cousin Athelstan concedes, the words wrenched from him, his unhappy eyes showing his sorrow. 'He isn't always honourable, as I well know,' he barks back a miserable laugh and shrugs his shoulders, his attention back on the map as though he's never spoken.

My cousin is my friend and ally, but his feelings towards his father have always fluctuated, dependent on my uncle's attention to him. His loyalty can be guarded and has always relied on his father's moods and political aspirations. I wish it weren't true, but even cousin Athelstan has admitted his contrary nature to me.

I don't pity him, after all, he benefitted from the love and care my mother and father lavished on me, and he always knew of their regard for him. But his relationship with his father could help and hinder me.

'You should go to the most northerly burhs, Nottingham and Derby. They are, after all, newly constructed. I'll go west to Chester, Runcorn, and Eddisbury. They're more established, especially Chester and will know what's expected of them.' Cousin Athelstan's voice is reasoned as he considers our next steps.

I feel I should have made the decision, but it's the correct one, and even Ealdorman Æthelfrith is nodding in agreement, and I see little point in starting an argument just so I can be the one to say the very words that cousin Athelstan has spoken.

'I'll escort Lady Ælfwynn to Derby and Nottingham,' Ealdorman Æthelfrith interjects. It would be good for him to go with cousin Athelstan, where he's well known. But as the most accomplished warrior within Mercia, it's perhaps better that he comes with me to the newer burhs with his well-trained eye and ability to elicit loyalty in all men and women.

'Agreed, and now I must write to King Edward.' The task is already weighing me down, but my decision to be the one to inform my uncle is also the correct one.

I'll not let him think that I rule only with the aid of men who could be construed as his own creatures to command if he wished to do so.

'I wish you luck with that,' cousin Athelstan mutters, tearing his eyes from the map. 'I'll go and sort out supplies, horses and divide the men to be most effective. Ealdorman Æthelfrith, I'd welcome your assistance,' he turns to the older man as he snaps his words, but he and Æthelfrith are old allies and friends. The other man thinks nothing of being commanded by King Edward's son, just as he thinks nothing of being commanded by the Lady of Mercia's daughter.

'My thanks,' I mutter, standing to leave the hall. Cousin Athelstan is only just returned, and already I'm sending him away again. I feel a moment of sadness. I don't want this new threat to come between us, but as a man, he has all the advantages in any coming battle. As the son of my uncle, the king of Wessex, he has even more, regardless of whether his father or he truly appreciate it.

CHAPTER 6

Settling myself at my lectern within the scriptorium, I think of the words I must write as monks robed in brown scuttle around me. They ensure I have the highest quality vellum and sharpened quills hoarded in their stores for only the most important of tasks. They check that the ink hasn't turned gloopy from lack of use in its tightly sealed pot, the wax seal supposed to prevent such an occurrence but far from assuring it. Only then do they leave me to my unwelcome task. If they resent my presence within their personal space, they fail to show it, and I'm pleased to be so welcomed.

The scriptorium feels like a church, its hushed softness a testament to the studious nature of all the monks here. Their labour is never ceasing, and their hands are always steady as they write and copy, copy and write. It's here that the paperwork of my rule is in its ascendancy, almost a secret world that few glimpses and even fewer understand. It's the ordered rule of my grandfather that preserves here, with his fastidiousness in ensuring that everything's recorded and written down for future generations to read. Anyone visiting here could, with the correct amount of patience, offer a full accounting of everything that's so far happened in my rule, from my acclamation as the Lady of Mercia to the number of shields in my armoury.

My writing isn't a new thing – I've often sent messages for my mother or in my name to the holy houses we support within Mercia, but this is my first official act as the Second Lady of the Mercians. Trepidation temporarily stays my hand, as I allow myself to be distracted by the men scuttling backwards and forward or standing as though motionless while their foreheads crease in concentration. Only their eyes and hands move as they scan and copy the work before them, sometimes double-checking before they finally commit the words to vellum and ink.

'King Edward,' I write first, holding back my long blue sleeve with my left hand and concentrating on forming the letters neatly and precisely as I hold the quill in my right hand. I'm dressed as a lady of the court today, and that makes my attire less than ideal for the task I've set myself.

I make the first letters of each word a flourish, as the monks do. Although I doubt I'll take the time or the expense to colour in the empty spaces that scream out for a depiction to fill the cavernous hole of the kicking feet of the 'K' and the open mouth of the 'E'. The monks would fill the letters with images of animals or holy saints. I find I don't have the desire to do so and never have.

'Tidings from the north demand that I inform you,' I feel myself relax with the use of that phrase. I know I sound like a ruler. I'm not asking for permission or agreement. 'Of a skirmish between King Constantin and Lord Rǫgnvaldr, grandson of Ivarr Ragnarsson, near the ancient wall. Your son, ætheling Athelstan, witnessed the altercation but kept his presence a secret from the forces involved. We'll now take action to secure the border with the north against a possible attack. The burhs are to be inspected and made ready for any attempted incursion into Mercia.'

I stop and think about what I'm trying to say without actually saying it. I don't want my uncle to decide I need his support, but neither do I want him to ignore my endeavours completely. He must be alert to the danger but not too alert. Mercia will stand ready, and so should Wessex, but this will be Mercia's fight, not Wessex's. Sourly my face curdles. Wessex has fought very little in the last twenty years.

Mercia has done all the fighting as Wessex basks in the peaceful reign of my uncle.

How do I tell my uncle what I don't yet know? Will there be war? Will Lord Rǫgnvaldr attack Mercia? Will King Constantin attack him once more? Does Lord Rǫgnvaldr only hunger for the hinterland between the kingdom of York and that of the independent kingdom of Bamburgh? Or are Lord Rǫgnvaldr's ambitions far loftier? Is he the second generation of Viking raiders who'll try to undo all the advances of my mother's rule?

I sigh deeply. My actions are far easier to explain when I say them out loud than when I commit them to vellum. I'm more assured when I think than when I write. When I write, I feel as though my soul is laid bare, and my uncle will infer my fear and worry and come to relieve me of my position. Dry words on a piece of vellum should be taken at face value and not poured over for signs of worry or fear, but I know that my uncle and his scribes will do just that. Should I make a mistake and ink splash the sheet of paper, I know my uncle will envisage me, all shaking hands and worrying as I beg him for assistance, even if my words don't say that. I must be bold with my words and with my approach to this message.

I don't wish it to sound as though I'm asking for his permission or agreement as I take actions to keep Mercia safe.

I groan. Perhaps I should have let Archbishop Plegmund send the message after all? My mother always used an imperious tone when communicating with her brother, one equal speaking to another, but I don't yet have the audacity and resolve to do the same. I only wish I could stop seeing my uncle as somehow wiser than myself because of his advanced age.

'My household will know where to find me for your reply,' I write only to wish I hadn't. My scribe watches me, his face inscrutable. I think he'd prefer to write the message himself, and I think I'm beginning to agree with him. Once more, thinking about writing the letter itself has proven to be far easier than its execution.

'I need more vellum,' I say to him, a little breathless with annoyance, crossing through the words I don't like on the page as though they've offended me.

'Tidings from the north demand that I inform you of a skirmish between King Constantin and Lord Rǫgnvaldr, grandson of Ivarr Ragnarsson, near the ancient wall. Your son, ætheling Athelstan, witnessed the altercation. We'll now take action to secure the border in case of a possible attack. The burhs are to be inspected and made ready for any attempted incursion into Mercia.'

He nods quickly; his eyes turned away from my discarded message as he pins a new, completely unused piece of vellum to my lectern. Only the best that Mercia has to offer for King Edward of Wessex.

'My apologies,' I offer him, handing him the tainted sheet. He nods his head, and I think he'll not speak to me.

'It's no matter. I'll erase the words, and we can use it again,' he mutters, only for me to realise that I need to copy what I've already written and was happy with.

'Sorry, I'll need that back for a moment,' I say, and understanding flashes across his face. 'Will you help me …find the correct words?' I finally utter, and his body deflates at the words, as though he's been holding his breath while I worked and can only now inhale again, now that he's assured that I won't make a total mess of my message and embarrass his scriptorium in the eyes of the Wessex one.

'It would be my honour,' he smiles shyly at me, and I feel the same reprieve he must feel.

'Here, this is what I've said so far. Is it adequate?'

'Tidings from the north demand that I inform you of a skirmish between king Constantin and Lord Rǫgnvaldr, grandson of Ivarr Ragnarsson, near the ancient wall. Your son, ætheling Athelstan, witnessed the altercation. We'll now take action to secure the border. The burhs are to be inspected and made ready for any attempted incursion into Mercia.'

His small, mole-like eyes scan the vellum, his lips moving slowly as he reads my words, ignoring those that have been crossed out.

'It's concise and to the point,' he offers.' I would perhaps use more flowing language and add another word here or there, but then, I'm used to sending long accounts of events in Mercia, not the possibility of an attack on York. I think it will suffice in the circumstances.'

I bite my nail in frustration. I want my message to more than suffice.

'How would you write it then?' I ask a little angrily. How can I fail at such a simple task?

'My lady,' my scribe stutters, 'I meant no criticism.'

'Oh, I know that I just want this to be right. I wish to give my uncle no cause to doubt my resolve or abilities. I want the words to be mine, and yet, they need to be the right words,' I finish a little helplessly. I don't know what I'm trying to convey to him.

The scribe looks pensive for a moment, and then he nods.

'Sometimes it's easier to send a messenger and not a message. A messenger could assess the situation and use the correct tone. It's harder to do the same in writing. But come, it can be done, and we'll do it together.'

I find myself nodding along with the man. In the past, I'd assumed him to be a severe character, his tonsure always trimmed sharply across his forehead, an unappealing look in a man who possesses such a large, broad forehead and small, beady eyes, but now I see his eyes are intelligent and keen.

The scribe's voice returns me to the more serious business at hand, and with his help, the message to my uncle is finally composed and sent on its way. The sentiment of the letter has been little changed, but the words are now couched in slightly more imperious tones with no trace of a request or hesitation in them.

'Edward, king of the Anglo-Saxon people in Wessex. News from the north of a skirmish between King Constantin, Lord Ealdred and Lord Rǫgnvaldr, grandson of Ivarr Ragnarsson, near the ancient wall, has reached Mercia. Ætheling Athelstan witnessed an inconclusive battle between the three men, and an accord between them has been achieved, of which the exact details elude us. In light of this, Mercia will secure the burhs and the borders.' I sign the letter as Ælfwynn, Lady of the Mercians and attach my seal to it, the double-headed eagle standard of Mercia standing alert in the red wax.

I thank the scribe, and he turns and offers a sharp nod of his head, all traces of our prior familiarity gone – well, all apart from the twinkle in his eye.

'Osbert, my lady, that's my name. Brother Osbert. I served your mother for many years. She relied on me for my discretion and ability to give words to her thoughts.'

He speaks plainly, without bragging about his relationship with my mother, and I grin at him.

'And I'm Lady Ælfwynn, and you have my sincere thanks for your help. I think I might need it in the future.'

'Very good, my lady,' and then he shuffles from my presence, the message in his hand. I hope to have found another ally for Mercia and myself in perhaps one of the most unexpected of all places, the secluded and enclosed sanctuary of Mercia's scriptorium, filled with holy men who usually eye the rule of a woman aghast and against their holy writ. The people of Mercia never fail to surprise me.

CHAPTER 7

Cousin Athelstan and I ride from Tamworth together, but still within sight of its wooden walls and walkways, we part ways. He and his household troops, numbering forty-eight, head west towards Chester, Eddisbury and Runcorn along Watling Street, Ealdorman Æthelfrith's two oldest sons, Ælfstan and Æthelwald, supporting him.

My warriors and I journey east first to where the ancient Foss Way meets the equally ancient Watling Street. From there, it's an easy ride to Derby. Ealdorman Æthelfrith rides with me, his two younger sons, Athelstan and Eadric, bickering as they bring up the rear of the party. The ealdorman ignores the youths, but I find myself listening to their argument and enjoying the banality of it all. To have nothing more to worry about than one-upping your sibling would be a fine way to ride on this bright summer's day.

The burh at Derby was only completed last year, along with Huntingdon further to the southeast. It was one of the last places my mother visited before her death. She always enjoyed seeing the earth ramparts rising from the mud and muck to support the wooden turrets and walkways. I confess I've never much enjoyed the smell of labouring men and women as they force the sticky mud from the earth. I must now hide my dismay at the aroma and the noise while praising them for their efforts in organisation and building craft.

The system of burhs, instigated by my mother and father in Mercia, although some say their original is older, is often credited as being my grandfather's invention. It has enabled the English parts of Mercia to stay whole against attacks from the Viking raiders hailing from Dublin or the north and east. They've allowed the farmers and coerls to feel some safety and to know that if an attack comes, they have somewhere to retreat to with their animals and possessions. No more will isolated steadings be prey to attack with no hint of help or refuge available.

As for the enemy, the complex tasks of the burhs construction have shown our would-be-attackers that the men and women of Mercia are now prepared to act together and to put aside any ancient petty arguments in favour of defeating a mutual enemy.

Mercia may currently be split between English Mercia and the Danelaw – also consisting of the former kingdom of the East Angles – but no more of the kingdom will become subject to the rule of others. And each year, Mercia grows in extent, first to the western lands around Chester and further north-west, and then to the north, where burhs at Derby and the new construction at Nottingham reveal my mother's passion and commitment to rebuilding the Mercia that kings Penda and Offa once ruled. The strong warrior kings of previous generations, one a pagan and one Christian, are both role models I'm keen to emulate, although perhaps not in the manner of Penda's untimely death at the hands of the Northumbrians.

The worrying nature of my journey is muted by the radiance of the late summer's day. It almost feels as though I travel to a rendezvous with a lover or to spend time with my women, spinning and chatting on a sheltered riverbank (or more likely, engaged in a mock battle) and not to announce that Derby should be maintained at a level consistent with an upcoming attack.

My message will convey that those responsible for the harvest should be alert to all rivercraft and horsemen they happen to spot on the River Derwent. It will mean that the reeve's men will ride further north each day, checking for any sign of advance from York, and that ship traders will be treated with suspicion. Far better suspicion than allowing an army to sneak inside the burh under cover of trading and then burn it to the ground and claim a victory.

Athelstan, Ecgwynn and I had a good education at the hands of the monks of Mercia at the request of my grandfather. I know of the Trojan horse and the fighting techniques of other races. Should the Viking leaders ever hear of such tactics, I'll be ready for them. I now expect subterfuge and guile, not the simple attacks that once took Mercia from the control of the Mercians and exploited the weak divisions of men tempted by the idea of power and leadership.

Cousin Ecgwynn has been left behind at Tamworth. She'll work with the reeve of Tamworth to keep the capital of Mercia safe and secure, and she'll redirect any response from my uncle to my message. I expect a lengthy missive from him, but I hope he'll not send more warriors than those already sent to do his bidding and ensure that Mercia rebuffs any attempts at conquest. It would undermine my warriors and the men of the fyrd if he were to do so. I fear it could cause more damage than if Lord Rǫgnvaldr were to appear with a host of two thousand men and attack the half-formed burh of Nottingham, my next stop after Derby.

I can only hope my uncle has more sense than that and understands the pride of the Mercians and the strength of Mercia. It's no longer weak and ripe for attack from unscrupulous men and women who take delight in killing and wreaking havoc over the tamed landscape that makes it so easy to circumnavigate.

Derby is bordered by hills to the north but is on relatively open ground as we ride toward it. My warriors are watchful, but we've received no intelligence to suggest the need for such vigilance. After Athelstan returned from his foray to the north, I sent fresh men to York, some via ship and some on horseback and others dressed as little more than slaves. It's a good idea to infiltrate as many sections of society as possible when treachery is feared.

They have instructions to provide details of events in York and to inform me if Lord Rǫgnvaldr makes any overtures of friendship or violence. I don't expect to hear from them anytime soon. Until Lord Rǫgnvaldr can claim some victory for himself in the northern lands of Northumbria, there's little to no point in trying to take York for himself.

No doubt Lord Rǫgnvaldr has allies and maybe even family in York, but it won't be the numbers he needs to claim it as his own to rule. Not yet, and hopefully, never. Not unless in the years since his grandfather was active, his descendants have proliferated like rats, to come streaming from a burning building at his advance.

The settlement of Derby comes swiftly into view, and I'm pleased to see men on the raised wooden walkways, although many work in the fields outside the safety of the rampart, busy with the harvest and minding ambling animals in the pleasant landscape.

As new as the defences are, it seems that the people of Derby have quickly come to rely upon its force of warriors to alert them to any danger. Few, if any, stop their tasks and rush back inside as we pass. I've sent a fast runner on ahead to announce my arrival, and I don't know whether to be pleased or concerned by the lack of worry and fear I see on the faces of the local inhabitants. But I know why they show no fear. We ride from the south. It's almost unheard of for an attack to come from the south, but then, even that wouldn't be enough for me to dismiss the possibility out of hand. The Viking raiders like to use the waterways to launch attacks rather than horses, and in Derby, the river runs right through the settlement, protected by even more warriors.

Riding into the burh itself, through the wide-open wooden gates, I'm greeted by a man of middle years, his hair disappearing from the front of his head like snow recedes from the touch of water. Here and there, clumps remain of his patchy grey and auburn hair, and although he's brushed what's left forward, he's fighting a losing battle.

'Lady Ælfwynn,' he greets me, staying my horse so that I can dismount. I've known the reeve here for many years, from long before Derby was a burh and safely returned to the control of Mercia. He's dressed far too casually to receive me without even a trace of his warrior's garb.

'Sigehelm,' I respond, my voice a little chill. While I'm pleased with the physical appearance of the burh, I'd have preferred to be welcomed by all the warriors stationed here, in their byrnies, helms, swords, seaxs and shields. This all appears a little too lax for one of the most northerly of my burhs, more likely to be a focus for any coming attack. I know a moment of unease. Do the people of Derby show so little concern for their safety all of the time?

Sigehelm gives me a pallid smile, his sparse hair floating in the gentle breeze stirred up by the passing of so many horses.

'My apologies, but your messenger's horse grew lame, and the man arrived mere moments before you did.'

Ah, he offers me excuses for the state of the burh. I see more men rush to join him, some almost dressed for battle, gripping their equipment as they struggle to fit into byrnies without dropping their shields and sword. I feel it would be churlish to chastise him when it's so obviously the truth. I try to drive the coldness from my welcome and be content with knowing that at least one of us here is dressed as they should be, my sword held down my back and my shield to the left side of my leg, hanging on the horse's reins. It bears the image of the Mercian double-headed eagle on its front, picked out in tiny metal bosses in black and red.

'Would you like to rest, or would you prefer to review the work first?'

I'd like nothing better than to be feted and feasted, my throat dry from the summer's heat and the dusty road, which my warm water bottle will not ease, but I've come here with an express purpose. The presence of Ealdorman Æthelfrith in my entourage makes that intention clear. He may not rule here, but his governance in the west of Mercia means that he's well respected, if not always liked, and his skills and prowess in battle are almost legendary. He'd not be here unless inspecting the construction of the wall was his intention.

'Show me the earthworks first,' I command, and Sigehelm's head bobs as though he expected just such an answer, one that he probably hoped for. I imagine that somewhere some frantic cooks are trying to find a meal worthy of the Lady of Mercia. No doubt there are also screeching women and desperate servants trying to scrub the wooden boards clean and sand down the priceless glassware, if not remove a season's worth of dust from the floorboards, as well.

My scribe, Osbert, accompanies me, as does Ealdorman Æthelfrith and all the members of my escort as Sigehelm leads the way back outside the burh once more. They're all warriors and are expected to tell me if they see any weakness or area of concern as we survey the building work. More publicly, they're here to commend the construction of the burh. As members of the Mercian household troop, their expertise and experience mean that their approval means a great deal to the people of the newly constructed burhs.

Sigehelm now has almost as many men battle-ready as I do, and I feel a little closed in as the men all break into small groups, discussing what they see and praising, if praise is required, and querying where they might see an oversight. The bubble of conversation explodes almost into the roar of battle.

The wooden gate across the road in and out of Derby is a solid affair, built of timber felled from the Mercian oak forests. It's speckled with huge metal bosses, similar to those found on the linden shields all warriors carry. But it's very new, not yet streaked with age and its yellow rawness contrasts with the more seasoned wood used further along the steeped embankment in the construction of the walkways and fighting platforms. It attests to the gates being the last piece of construction, and if I were a Viking raider, I'd think them the weakest part of the line of defence.

I consider that the gate would benefit from a coat of darkest resin to try and hide its rawness. At the moment, it proclaims itself as the entrance even more than the snaking road we've travelled along does. Before I can comment, I hear another discussing the intentions to undertake the work soon. I save my breath. It's not politic to comment on an oversight when it's already been identified.

Sigehelm is deferential and yet eager as a child at the same time. I find myself keen to be impressed, and luckily, he soon finds something that does impress me. We entered Derby from the south, but by the time we've ridden to the northern entrance, tiptoeing our way across the river snaking through the centre of the settlement where it runs flat and sullen in the summer's drought, I'm aware that the defences here are far superior.

The wooden palisade has been twice reinforced, and the attendant ditch is filled with the most vicious spikes I've ever seen, the pieces of wood jabbing upwards like splintered bone, the ends tipped with the stench of excrement. The very same ramparts mark the path across the river, a sunken ship visible as well until the river returns in spate.

I wrinkle my nose at the smell but keep my face as bland as possible as I examine the northern gate.

It's much smaller than the Ssouthern gate, barely wide enough for a cart to enter. I raise questioning eyebrows at Sigehelm. He watches me with the hopeful expression of a child who's performed a task well but waits for another to voice the words to cement that hope.

'We expect any attack to come from the north. We rarely even open the gateway for our people. They've become used to using the other gates. It's a small extra precaution, and none mind the minor inconvenience.'

I can see that it also has an additional tower above the gate, from which the men on duty can attack any who try to breach it. It's much higher than the gate to the south or the west. It must allow those on watch duty to see even great distances on a clear day and to gain precious extra moments when the enemy is sighted.

'It's a clever idea,' I concede, his cheerful face glowing with pride. 'Better to be safe.'

'Indeed, my lady. When the border is pushed further north, we intend to extend the gate to the same size as the others, but for now, it's an extra level of protection for the men and women of Derby.'

'Let's hope that more burhs are built further north then and soon. I know my mother and my uncle, King Edward of Wessex, are keen for such an eventuality. This year we build at Nottingham and Headington to the east. Perhaps next year it'll be elsewhere.'

'Once Lord Rǫgnvaldr has been defeated?' he asks breathlessly, and I glance at him sharply.

'Has Lord Rǫgnvaldr made any forays so far south?' I quiz him abruptly, but he's already shaking his head.

'No, my lady, I'd just assumed that this inspection was the beginning of an attack upon him, a desire to ensure that should the need arise, there were strongholds for warriors to launch strikes from. Apologies if I was wrong.' He almost falls over his tongue with the speed of his apology.

My heart sinks at those words. I don't wish to send the men of Mercia to war against Lord Rǫgnvaldr, but it seems that they're keen to go. It might be that my endeavours to issue cautions and raise the possibility of war could soon become the command to make war on our enemy, and no one will be disappointed. Rather, they'll be disappointed if peace reigns supreme. I shake my head and swallow back my sorrow. The time for peace is many years in the future, but I had hoped, as my mother always did, that I'd be the one to bring it about.

It seems I was wrong.

CHAPTER 8

The rest of the inspection of the earthworks proceeds with no problems, and then it's the turn of the warriors to be scrutinised.

A jovial atmosphere has infected those showing off their accomplishments and those inspecting them, but as we return inside the ramparts, the gate being smartly guarded by a small force of five men all in full battle gear, the mood turns a little more pensive.

These men have chosen to live in Derby and to be the permanent members of its defence against any attackers. They're a mixture of Mercians and descendants of the Viking raiders who came arrived fifty years ago and decided to remain when my grandfather and King Guthrum made peace. The settlement of Derby has long been a split community, half Mercian and half Danish, but even those Danish who live here have recently been reconciled to it being ruled by the Lady of Mercians. I can only hope that they're as happy to be ruled by me.

I feel as though they've proved themselves, and now I must return the favour. A bare three months ago, my mother was bolstering these people, ensuring they were firm in their resolve while fighting for Nottingham's freedom as well. Reclaiming the Mercian lands from total Viking raider domination is an intensely personal matter. Towns are won and lost on the roll of a die and on the sort of mood the men and women of the town and my mother brought with them to the bargaining table.

I know I need to make a speech; regale them with their strengths and accomplishments, and yet my words must also be tinged with caution. They've achieved much, but there's still plenty to do. They can't think of themselves as indestructible because that way lies disaster.

Still astride my horse, I look around at Derby, my eyes meeting those of Ealdorman Æthelfrith's. He nods sagely at me. He knows how important my words will be to these men and the few women who've also come to listen. My physical appearance, as a warrior woman, will have won me the respect of those with Viking raider blood in their veins, but now my words must assure them that I can produce the promise in which my garb cloaks me.

I breathe deeply, taking the time to slow my frantic heartbeat as I slide from my horse.

I am my mother's daughter. I must remember that in all my actions. She was a fair woman but harsh when she needed to be, and she was also a warrior, even if she was never allowed to fight in a battle.

'Good people of Derby,' I finally call, my voice not overly loud as my horse is led away to the drinking trough by a small boy who gives me a cheeky grin as he offers my horse an apple for her good behaviour. I watch him walk away with the confidence of childhood. This little boy, at least, believes in me as he shows no trace of fear at having so many armed men and women surround him.

'Good people of Derby,' I start again. 'I've examined your defences and declare myself well pleased with them. You must congratulate yourselves on accomplishing so much in such a short space of time.' The small crowd is silent, watching me intently. I find I want to make the harsh faces of the crowd more amenable to me, but I also know that not everyone can live their lives with humour as a constant companion. For a moment, I flail, the tracks of my thoughts disappearing when my words elicit no cheering or self-congratulations. Perhaps the people of Derby are more worried than I thought.

'The burhs have, for decades, allowed the king of Wessex and the lord and lady of Mercia to counter the threat from our Viking raider neighbours. And then to push back the boundaries of Wessex and Mercia, in order to reclaim the lands that once were ruled by the kings of Wessex and the kings of Mercia.' It's always difficult when addressing such a mixed heritage to remember not to insult the Viking ancestors of some of these people. For all that my grandfather, uncle and mother devoted their lives to regaining control of their ancient kingdoms, equally, there are men and women here who've spent just as long trying to ensure that doesn't happen. Many of the Danish will be the proud descendants of the army from fifty years ago, and for all that they may have chosen to ally with my mother in recent years, their pride in the accomplishments of their fathers and grandfathers will never leave them. And neither should it.

We're all warriors here, even if we once fought on opposite sides of the same great divide.

'The burh of Derby is almost the newest one of them all, apart from your neighbours in Nottingham. I'm now sure of its ability to protect all of its inhabitants from any attacks that might yet come.'

'From York?' I hear ripple through the crowd, and although I'd almost hoped not to mention my worries, I find myself nodding along with them.

'Yes, from York and Dublin and even from the homelands of your forebears.' Now I find I can't keep the smile from my face as I remember words my mother often spoke.

'It would be much easier if the Norse amongst us could prevail upon their extended families not to attack England anymore, but I understand that it would be simpler to raise Christ from his slumbers.' My words finally draw small smiles and smirks from those assembled before me, and Ealdorman Æthelfrith chuckles loudly. He and my mother often discussed matters in such a way. Those who live in

England might still count themselves as Viking raiders, but those from Denmark, Norway and Sweden would call them English. It is a matter of name-calling, little else.

'Now that you can defend yourselves from wherever the enemy might come from, I would ask for your vigilance; your attention to even the smallest unease you might feel and know this, your watchfulness will be rewarded. Should an attack come, the Mercian fyrd will march to support you. Mercia will continue to grow outward; to reach the boundaries it filled during the years of kings Penda, Æthelbald and Offa's rule when Mercia was at the heights of its power.'

These words, so often said in the quiet of a council meeting, take on such great intensity when I speak them to these men and women, the crowd swelling with each passing moment, that I feel emotion clog my voice. I stop, horrified. I'm a woman, but I must not cry before these men and women or my assembled entourage. A thunderous roar of approval luckily saves my embarrassment from the largest man I've ever seen. His beard overflows a gigantic chin and reaches almost to his waist, where he's tucked it inside his weapon's belt. I don't know the man, and yet I feel I should.

'Mercia,' the giant bellows, his voice echoing around the enclosed space created now that the outer gates have been pulled tightly closed to show me how quickly such a task can be accomplished. Immediately other voices join his own, and I find myself, a stray tear trickling down my face, surrounded by people who evidently share my view of the future.

Unbidden, I find the man before me, and on his knee, head bowed.

As the crowd continues to swell, I hear a much softer voice.

'My lady,' the large man calls. 'I'd pledge myself to you, as your oath-sworn warrior, to protect you in these perilous times and to ensure that none personally attack you.'

I didn't come here to add more men to my entourage, but neither can I ignore this show of utter loyalty, even if it serves to highlight that I might be a woman in need of a champion.

'And I'd be honoured to take your pledge and have you ride with me as I visit my burhs and keep my kingdom safe.'

The gruff giant is pleased with my response, and he begins to speak the words that my ealdormen said to me only a few weeks ago when my mother died. He speaks them clearly, and a reverential silence fills the gateway once more as the man gives voice to the well-known words of a personal oath. I hope that the image of this man giving me his pledge will inspire even more loyalty in the people of Derby.

'I pledge to be loyal and true to Lady Ælfwynn, and love all that she loves, and hate all that she hates, in accordance with God's rights and my noble obligations; and never, willingly and intentionally, in word or deed, do anything hateful to her; on condition that she keeps me as was our agreement when I subjected myself to him and chose her service.'

When the man stands, as I said, he's a giant, he looms over me, and I feel small and almost insignificant. I hope that the picture we present together isn't a vision of the future. I'll not be overshadowed by the men in my life. Mercia is mine to rule, and although I know I can't accomplish it alone, my mother never did, I still hope to be a strong ruler, one to be feared and revered in equal measure. The crowd cheers once this show of loyalty has been concluded, and I can feel the pride bursting through the man's massive chest that he's accomplished his task.

'My lady,' Sigehelm speaks quietly at my ear, and although I'd expected to have to say much more, it seems that the giant's show of loyalty was worth more than a thousand words. 'We have a meal prepared for you.' At the words, I realise how thirsty and hungry I am, almost as dry as my horse, who still drinks from the water trough as the young boy hops from side to side, trying to watch and hear everything that's happening within Derby.

'Lead on,' I indicate with my hand as my men and women, including my new oath-sworn warrior, rush to follow me, staying close to my side. It seems that some within my entourage fear even the warriors of Derby, who are our allies and our countrymen, now that they're armed and ready for combat. It appears I have an almost insurmountable task to accomplish in ensuring that Mercia remains physically united in the minds of the men and women of Mercia, as well as our enemies.

CHAPTER 9

I'm feasted well within Derby and when I leave the following day, having spent the night in the reeve's hall, positioned close to the gently flowing river, I feel relief and apprehension.

Derby is a finished burh. For all its newness, it's still complete. The task I've given myself next, to visit Nottingham, may not go as well. Nottingham has only been reconciled to Mercia for a handful of months.

I've had a small detachment of men on continuous duty there throughout the summer. Officially they're to aid in the construction of the burghal walls, but unofficially their task is to ensure there are no second thoughts, no desire to return to being a member of the Five Boroughs only and not a part of a wider Mercia.

The people of Nottingham must watch what happens in Derby with interest, deciding whether they wish to follow suit or change their minds and return to being ruled by themselves. Hopefully, Derby stands as a good example of the benefits of being part of Mercia. Certainly, I've had no reports of any burning problems, but then, a Norse Viking raider hasn't been on the loose with twenty shiploads of warriors for some time now. That sort of temptation might prove harder to ignore for the former warriors amongst the inhabitants.

We ride along the banks of the river from Derby to Nottingham. Nottingham is on the banks of the Trent, Derby on the Derwent, but the two great rivers of Mercia join, not far from Derby and to many, it might appear to be the same river. I imagine that those who know the difference are the people of the waterways – no doubt most of them more than half Viking by birth, with parents and grandparents who might once have slipped into Mercia along these self-same waterways.

My new oath-sworn man, I've finally determined that his name is Osgod, travels at the front of the train of people and horses. He's attempting to insinuate himself into the ranks of my chosen warriors. I don't know if they'll have him because they've not seen him fight and have only the man's own words to attest to his battle deeds. Still, some of them seem content enough to share stories, and their laughter often reaches me as I ride with Ealdorman Æthelfrith and his two sons for company. One of the youths shares my cousin's name, Athelstan, and every time his brother speaks it, I look up expecting to see my cousin. I've done it so often that my neck is sore from the constant swivelling.

For all that, I find myself enjoying the company of the two and joining in their conversation about Derby, horses and swords. Athelstan is pleased to include me in the conversation, even when it turns into a long debate on fighting technique and the advantages of a seax over a long sword. But his brother doesn't seem to want my input, and in the end, I tire of his constant comments that purposefully counter mine and take my horse forward so that I ride between the main body of my warriors with the ealdorman and his sons behind me.

My thoughts turn to the future. Cousin Athelstan hasn't sent word of how his journey progresses, but then, we only parted company yesterday. I must hope that everything is going according to plan. I've yet to hear anything from my uncle, King Edward, and for the time being, I think that's probably good news. I expect to meet his three hundred warriors in Nottingham or close to Nottingham, but I imagine they'll be doing little more than pretending to guard the burh in the heat of late summer.

So far, there's no intelligence that Lord Rǫgnvaldr has been to York, let alone attempted to travel further south. Although the thoughts of those twenty ships plague me as I gaze at the open expanse of the river, I try to consider only the implication that he'll ride overland to take Mercia if he decides to come at all. But the rivers are a problem. The mighty River Trent flows almost all the way through Mercia from near to the Humber estuary. And that estuary is too close to York for my liking.

I find the situation unpleasant. The not knowing is constantly forcing me to reassess my actions if an individual event unfolds. If there's trouble to the north, do King Edward's warriors have instructions to assist my warriors, or has my uncle not even considered the eventuality? If Lord Rǫgnvaldr has other allies, might they attack the west? And if they do, how quickly will I know about it, and how swiftly will my warriors ride to support cousin Athelstan? Or should I leave them where they are? Perhaps a two-pronged attack might be coming, in which case I'd need warriors all along the Mercian border. Have King Constantin, Lord Ealdred, and Lord Rǫgnvaldr made an alliance? And what about York? Will the archbishop side with the Viking raider warrior, or will he determine to hold the settlement aloft from the fighting?

Would York attack Mercia? Would the Danelaw rise against Saxon Mercia?

Not all of these questions are new. They've plagued me for many years, and only my mother's calming voice could ever disperse the worry and the fear once I understood the true nature of Mercia's predicament. She knew that much was uncertain and likely to change on the whim of a warrior or a king. She believed in being constantly alert and taking little for granted. She didn't believe that peace and unity were ever a foregone conclusion. I confess that I've always preferred the belief that we acted to fulfil my grandfather's vision of a united 'England' but sometimes, as of now, I think that hope is very far from being accomplished.

I'm not left alone with my thoughts for long, though, before the ealdorman's son rides to accompany me.

'Sorry, my brother likes the sound of his voice above almost everyone else's.' The words are tinged with humour and warmth – a brother very aware of but tolerant of another's foibles. It reminds me of the sort of conversation that cousin Athelstan and I have with each other.

'And you prefer the sound of your own, I assume?' I speak with humour in my voice, but not enough because, for a long moment, the young man looks at me as though unsure of my response. His eyes swivel to meet his father's, seeking comfort. I wish I could take back the words, but then he grins, and his youth and intelligence are evident to see.

'No, I prefer the sound of yours, and he wouldn't let you speak because he was too busy disagreeing with you. He's welcome to continue the conversation with himself.' At that, he turns to look at his brother, who is still speaking, although no one's listening to him as he rides alone.

He grins again and turns back to me.

'The burh at Derby was in good condition. What do you think Nottingham will be like?' He speaks as though we talk about meals or jewels and not life and death.

'I hope it will be complete, or nearly so,' I offer my voice low. I don't know if I like offering my opinions to someone outside my usual close circle of allies and friends.

Does he ask only for curiosity or because he hopes to tell someone what I think? I've become so used to second-guessing my thoughts that even this seemingly simple question has me reaching for a response I'm comfortable with.

Again, uncertainty flashes across his hazel eyes and I wish I'd sounded more confident and less as though I was answering a question with another question.

When he leans toward me, I almost force my horse to ride away, but instead, he speaks softly, and I listen.

'I'm no man of politics. I'd just like to talk to you about anything.'

He covers his unconventional approach by pretending to reach down and tighten something on my horse's harness, and while he looks away, I think about his words. Could it be that he only wants to try and be my friend? If so, I think I could agree to that.

I have many acquaintances, and my cousin Athelstan and his sister and my female warriors are my friends, but other than that, much of my life has been spent in self-imposed isolation. My mother was the same, and I followed her example. When ruling, it can be too easy to mistake the self-interests of others for genuine friendship. But I genuinely can't see what Athelstan has to gain by speaking with me now. His father is an ealdorman. No doubt he'll be an ealdorman in time himself, although it won't be his birth that accords him the distinction, but rather his skills. He'll have the maximum amount of influence and power that a man born outside the tight circle of the House of Wessex can ever hope to hold within England.

'In that case,' I say, as he straightens, 'I think we should talk about what might happen now. I've been trying to devise a plan of action based on almost every possibility, but no doubt I'll have overlooked something. Tell me how you see events unfolding?'

His right eyebrow quirks at my words. Perhaps he only wanted to speak about seaxes and shields, horses and ships, but in that case, he should have talked to someone with fewer worries on their mind.

'As you will,' he bows once more and then turns to look at the river we ride beside.

'The rivers have always been Mercia's weakness. There's an assumption that a land-locked nation, such as Mercia, has nothing to fear from the water, but that's to overlook an evident and easy way into Mercia.'

'You think an attack would come along the rivers again?' I ask the question with interest, for once my worry banished. This isn't a discussion of war but possibilities and will centre on strategy, not actualities.

'I do. I think it would be the safest option and much easier to retreat from if everything went wrong for the attackers.'

I consider the idea. Mercia has trading vessels that routinely travel along the rivers. Even now, there are slow-moving ships and ever slower-moving people on the River Trent beside us. But Mercia doesn't have fighting ships centred at its core. We would be more likely to block a river with whatever vessel could be found, such as at Derby, than face an attack full on, ship to ship. Is this an oversight that should be corrected? There are ships near Mercia's coastal posses-sions to the west protecting the river there from attack from Ireland or further afield. Should they be brought to the Trent and the Derwent?

'Do you think Mercia should have shipmen then, as well as warriors, to stop attacks?'

Athelstan's eyes flash with surprise at my words, and I hastily replay his brief comments to me in my mind. Perhaps I've misunder-stood his intent.

'I've never considered it,' he offers with an apologetic shrug as he watches a trading vessel glide along the river. The horses are moving quicker than the ship today, but that's not always the case. 'Mercia might well benefit from shipmen. I was thinking more that Mercia needed to protect its waterways by having the ability to block them if an attack should come. London has its walls, but they happily sink anything into the River Thames if they fear an attack. Perhaps a small fleet of Mercian ships would be better here. Although, where would they be kept to be most effective?'

I consider that answer. Mercia is beset by rivers. The Trent, The Derwent, they're just two of many. The Mersey, The Severn, The Thames, and even The Calder, which runs closer to York and is almost not a Mercian river but could be a way for the Viking raiders to infiltrate Mercia.

None of this should be new thinking; I ponder with some annoy-ance. When the attack happened on Mercia fifty years ago, they used these rivers. In fact, they used any river they could traverse with their ships, and even then, the river's end didn't stop them. They'd fish their ships from the water and carry them to the next stretch of water or abandon them and steal horses. I think there must be a reason my mother didn't consider ships necessary to protect Mercia. I just wish I knew what that reason was.

'We'd need a fleet on each river, running patrols. But then, we could never have the coin to provision so many crafts. Unless of course, we stole them from Lord Rǫgnvaldr.'

I laugh at my outrageous suggestion before realising that Athelstan doesn't join me but rather looks at me with incredulity on his face. I feel a little self-conscious under his glare but meet his eyes all the same. Does he think my suggestion is a stupid one? Have I just said something that will haunt me for many years to come?

Only then his mouth opens in an 'O' of wonder, and he nods.

'That's not a bad idea, you know. If Lord Rǫgnvaldr comes for Mercia, we could attack his ships, kill his warriors, and keep the ships and use them as a future deterrent. It would make the bastard reconsider his plans.'

I feel relieved at his words, pleased I've not said something idiotic. As I begin to consider what I want to say next, enjoying our discussion as though it's a game and not a possibility, the arrival of a small selection of horsemen drives all thoughts from my mind. These men look serious and intent. I ride forward urgently, Athelstan accompanying me.

The leader of the five is speaking in a rush to my guard, and I curb my annoyance that he hasn't immediately sought me out. Already, I can see some of my guards making quick changes to their clothing and equipment, and my stomach sinks. This must be news of a battle.

'My lady,' the lead horseman finally notices me and acknowledges my presence. 'I ride with news of an attack on Nottingham. We don't know who leads it, but they must have been watching closely for some time, for they've chosen the very part of the burh that's yet to be finished. King Edward's men have taken up a defensive position, but we need your assistance to drive the attackers from Nottingham's walls, or the burh will never be finished.'

News of battle worries me, and yet I find myself not only calm but fingering the edges of my shield with an appetite I didn't think I possessed.

'Are they Lord Rǫgnvaldr's men?' I think to ask, but the messenger shakes his head.

'We don't know. We weren't close enough to determine who they are, and their shields are simply plain black. They don't indicate who leads the attack.'

I look to my warriors, male and female. They're all waiting expectantly, my new oath-sworn warrior amongst them, the huge man licking his lips with a desire to be instructed to battle.

'We ride with all haste to Nottingham.' But I pause before I continue, a new thought running through my mind. We need to do more than just defend Nottingham.

'Do they attack to the north or east? Can we ride around Nottingham and cut off their retreat?'

'The northern gate, my lady,' the man answers quickly, a nod to his head as he does so, confirming what I thought.

'Did they see you leave?' I think to ask.

'No, we came through the southern gate.'

'Good, then we ride for the north of Nottingham. We'll encircle them and stop any retreat. Warriors,' and I look to the five who've ridden with the news. 'Return to Nottingham the same way you came, provided it's safe to do so, and even then, perhaps take a few risks. Tell Nottingham that reinforcements are coming. Tell them to expect to be relieved from behind the enemy.' The five warriors all nod encouragingly as I speak, and I realise that this could have been my first command that sends men to their deaths. But I swallow my fear, distracting myself with ensuring I have my weapons where I need them and that my byrnie, worn only ceremonially until now, is ready to face the cut and thrust of battle.'

'My lady,' it's Ealdorman Æthelfrith's voice that cuts through the hasty preparations, and I know what he's about to say even before he says it, or at least I think I do.

'You'll direct us from the rear,' he offers, his tone bland as he speaks. I look at him in surprise. I'd expected him to tell me that my place was to be as far from the battle as possible.

'I will?' I ask, the question hovering on my lips, even though I meant it to sound like confirmation.

'Yes, my lady. I'll command the men with the aid of my son. Athelstan will assist you with your women warriors and pass on your instructions. If the need arises, I'm sure you'll know when to intervene.'

For a moment, I pause, unsure how to proceed. It almost sounds like the ealdorman is ordering me, even though I'm his commander. Quickly my mind replays previous clashes I've witnessed with my mother, and I understand that Ealdorman Æthelfrith has usually behaved in such a way.

'Very good. We'll ride swiftly to stop the attack, and in the process, we'll demonstrate to Nottingham what it means to be a part of Mercia.' As I finish speaking, I grab my sword from across my back and hold it in the air, testing its weight as I hear the whistling slash of it through the air, a statement of my intent. My women cheer me, and so do the men. I urge my horse to battle. It's a warm day, and a gentle ride through the countryside would be welcome, but where the integrity of a kingdom is concerned, it seems it doesn't matter if the sun shines, if it rains or if snow lies along the ground. Foolish men will still try and steal what isn't there.

For the first time as Lady of the Mercians, I ride to battle, and any fear I might have has disappeared, a fleeting shadow discarded by the swiftness of my ride along the level ground.

CHAPTER 10

I fancy I hear the sound of the battle long before Nottingham is glimpsed in the far distance. It's a still day, and the noise of a struggle reaches my ears quickly over the flat landscape. There are the faint shouts of warriors battling and the snatched sounds of metal on wood.

Ealdorman Æthelfrith, his son Eadric, and the rest of the male warriors have rushed ahead, driving their horses at greater and greater speed, fearing the worst. Not that I tarry, but I know they wish to get there first. If I hang back a little, I hope they'll forget their responsibilities to protect me, and will focus instead on ensuring that Nottingham rebuffs the attack. Only then might I have the opportunity to join the affray.

As such, when I arrive to the north of Nottingham, I'm greeted with a skirmish that already seems to be well under control. At my side, the ealdorman's son, Lord Athelstan, squints into the bright sunshine, hand shielding his eyes as he mutters sourly under his breath.

Neither of us is happy at being forced to stay behind. I might nominally be in command of my army of warriors, but I believe any fighting will be accomplished without my help. Ealdorman Æthelfrith is a survivor of so many battles that I imagine he no longer keeps a tally of the times he's fought for Mercia or the number of kills he can claim.

'The two forces have clashed,' Athelstan offers, more loudly this time, his words intended for my ears and those of my six female warriors, and not those who escort him.

I'm squinting toward the unwelcome sounds but can see little in the harsh summer glare.

'Do they prevail?' I query, my voice rough with excitement. Ideally, I'd be among them all, as would my women warriors, who, like me, grip their weapons, faces taut at being kept so far away from the actual attack.

'I can't tell, but I think so. I can see my father, my brother, and that huge man from yesterday. Their swords are constantly moving. But I can't see the gateway clearly, so I don't know if the attackers are inside or out.' I can see the fortifications around Nottingham, and the haze of smoking cookfires from the houses inside rises as a strange grey cloud into the otherwise cloudless summer sky. But greater details are beyond me.

My horse, clearly annoyed at being forced to work so hard to get me here so quickly, is fractious beneath my hands. She would rather still be galloping or drinking at a water trough, not waiting here like I am. I yank on the reins, my pent-up frustration evident in the move-ment as I try and force her to behave while sidling slowly forward to gain a better view of events that I can't see.

'My lady,' Athelstan turns to look at me for a brief moment under-standing my intent far too quickly. 'We should stay here, not go any further forward. They might make a break for it, and we need as much warning as possible to prepare if they try to retreat.'

His words make sense, but they frustrate me all the same. My sword is in my hand, without volition, and I'm keen to play a physical part in the battle. My women, too, are avidly tracking the action, eager to put their days and days of practice to good use.

'I can hardly command from here. I can barely see anything.' My eyes are streaming with tears from the sun's glare, and I think Athelstan takes a little pity on me, for he nods and shuffles his horse forward.

'I'm sure another ten horses' lengths forward will be acceptable,' he half utters, more convincing himself than anyone else. 'I'm sure my father would approve of you seeing as much as you can.'

And so we slink forward, our horses still beneath us, although Ealdorman Æthelfrith and the rest of the force have discarded their horses. Five nervous-looking squires are now watching those horses at an even greater distance than ours from the fighting. They shelter in the corner of a field of half-harvested crops, valiantly trying to prevent the horses from cropping away at any stray piece of greenery that takes their fancy. I spare them a thought, ensuring their position is safe. I don't know the area well, but it looks like the ealdorman chose a good place to discard his horses.

From my vantage point, I can just about make out the gateway to Nottingham in the distance. It nears completion, but the wooden gate remains unhung, and so, although men fight from the raised wooden platform above it, there's nothing but a thin line of men to prevent the Viking raiders from getting inside Nottingham. Not that the enemy seems to be having much success. Not now they face an attack from their rear and their front.

I count over a hundred attackers against a force of no more than fifty warriors from Nottingham and the fifty warriors that Ealdorman Æthelfrith has under his command. I consider briefly where King Edward's warriors are but quickly conclude that some of them must be fighting with the people of Nottingham. I can just make out the colours of Wessex on the shields the defenders carry.

This isn't my first sight of the battle. Far from it, in fact, but this is the first time that it could be up to me to issue commands to attack or kill. If there are prisoners taken, will I order their death or allow them to live? These thoughts tumble through my mind as I try to determine which side is about to win the battle.

Only then, the scream of a horse pierces my thoughts, and I turn in horror to see that enemy warriors are emerging behind me, attacking the five young men and the many horses of Ealdorman Æthelfrith's warriors. In dismay, I watch one of the boys encouraging the animals he guards to scatter with a firm whack on their behind, only for a hulking enemy warrior to rush in his direction. The enemy warrior is armed. His seax is raised in his right hand, his shield in his left. The youth has no weapon drawn and is a fraction of the man's height, weight and girth. The man's eyes glitter with the joy of what he thinks will be an easy kill.

'Athelstan,' I cry in alarm, but he and my female warriors are already alert to the danger. The twelve of us hurry to protect our own.

My horse rushes me toward the fifteen or so warriors emerging from whatever hiding place they've found. I slide to the ground, feet firmly planted, shield and sword in hand, ready to face an attack when I'm close enough. My mount has skillfully woven her way through the panicking horses trying to go the other way, but I release her just as quickly and send her to follow them. I don't want her wounded unnecessarily.

The young lad I first saw under attack is lying on the floor, his hands upstretched as he tries to protect himself from a savage assault. His screams of terror have me rushing to his aid as quickly as my legs will carry me. I barely notice my horse rushing to encourage the other horses to flee the smell of spilt blood and the cries of terror from my squires mingling with those of the enemy's rage.

I know Athelstan and my female warriors follow my lead, and so I'm confident, as I slash my sword downwards and across the hulking giant's back, that they'll aid me should the man prove too much for me. I want to rescue the boy, but I fear I'm too late. Finally, I feel the satisfying thud of impact as my sword strikes the man so keen to attack an unarmed youth.

The warrior turns to look at me, a leer on his unhelmeted face, a sneer of derision as he realises I'm a woman. I remove his sneer with a sword slash across his exposed hairy chin. Quickly, I reverse my attack so that the sword's hilt smashes into the man's nose.

He crumbles to the floor, to the boy's side, allowing me to continue my attack on his back. I find a weakness in his byrnie to plunge my sword through his back, my battle rage making the action much easier than it should be. As I yank my sword clear again, blood shuddering from its shimmering blade, I feel eyes on me. The startled eyes of the young boy meet mine, blood dripping from his outstretched hands onto his white face.

'Are you well?' I manage to gasp quickly. He nods as I offer him my hand and yank him to his feet. Around me, my women fight the remaining attackers, but we're outnumbered.

I turn to the boy.

'What's your name?' I'm aware I should probably know. At the same time, I scan his hands to determine the severity of the injuries. Blood oozes from deep cuts to the inside of his hands, put there by the sword of the hairy warrior.

'Eadig,' he pants, his eyes about to drop to his hands.

'Tear a scrap of cloth from your tunic and wrap it around your hands. Then run to the Ealdorman Æthelfrith. Or take one of the horses if you can catch one. Tell him that we're under attack.'

He nods, his face turning even white. I fear he'll tumble to the ground in shock. Only at that moment, I feel the thud of steps behind me and turn, my shield raised and my sword ready to face another enemy. This explains Eadig's fear.

This man is far younger, leaner and smaller than the one who lies gurgling his last breaths near my feet. I imagine he'll fight more like I do, taking advantage of greater manoeuvrability instead of increased weight.

He carries his shield, but rather than a sword, my foeman, has an axe. I watch as he lightly tosses it into the air and catches it again without cutting himself with the sharp blade.

He thinks himself a skilled warrior. I'll show him the truth about his thoughts.

'Let's see if you fight as well as the shieldmaidens of my homeland,' he taunts in the Saxon tongue, but I ignore his words. I've trained with shieldmaidens. I know their skills are legendary.

I position myself before the man, hoping that Eadig has managed to do my bidding. Around me, the rest of my warriors and Athelstan are engaged in a fierce fight for their lives. We're unevenly matched. I hazard a guess that there are at least two men to every one of my warriors. They're not odds I feel uncomfortable with, but until reinforcements arrive, we'll have to hold against the attack.

My opponent darts forward as I raise my arm. Although his axe impacts my shield, it does little damage, shearing off on one of the smaller metal bosses with a harsh shriek. He steps back to try again, but I follow his movements. I attack into the confined space between us. My sword's ready to strike as I track his eyes following my sword hand. His preoccupation allows me to use my shield instead.

Once more, it's the heavy edges of my shield that cause the most damage, crunching into the lower part of his face. It knocks his exposed chin, and it's the shock of that pain more than anything that allows me to use my sword to slice across his chest. Then I turn the blade to embed it in his byrnie. He sinks to his knees at the bite of my sword, a surprised expression on his face.

I've been taught that thinking in battle is more important than instinct. Instinct is vital, but it's easy to outthink a man who only acts instinctively.

He dies before me, joining the larger man at my feet. I blink in surprise, amazed to find that I've killed two men in such a short space of time. Only the battle is far from over, and as of yet, Ealdorman Æthelfrith hasn't come to shore up my defence or assist my attack. I'm not sure what this skirmish should be called.

I pause for a moment and catch my breath with my hands on my knees. I swallow down bile. I've never killed before. But I'm not left alone for long, and even though I want to know how my warriors fare, I'm soon facing an attack from two men.

These two are opposites, one short and fat, the other tall and lanky. The pair watches me with crazed eyes as though I'm a beast to be caught and slaughtered for an evening meal.

My sword is tipped in red, and its handle is smeared in yet more blood. I wear gloves to keep my grip firm. My shield reveals the scars of the battle. A piece of what might well be a tooth sticks into its rim, and magenta covers the shield boss, while some scratches have gauged the colour from it.

I heft my shield, pleased that its weight hasn't been compromised and that my arm feels robust enough to hold it. The fury of battle pounds through my chest.

Both men stand in front of me. Not the cleverest of approaches. They'd have done better to split their strategy, one from the front and one from the back. Or even one from either side. Instead, they've already compromised their chances of success. It'll be easier to fight two men who stand in front of me. I can use my shield on one and my sword on the other.

I hear the grunts and strains of battle to either side of me, the shouts of men and women fighting for their lives. But I don't have time to glimpse how the battle is progressing before the smaller man steps before me. His eyes glint behind huge bushy eyebrows, his head unprotected. His long hair flows in a messy tangle to either side of his balding head. But in his hand, he carries both a seax and a war axe. He does not need a shield. Uncharitably, I think his enormous girth will protect his body from any frontal attack. It would take more strength than I have to pierce so much excess weight.

His comrade cheers him on, his toothless mouth gaping open.

'A Saxon woman! Kill her, and do it quickly.'

I'm surprised by that. I thought the Viking raiders respected their female warriors, but perhaps not all men can see the advantage and skill of shieldmaidens.

Annoyed, rather than amazed, by the warrior's skills as he swirls both weapons in his open hands simultaneously and aware of frantic cries coming from behind me, I attempt a similar attack. I step smartly into the space he needs to swing his weapons, hoping to crowd him out. Only he seems to expect the manoeuver, and despite his massive bulk, he manages to swerve out of my way before I can even complete the arc of my sword. Instead of meeting the small man, I face his ally, his tongue sticking through the gap where his teeth should be, a grin of delight on his face. Did the men plan this, or are they so used to fighting as a team that this is commonplace?

The taller man, totally bald and without headgear, carries a shield and a giant sword. He also has a shoddy-looking byrnie covering his chest that's littered with cuts and old dried blood. I see his tattered belt that holds even more weapons. He might be a decent opponent as opposed to his comrade.

Raising my shield, I accept the challenge in his eyes but wait for him to decide to attack. I'm aware that the other man now watches, threatening to take no advantage of the fact that I'm outnumbered. That worries me. Does he believe the larger warrior is more capable than me?

As I worry at the grip on my sword, the tall warrior chuckles with delight and dashes in to try and slice open the front of my byrnie. My shield's raised and ready, but the force of the blow forces it tight to my chest, crushing my arm between the shield and my body. It's uncomfortable and makes it impossible for me to move with the sort of freedom I need to be successful. The warrior's sword scrapes down the left side of my body, its edge trailing through my byrnie so that it reaches my skin but doesn't draw blood. Still, the bruise will be bad enough without the threat of itching from a healing wound.

As he steps back to consider another blow, I free my shield. Thrusting it against his face, where his tongue still pokes through his toothless mouth, it makes a decent impact. He howls with hurt and surprise as blood trickles down his bearded chin.

An uglier Viking raider would be difficult to find, but then, warriors aren't known for their beauty, only their battle scars.

Seeing his comrade in pain, the short man makes a movement to come toward me. But my plight isn't mine anymore. Lord Athelstan distracts him with a sharp slice down his back from his sword and engaged him. I vow to finish the tall warrior as soon as possible.

He's still growling as I swing my sword wide, looking to attack where he's most often exposed by his shield. No one can carry a shield evenly in front of their body, especially not such a large man with only a standard-sized shield. He'd have done better to equip himself with a much bigger shield.

He mirrors my movements. As he does so, I see the opportunity I need. The next time I swing to his right, his right side is left unprotected. Quickly, I reverse my action and use my sword to slice his byrnie once more. As I do so, I manage to cut through the thick leather of his weapons belt. It's that he feels first as it begins to slide to the ground. He reaches to grab it, his shield tangling in the leather strap, and I score my shield down the right side of his body.

His byrnie stretches with the movement. With a cry of fury ripped from my throat, I sever the bulging padding of his byrnie. He rushes to counter my move with his sword, but I've seen the telltale sign of blood and know that my strike's a good one. He fights on, swinging his sword in anger, his weapons belts forgotten about on the ground. I use my shield to counter his attack.

His weapon clatters against my shield, and initially, the force is phenomenal. But his next strike is already weakening. I know he'll soon falter. When that happens, I lower my shield as he sinks to his knees. Blood soaks his dirty byrnie, shining thickly black in the bright sunlight. I can already hear the buzz of a fly hovering close to him, ready to feed on his death.

My opponent's eyes are almost rolled back into his head. I don't need to meet his gaze as I plunge my sword through his thin neck. It's not a pretty move, but it does the job quickly. Yanking my sword clear of his neck, with a red sweep of gore, he tumbles forward, spread out on the dry ground where his lifeblood flows into the cracks of high summer heat.

But I don't have time to celebrate, not yet. Lord Athelstan still fights the fat little man. It should be an easy fight, but it seems Lord Athelstan carries an injury to his left leg. A thin scratch of blood snakes from his thigh. I know a moment of fear. He could be mortally wounded. The fat little man somehow manages to skip around him, his great weight, which I thought would be his downfall, hardly hampering him at all, as he roars in fury at his comrade's death.

I rush toward Lord Athelstan, suppressing a shriek of fear when his left leg slides out beneath him on the slippery surface, causing him to fall to his knee. Only his shield stands between him and his attacker.

Time slows even though I rush forwards. I wince to see the axe and sword of Athelstan's enemy snaking out toward his head. He can't see the movement because his eyes remain on his shield in front of his body as he tries to angle his sword to make it useful.

Lord Athelstan won't manage it in time. I fear that I won't either.

That doesn't stop me as I spur myself to even greater haste, my eyes watching the rotund little man as I decide how best to attack.

Lord Athelstan has fallen side on to me, which means his enemy is also side on to me. I can aim for his back, his head or his legs. As he looms over Athelstan, I must decide which is the best place to attack. He's a round man, and I think any attack on his back would be worthless. There's no way that my sword would penetrate his byrnie and his excess weight.

It's his legs that are the most exposed. He wears leather trousers and boots, but other than that, there's no protection on his lower body. I could hamstring him and distract him from his easy target. But it might not work. He, like the man I've just killed, could carry on attacking as such an injury takes time to register.

No, I change my mind. I need to aim for his neck and slice it almost from his head. Only then will I know that LordAthelstan will be safe. I orientate myself so that I can angle my blade and have it in the correct position for when I arrive. I school myself, hoping against hope that I won't be too late.

My screech of rage as I swing my weapon is so loud, I suddenly find both Athelstan and his enemy watching me, their individual attacks arrested in the face of my countermoves. But it's too late for either to change their course of action. The enemy has his axe to the left of Athelstan's shield, and Athelstan is cowed beneath it.

No matter what, I think the axe will bite into Athelstan's shoulder. But neither can the warrior stop my blade as it swings before me. I pull my arms in, holding them tighter to my shoulders than normal. The blade slices across the man's throat with an arc of magenta fluid. The sword's weight carries it just deep enough. Although Lord Athelstan crumbles beneath the swipe of the axe, I know that its speed and force have been tempered by the death of the man that holds it.

Once more, I watch a man die and this time, I find myself impassive to the whole thing.

I finally hear the yells of others rushing to our assistance, and I look to Athelstan to see him bleeding profusely from a shoulder wound while his leg bleeds continuously. A glance to the left and right tells me that the enemy is all either dead or captured. I sink to the grassy floor, ripping the bottom of my tunic free as I do so and forcing it against Athelstan's shoulder wound, which leaks grotesquely.

He watches me with weary eyes, thanks on his lips, but I shake my head.

The exertion of the battle has finally caught up with me, and slowly I allow my head to sink between my knees as I think of nothing else but breathing in and out.

CHAPTER 11

I t's with the feel of a hand on my shoulder that I finally come to my senses. I don't know how much time has passed. Bleary-eyed, I look around. The battle site is flooded with my warriors who fought with Ealdorman Æthelfrith. Eadric is talking to his brother, who seems to be well, although his face is bleached of all colour, and he keeps glancing anxiously at me.

I swivel my head, taking in the view of the ealdorman giving instructions, and I squint at those who walk or stagger, trying to determine who still lives.

Ealdorman Æthelfrith must feel the weight of my gaze as quickly he's beside me, offering me his hand to stand and also his water bottle. I take both gratefully, and when I'm standing, I swish warm water into my mouth. It feels good to do something as simple as swallow and ease my thirst.

I hand him back the bottle and wipe my mouth with the back of my hand, freed from my gloves. They're blood-stained. I wrinkle my nose as I look at them. I doubt I'll be wearing them again.

'My lady,' the ealdorman bows low, his brow creased. I notice that he also wears a faint miasma of blood on his clothing. 'The fighting is finished. There's only one survivor, and he's under guard in Nottingham. None of the men who were to be reinforcements has survived. You and your warriors have seen to that.' He sounds both pleased and censorious simultaneously. We both notice that he just says warriors without mentioning that many of us were women, apart from his son.

'How many were there?' I ask, taking stock of who I am and what I've accomplished. I'm also trying to check that I've suffered no injuries of my own.

'About a hundred attacked Nottingham, and there were near enough twenty left here.'

'Twenty against my twelve,' I nod with pride.

'Yes, you were outnumbered but won the day. Their men are all dead. You have some wounded, a few serious ones, but nothing that seems to be life-threatening.'

I nod to hear that.

'And Lord Athelstan?' I ask, indicating his son with my gaze.

Ealdorman Æthelfrith winces at being reminded of his son's injury.

'He'll be fine, I think. But we need to get him to Nottingham and have someone look at his leg and arm.'

'Then go. Take him, and I'll finish up here.'

'If you're sure?' he says, a moment of hesitation in his reply, but his worry for his son overrides everything. Quickly he's calling for a horse to carry Athelstan and himself. I wish I felt quite as robust as I've just implied, but I understand the need for Ealdorman Æthelfrith to care for his son. Even I feel a twinge of sorrow and remorse as I watch the younger man being carefully lifted onto the horse.

I try to catch his eye, but Athelstan's face is scrunched in pain, and instead, I turn to survey the battle site. It's the men I killed that I look at first, a brief moment of remorse for their deaths. My attention is then drawn to where my warriors work together to pile the bodies together, strip them of their valuables and place them in a hastily dug grave. The five lads who'd been left to guard the horses are all trying to rein in their beasts. Even the lad I saw being injured is limping along with a huge dirty bandage around his face, circling his chin and his forehead but grinning all the same.

He has a few horses gyrating around him, and others are meandering their way back to him. He's reaching for their reins but keeps missing them with his hand. I think he must have hit his head, and so I rush to him, grabbing reins as I go. I hand them to him, and he offers me another grin.

'Thank you,' he says, far too loudly, startling the horses again. I want nothing more than to ruffle his hair, but I don't want to make his injury any worse.

'Calm down,' I mutter to him, and he nods and then sits abruptly, his legs sliding from beneath him. Many inquisitive horses suddenly surround the pair of us, and the smell of sweating animals is overpowering on a hot day. Not that it makes a jot of difference to the squire. His eyes are closed, and his body limp, the reins of the horses tangling together.

I bend down to shake his shoulder, relieved when his eyes open, and he squints at me. Now it's my turn to stoop and help him to his feet. As I do so, I wiggle my way free of the horses and look around for someone to help us. I can't manage all the animals and the boy at the same time.

I don't have long to wait. One of my warriors, Leofgyth, sees my predicament and calls another to assist her in regathering all the reins. I try to help the lad into one of the saddles. He needs to get inside Nottingham and be seen by the same healer as Lord Athelstan.

Ealdorman Æthelfrith didn't return with all of his warriors from the battle against the Viking raiders near to the half-built wall, but there's enough to help me. Two of the bigger men assist me in boosting the boy into the saddle. I consider taking him myself, but in the end, I delegate the responsibility to one of my warriors. Coelflaed has a weeping gash across the side of her face that needs treatment.

'Take him inside Nottingham,' I order her. 'Find a healer for you and him.'

'My lady,' she argues, her words rough and edged with pain. 'My place is here, with you.'

'Your place,' I counter, 'is where I tell you it is. Now, go.'

I slap both horses on their rumps before the argument can

continue. One or other of them will need to pay attention and direct the horses, or they'll both end up halfway to York. I watch them go and then return to the grizzly task before me.

I want to see the men who died. I want to look at their cooling bodies and understand that the destruction I see, and the devastation I carried out, is of their devising. They came to Nottingham and attacked it. They didn't have to. It could just as easily be me who lies here dead. That thought sobers me and stops me from worrying about the men I've killed.

The naked bodies of the warriors are rolled or thrown quickly into the mass grave, the thunks of cold flesh hitting mud, sounding thickly in the air. I swallow back my revulsion.

These were men this morning, with families and children and a future. Now they're nothing but an inconvenience to my warriors, already tired from their exertions during the attack. The lack of care shown should concern me, but I can understand it.

Resolutely, I turn my attention to the steadily growing stash of weapons and riches that men carry with them into battle. The pile is surprisingly high for only twenty or so men. It appears that my enemy all carried shields and at least three or four different weapons, not to mention byrnies. Some had helms as well.

'How did they get here?' I ask of no one in particular. Are there more warriors nearby or a ship?

'Ealdorman Æthelfrith has sent out scouts. They're to go as far as the river to see if any more are hiding out. Those that attacked came on foot.' It's the voice of my newest warrior that speaks to me, Osgod. He's battle weary but seems buoyed by his taste of blood. I wish I had his vigour.

'Tell me what happened by the gate?' I finally think to ask, and he grins sheepishly. What great feat has he accomplished that makes him so proud, I think to myself?

'We raced to Nottingham. We could see that there was already a fight at the wall, so Ealdorman Æthelfrith had us ride close to it before he ordered us to dismount and hand the horses over. The squires were ordered to bring them back here. They chose this place,' he offers in a bluff voice, not so much dripping with disdain, but not far from it. It seems he'd have chosen somewhere else. I don't argue with him just yet. Indeed, I'm surprised that the ealdorman took such a risky gamble. He must have feared for Nottingham's survival much more than he implied.

'There was a large force of Viking raiders. They were fighting hard, and already some bodies littered the ground, both the enemy and some from Nottingham.' His voice turns quiet. 'But they weren't expecting us,' he adds, the grin back on his face. 'In fact, we took them completely by surprise. But they rallied quickly, half their force turning to face us and half still trying to overpower Nottingham's warriors.'

'They could never win. Your warriors were much better provisioned and trained. They were ramshackle by comparison. Some had good weapons, with sharp blades and deadly edges, but others had very poor weapons. Few of them wore byrnies. They were strong.' Now he sounds admiring. I smirk at him. Warriors are never above appreciating their enemy if they put up a good fight. Especially ones they've beaten in a fair battle.

'But once their strength started to wane, victory came quickly. They were swiftly overcome. And the warriors from Nottingham were able to leave their defensive positions and help us finish them off. There's another grave being dug over there,' and he points in the direction I've just sent the young squire and my warrior. 'It'll have many more bodies in it than this one.'

'Do we know where they came from?' I finally think to ask.

'They were Danes,' he answers without hesitation.

'All of them?' that surprises me. I'm used to ships sailing with a mixture of men from the different Norse kingdoms, all desperate to make their fortunes elsewhere or just sate their blood lust. 'Not Irish Norse?' I think to ask. I'd been anticipating the men being in the employ of Lord Rǫgnvaldr.

'As far as we know, they were Danes,' Osgod speaks confidently.

'So just an isolated ship?' I think out loud, and he nods before beginning to move away. Then he pauses and looks back.

'They're expecting you in Nottingham. You should go. We can deal with the bodies and the plunder.' Once more, I look toward the half-completed burh. I know I should go there, but I'm strangely reluctant. Not that standing on a bloodied battlefield is much of an alternative, but for now, I'm a warrior. When I enter Nottingham, I'll have to resort to my usual guise as the Lady of Mercia. I'm not sure that I'm ready to make the switch yet.

'What of King Edward's men?' I suddenly call, and Osgod turns once more.

'Not a great deal of use,' is his less than helpful reply, and I ponder the meaning of that. Surely, they were sent to ensure the safety of Nottingham, only recently won back from the Viking raiders?

A shout of my name stops me considering the words of my warrior. I turn to see that Ealdorman Æthelfrith has sent his son, Eadric, to me.

I can, if I look very carefully, just about tell that he's recently been in a battle. But he has none of the blood, muck and sweat adhered to his clothing that I do. Either his battle was much cleaner and quicker, or he's taken the time to change and slick the filth from his body.

'My lady,' he mumbles. 'My father and the people of Nottingham require your presence. They wish to thank you and your warriors for all that you've done.'

I nod decisively. I should have known I'd get no time to recover my wits before I was plunged back into the world of politics.

'Very well,' I respond, signalling for a horse to be brought to me. Somehow, despite the rabble of the impromptu battle site, one of the squires manages to bring me my horse, complete with saddle and all my belongings. And more. He's ensured she's been watered and brushed down. She looks in much better condition than I do.

Should I go into Nottingham as I am? As a warrior woman? Or should I find the time to change and wrap a dress around my skinny frame?

'My father says come as you are. He tells me you look more like the Lady Æthelflæd that way.'

I nod again. It feels nice to have someone else decide for me, and more, to note a similarity with my mother.

The ride to Nottingham is accomplished quickly. I barely have time to enjoy the passage of the cooling wind over my face, before I'm escorted to the site of another battle.

The ground is heavily trampled, and the bodies of the dead are being stripped and buried. However, here, the bodies are being dumped onto a wagon and pulled away from the main entrance to Nottingham. In the near distance, I can see a group of ten or twelve men labouring away to dig a grave and dump the bodies in it. I shudder as I watch the lifeless grey limbs of a young man being thrown into the pit. It's no way to end a life, with no one to mourn at his grave side, but then, these men made their decision long ago to come raiding. I shouldn't pity them, and yet I do. I resolve to ask for a Mass to be said for the souls of the dead. It doesn't sit well with me to abandon the bodies with no ceremony at all.

Eadric quickly explains the ebb and flow of the altercation here. I can tell that it was a more orderly affair than the brief skirmish I was involved in. But still, for all that we had the victory, there are some men who've lost their lives. I feel a moment of remorse for them. There will be weeping tonight and children forever orphaned. It fills me with fresh desire to stamp out these stray pockets of attack once and for all, but with Lord Rǫgnvaldr hovering somewhere to the north it seems unlikely that I'll ever manage it.

Neither has the wooden enclosure around Nottingham escaped unscathed. Repair work will need to be carried out before the gate can be put into place, and all the time, it'll leave Nottingham vulnerable once more.

I'll need to make provision for that, perhaps instruct Ealdorman Æthelfrith and his two sons to guard the border for me, especially if King Edward's men have already failed in that regard.

The stench of battle leaves me quickly as I ride through the gaping hole into Nottingham. There are scuff marks on the ground, the odd discarded piece of clothing and a single body lying in the road, a few stray hens pecking at it.

It seems that the Viking raiders were able to gain entry before they were stopped. That knowledge reinforces my resolve to leave Nottingham with a larger contingent of warriors than normal.

Apart from the body and the missing gate, Nottingham seems very much as I remember it. No crowds hover by the gateway, peering out at the work of the gravediggers beyond. Either the people of Nottingham have no fears, or, and this is more likely, they're huddled in their homes, waiting to see who yet prevails and who'll command their futures.

'Where are the Wessex warriors?' I demand. Eadric takes a moment to sit a little straighter in his saddle, bracing himself for imparting news I might not want to hear.

'One of their finest warriors died in the attack. They're mourning him now and will arrange his burial soon. My father has instructed our men to fill the breach in the meantime, but they're drinking and feasting, or picking over the dead bodies.'

This isn't what I expected to hear. Not at all. My warriors should know better.

I open my mouth to voice my anger, but there's no need. Eadric already knows I'll be vexed. He's tried to right the wrong, for many of my female warriors are riding in behind me, encouraging their mounts to trample through another gore splattered field before filling the space that so worries me.

'Where's your father? Take me to him,' I command, with only a little less tension in my voice, and Eadric leads me deeper into Nottingham.

Along the narrow streets, I begin to see a little more activity. Some children are chasing a large black dog, and a small girl stands and sucks her thumb as she watches the older children. Her face is tear stained, and she clutches at her tunic so that it rides high above her knee.

I turn away from the fear in her eyes as she watches the tall horses' approach. I don't want small children to live in terror anymore, and yet, as Nottingham has shown me, my own wishes are irrelevant to the raiders who still try and claim Mercia as theirs. I only wish I could build a giant enclosure around all of Mercia, as King Offa once tried to do to stop the various Welsh kingdoms from encroaching inside Mercia. All that remains now is a deep ditch, mostly grassed over but never filled in.

It's a thought I should consider. Should Lord Rǫgnvaldr secure York then I could have Mercia build a dyke across the boundary – it would be a clear demarcation of power then. Only, I have ambitions to claim York and Northumbria for Mercia, to make the 'England' my grandfather so often spoke and wrote about. I wouldn't want the people of that kingdom to feel excluded by the building of such a dyke.

I sigh wearily. There are no simple solutions to keeping my people safe and expanding the 'saved' kingdoms of Mercia and Wessex. I sometimes wonder how my grandfather dealt with the apparent futility of it all. But then, he had faith that was much stronger than mine, and in every action, he saw the hand of his God. I see only the meddling interference of greedy and power-hungry men and women in the chaos that surrounds my kingdom. I don't, and never have, believed as firmly in my grandfather's God-given duty to protect and keep the Saxon kingdoms of England free from Viking raider attack.

I only want to kill the bastards for all the suffering they've caused, and continue to cause.

I'm led almost to the centre of Nottingham, where a wooden hall sits proudly on a small rise. It's a relatively small building for such a large settlement, but, I reconsider, there isn't much room for expansion, as other buildings crowd it out.

Inside I can hear the scrape of feet on wooden floorboards and know that my warriors, who should be guarding my gaping gateway, are drowning their sorrows inside.

I slide from my horse, determination on my face as I march through the flock of ducks and goats that have come to investigate my purpose, far more curious than the men and women inside the hall. Only Eadric rushes to catch up with me.

'My lady,' his tone is humble but also urgent. 'My father isn't in there. Come with me. Let the men have their moment. Your own warriors are currently far more able to protect Nottingham than the rabble in there.'

I consider rushing past him, storming into the hall and demanding an explanation, but Eadric looks desperately toward another building. Reluctantly I follow him. I'm all for mourning a lost one. I understand the need but only when my kingdom is safe.

My horse is led away by another small boy, who gives me a cheeky grin as he takes the reins of the 'pretty horse' a fair way to win the approval of my mare. I stride toward a smaller building. This one is in a much better state of repair, the thatch bright on the roof, with some new struts to support the walls and roof. The stark blond of the newly cut wood makes me consider that these struts have been discarded from the building of the burh walls.

I duck my head, and inside there's a light smell of herbs and Ealdorman Æthelfrith and a young woman bend over the inert body of Athelstan.

They've removed his byrnie and cut away the fabric from his leg wound. I gasp in surprise. I'd not expected to see quite as many bruises on him or quite as much naked flesh. His body is riddled with the green of older injuries and the purpling of fresh ones.

Ealdorman Æthelfrith hears my intake of breath and nods at his other son, who quickly walks away, his task accomplished.

'My lady,' Ealdorman Æthelfrith half apologises without moving from his task. 'The men are grief-stricken. The bloody fool was trying to prove he was the better warrior than your new man and was struck down by a lucky spear throw. He'd forgotten his shield, or he might have survived. I apologise for their dereliction of duty, but I needed to tend to my son. They're already too drunk with grief to listen to Eadric. Can your women hold the gateway until the men are recovered?' He sounds weary and worried, and I step closer to Athelstan.

The wound on his leg has stopped bleeding, but his skin is strangely blue and mottled around it, as though there isn't any blood left in his body. His head wound pulses angrily. His eyes are closed, and when the healer steps closer to examine him, she forces his eyes open only to be greeted with the whites of his eyes because they've rolled so far back in his head.

I nod, just once, aware that my female warrior is also being cared for as she drowses by the fire under some furs, her face a healthier colour.

'I understand. There'll be time for recriminations later,' I mutter softly, just about stopping myself from reaching out to sweep Athelstan's fair hair away from his deathly white face. He moans softly at the healer's touch. I understand the concern and inattention of Ealdorman Æthelfrith. But I'm here now, and I'm fit and healthy. I turn to stare at the hall, where an eruption of noise no doubt indicates some new disaster.

'I'll go and sit with the men,' I announce, but the ealdorman shakes his head.

'Not yet, my lady. We must speak with the leaders of Nottingham. They're waiting to meet you.'

'What, in the hall?' I squeak, appalled to think that the traumatised people of Nottingham might even now be being forced to witness the drunkenness of the Wessex warriors.

'No, that's more a tavern than a great hall. Remember, Nottingham is more than half Norse. They're waiting for you outside the church.'

This makes a lot more sense to me, but as I watch the healer work, I'm torn once more. I would prefer, as the ealdorman clearly does, to sit here and wait for Athelstan to wake. I don't like to see someone so still. It reminds me of my mother just before her death.

But the ealdorman understands his duty as well as I do, and with a look at the healer, who only nods as she works, he stands and leads me from the smaller building.

'Come, we'll meet with them, and then, we might get bloody fed.'

He winces at the raucous noises coming from inside the tavern as we walk past it and into a quieter street until we reach the church. It's of new construction, the wood, like so much of Nottingham, not yet holding the stain of years of rain and muck, although it does have a firm stone structure at its feet.

Here more people are milling about, and I think this must be where all the missing people from Nottingham's deserted streets are waiting. The hush in the murmur of conversation is apparent as soon as news of my arrival spreads. I walk with my head held high, aware that I still carry the stain of battle around me.

Slightly behind me, Ealdorman Æthelfrith walks patiently. He's used to the aftermath of a battle, when high emotions are suddenly drained, and when the dead need burying. I wish I were as calm as he appears, although his worry for his youngest son is evident to me as well.

The church's interior is just as crowded as the exterior, only with a more demarcated path for me to walk through. At the front of the church, I see the holy men of the city talking amongst themselves as they wait for me, their robes making it clear who is a monk, priest or bishop. It's beginning to feel as though I'm about to be judged again, a replay of the Mercian witan which proclaimed me as the leader of Mercia, as my mother was before me.

It's only as I take my place at the front of the church that I finally catch sight of some of the Wessex warriors my uncle sent north. There's a small selection of about ten men, all in immaculate clothing. I can't see that they've just fought a battle. Why did my uncle send these men north if not to fight? Did he do it to gain a foothold in Nottingham? Did he do it because, like London, he wants Nottingham for himself?

I try to ignore the penetrating gaze of the men as I survey the people of Nottingham before me. There's some concern, anger, and contentment on the faces of those who watch me in near silence. I don't miss that many of the women are looking at my clothing with respect on their faces. Even some of the men look a little impressed.

'People of Nottingham,' I begin, hoping that this is the correct tone to use. I need to be conciliatory in the face of the attack. I also need to press home the important fact that it was my warriors and my intervention that saved Nottingham this time. This is what the people of Nottingham agreed to when they rejoined Mercia. It's not my fault, just as it's not the fault of the people building the wall if it's not completed yet. Like Derby, they should have concentrated on this aspect of the work first. But then, none of us expected Lord Rǫgn-valdr this year. None of us.

'I wish I'd arrived under better circumstances, but I'm pleased that my warriors have gained your freedom from the attack.' There's a faint rustle of 'something' from the audience, but I press on. I'm a warrior. I'm their leader. I need not apologise for both leading and fighting for them.

'My intention today was to inform you of a new threat to the north, but it seems there's no need for my warning anymore. The threat has made itself well known to you. Mercia is once more under attack,' this honest statement is greeted with a hiss of anger. Perhaps some are regretting their decision to side with Mercia. 'But we have the means to defend ourselves, and to beat back, and kill any who try to take by force, what is ours by right as we have shown today. My warriors have bled for you. I've bled for you, and Ealdorman Æthel-frith's son has suffered for you. And we've lost friends today, as my warriors' grief shows. We've done our duty to Nottingham, and now, Nottingham must do its duty for Mercia.' I expect some anger from my words, but gentle acceptance sweeps through the hall, the nodding heads and respect clear to see on the faces of many if not all.

'Nottingham must hasten to finish its walls. Nottingham must have its warriors ready to defend and attack at any moment, and Nottingham must be alert to the danger facing Mercia. Only together can Mercia grow strong and overpower all its enemies.'

With no time to think about my words before being put in this situation, I can only hope that those I've cobbled together aren't met with derision or anger.

The Wessex warriors watch me intently. There's something on their faces that I don't quite understand. Like my uncle, they seem ambiguous toward me, my intentions and my accomplishments. I wish cousin Athelstan stood at my side. I wish he could interpret this current chain of events for me, but I must stand alone and make my own decisions.

The inhabitants of Nottingham still nod or mouth their agreement. They see that the future must lie in working more closely with me. Their response emboldens me.

'Today, a great victory has been fought. Your warriors and Ealdorman Æthelfrith's warriors have overcome the enemy, the Viking raiders. The burghal fortifications are not even complete, and still, they've kept Nottingham secure.' I laugh a little as I speak. I want them to understand how well they've done and also, more importantly, how much more they can accomplish in the future.

There are growing looks of triumph on faces now, and I know my work is nearly done.

'We must work all day, every day, until the gateway is completed. In that way, you'll ensure your safety so that next year, when the crops are ripe, you'll be able to leave the shelter of the walls and venture out and harvest all you can. You'll know that should the worst happen, there's a sanctuary for you and for the people who live outside the walls all year round.'

'This is just the beginning of ensuring Nottingham's security and your own. In a generation's time, you might well wonder what all the fuss was even about,' again, my tone is light. I've fought and bled for these people, and now they must do something for themselves, but they need to think it's more than half their idea. Politics is a strange business. Tell people what to do, and they'll refuse. Give them an idea, and it's to be hoped that they'll grasp it and fully embrace it.

I can see a quirk of a smile on the ealdorman's face as the reeve and the holy men all look at each other, no doubt determining how many people they need to complete the task and how long it'll take. There'll also be some considering the profit to be made in providing materials for the wall. Still, I know how much the wood should be costing, and I do not intend for Nottingham to pay over the odds to ensure their future safety.

There's a relieved flutter of laughter at my words. Like my mother before me, I dream of a time when it's possible to ride throughout Mercia without fear of attack. In the heartlands, near Tamworth and Lichfield, Mercia is as safe as it's been for more than two generations, but only this short distance to Nottingham, it's still lawless. And there are still opportunistic Viking raiders hiding in coppices, snaking their way along the rivers and making a nuisance of themselves.

For now, I need to ensure that these parties aren't sent by Lord Rǫgnvaldr. I need to understand what the contingent of Wessex warriors is doing here. But first, well, there's a Mass to be said and a feast to enjoy.

As Lady of the Mercians, I have a duty to protect my people. And that's what I've done, and will continue to do.

CHAPTER 12

I sleep where I fall, surrounded by my fellow female warriors and also some of the inhabitants of Nottingham. None of us knows when to stop drinking, even though we should.

Sloshing water over my sticky face, and grimacing at the smell of my body, still encased in the clothes of a fighter, my newest warrior seeks me out as soon as I'm awake.

Osgod looks suspiciously fresh, and I know for a fact that he's not gorged himself drinking and feasting all night long. I wish I could say the same. My head pounds, and my mouth tastes like horse shit.

'My lady,' he greets me, his face staying suspiciously free of all judgment at my current state. 'We captured a man alive during the night,' he informs me conspiratorially.

'And?' I ask, fearing what he'll say next.

'He said he came here with Lord Rǫgnvaldr. He knew nothing of any skirmish between Rǫgnvaldr and Constantin. He seems to have been hiding on the borders for some time.'

I fear to ask how Osgod extracted the information, but I know it's both important and damning.

'Does he still live?' I ask hopefully, and he nods a little, a strange smile on his face. I assume the man lives but will not for much longer.

'Take me to him. I'd speak with him.'

'My lady?' he tries to argue, but I'm already striding away, keeping my steps even for all the world sways alarmingly. I expect him to follow me. He does so, a grim silence hanging in the air.

We walk, or rather march, all the way through Nottingham. Only when we return to the already busy work site at the unfinished northern gate does he lead me away from the main street and into a dark and dingy little wooden hut. It looks like a prison to me, and it smells like one too.

Two men guard the door. They stand abruptly on seeing me and look to Osgod in shock. I sense his massive shoulders shrug rather than see it.

'Show me the prisoner,' I demand, and they quickly open the doorway and let me inside.

The hovel is small but well-maintained, just light enough to see. Why else have a prison if it won't keep the prisoner inside? That said, it does lack certain niceties and is complete with many sets of chains. It has a feeling of hopelessness about it.

The man I see shackled to the floor is a mess. His breath is ragged, his clothes torn, and his face a welter of bruises. If he ever sees daylight again, he'll be a rainbow of hues and might even make money from displaying them. I'm sure that skin shouldn't turn such a deep greenish tone.

I swallow back my unease at this and nod to Osgod.

'Wake him,' I command, and he leaps to do as I've bid as though pleased this is all I've said. A handy jug of water is dashed over the slumped man's form.

The face that greets me, with just one eye peeled open, is far too young and innocent for my liking. I see a young boy, not a warrior before me, and consider who he is.

'Do you speak the language of the Saxons?' I ask him. He tries to nod, wincing and then opening cracked lips. 'Yes,' he coughs.

'Give him some water,' I say imperiously. I need information from the youth and don't want to listen to him constantly trying to extract some moisture from his dry tongue to moisten his lips.

Again, Osgod does as I ask without comment, holding the jug in front of the man's eyes so that he knows he can take it. A look of surprise crosses his broken face as he fixes his one eye on me. He wasn't expecting to see a woman before he met his fate or be given any comfort.

'Tell me all that you told Osgod,' I command as soon as he's emptied the jug. He flinches at my tone. I don't want him to think that I'm a soft woman, but he nods all the same. His wrist chains clink as he lowers the jug back to the floor, almost reverentially. It seems he fears that if the jug's broken, we'll allow him to die from thirst. But I don't intend to allow him to die at all.

'I'm from Dublin,' the youth gabbles, keen to be speaking. 'Lord Rǫgnvaldr put out a call to arms to come and retake York. My father told me to come. He said we had family in York and that Lord Rǫgnvaldr would reward me well.'

I observe the man. How will I know if he's telling the truth?

'And where did you first come ashore?' I ask, all the time thinking that he lacks the accent that the Norse Dublin warriors have adopted. To me, he sounds as though he comes from the far northern kingdoms, not from Dublin at all.

'To the north,' he offers, his face scrunched in pain as he bends his head low and rubs a grimy hand across his broken face. He hisses with pain.

'Where to the north?' I press. I feel he's lying to me, but I don't know why or even why I'm convinced of his lies.

'Along a river, a big one,' he offers, a shrug of his shoulders bringing back a wince to his face.

'You didn't think to ask the name of the river?' I continue to interrogate.

'Whose name would I use, my lady? The correct one in Norse or the one the locals give to it? It would mean nothing to you Saxons.' A clever boy, then. And that has me doubting his words even more.

'What happened when you came ashore?' Will he tell me of a battle, or doesn't he know about it?

'Lord Rǫgnvaldr sent two ships to the south, along the river that runs from the Humber. To raid Mercia. He said that you needed to be distracted so that he could reclaim York as his birthright.'

Again, the words sound right, but there's something off in the prisoner's demeanour, even though he faces death. I know he's lying to me. But the reason why he'd lie is unclear.

'Where have you been on your journey here?' I ask, hoping to pry something from him to feed my concerns.

'Along rivers, into steadings, laying low, just waiting for the right time to attack.'

'Didn't you think that it might be better to attack somewhere smaller than Nottingham? After all, there are only two shiploads of warriors in your group.'

For a moment, I see a flicker of worry cross his face. This seems to be the core of his lies. It seems that the intention was always to attack Nottingham, which makes me suspicious. Nottingham is a large settlement. Why wouldn't ragged warriors simply try their luck with smaller settlements and outlying farms?

'Nottingham is a prize,' he offers, half hopeful, and for the time being, I decide to leave him be.

'And you've been paid for your work already?' I ask. I can see that although his clothing is ragged, he wears a chain of thick gold around his neck. No doubt there's a pagan symbol of the Old Gods beneath his tunic. I'm surprised that it's not been taken from him by his captors.

'No,' he stutters, his restrained hand unconsciously trying to reach his neck, revealing the falsehood.

I turn away from him, contemplating what I should ask him next, only for the limited amount of daylight in the room to be blocked by a massive warrior.

I glare at the man.

'My lady, Ælfwynn,' he stutters, and I recognise him as one of King Edward's warriors. He should have been fighting for the good of Nottingham yesterday, but as far as I know, he made little or no attempt to rebuff the attack. This is the first I've seen of him. That, coupled with this latest piece of news, is worrisome. What's the man playing at, and why has he come to question my prisoner?

'Yes, Aldred.'

I wait for him to speak, enjoying the uncomfortable expression on his lined face.

'I … I'd heard there was a prisoner,' he stutters, and I turn from him. What does he know about my prisoner?

'There is, but I'm interrogating him. You may go.'

'King Edward asked me to speak with any prisoners,' Aldred attempts, and I turn to gaze at him once more.

'The king, my uncle, was expecting there to be an attack, or attacks, then?' I growl. The haunted expression on Aldred's face tells me all I think I need to know. 'It's none of your concern, Aldred. This man and I are talking about the attack yesterday and the past. There's no need for you to be here. Osgod can protect me well enough.'

Aldred doesn't want to leave, even going so far as to finger his seax at his waist. I understand his intent here.

'Osgod, arrange for the guard on this man to be trebled. I don't wish him to die, not yet. I have more questions for him.'

Aldred's face falls at my words. What sort of warrior is he? Certainly, he lacks all guile to play the game of politics.

The prisoner's watching all of this intently, but his body has stilled, an animal caught in a trap. I know what I'm witnessing, but I wish I didn't. I need Aldred to leave now so that I can spirit the man away to safety, somewhere where Aldred can't get to him but first, I have a pressing question.

'You were paid to say that Lord Rǫgnvaldr sent you?' I demand. My prisoner manages to tear his fearful gaze away from Aldred and glance at me.

'No, my lady. Lord Rǫgnvaldr sent me and will pay me well with more plunder when York is recaptured.' The words are softer now, more persuasive, and the tang of the Dublin Norse has lilted back into his voice. I don't find it surprising that all this happened while Aldred watches. As he still does.

'Aldred, you're dismissed,' I say to him, turning and indicating with my hand that he should leave. He doesn't want to, but I've had the prisoner say exactly what he's clearly supposed to say. Aldred has no choice but to obey my words. As he shuffles from the room, I bend my head low to the prisoner.

'Who's paid you, good friend?' I query, my hand on my seax. I'm more offering to protect him than threaten him, but it remains to be seen if he understands my intent. He swallows, considering my words. I have half an ear listening for Aldred's retreat, but it's only the shocked eyes of my prisoner that give me the warning I need.

With a cry of rage, Aldred advances on us both with his seax raised threateningly. It's only the quick reflexes of my prisoner and Osgod that save me as I fall back into the dirty straw, my hand coming free from my seax. I hear Aldred's hoarse cry of, 'beware, my lady,' just before his weapon cleanly impales my prisoner. His hot blood gushes from his broken throat as the looks at me with panic in his eyes.

Outraged voices can be heard inside and outside the prison, but it's the pleading look in the eyes of my prisoner that has me moving forward toward him while Osgod tackles Aldred to the floor. Hot blood pools on the floor as I crawl toward the boy whose name I don't yet know. I cradle his broken body as his chained hands try to stem the blood flow from his neck. He has something to tell me. Something urgent.

In the confusion and terror of Aldred's act, I reach the boy and clasp both of his blood-stained hands, mine slipping in the gore. I have to hold them tighter and tighter still. I pull myself close to the boy, sadness on my face for such a despicable act.

The boy whispers two words repeatedly, so softly that I can't hear them until I put my ear to his lips. With his final breath and a pleading look in his eye, he says two words I hoped I'd never hear from him. 'The Saxons,' he exhales, and then he's dead, his body lifeless, his eyes forever staring, his bruises even starker on his pale face.

Exhausted from this terrible action, I settle back on my knees, reaching out to close the eyes of the dead boy.

His death is a tragedy, but more, what he tells me is horrific.

He's been paid and paid well for this attack on Nottingham. But not by Lord Rǫgnvaldr. His lack of knowledge about the north points to one thing and one thing only. He's never been to the north. Neither, I suspect, has he ever been to Dublin, although he speaks with the inflexion of the Dublin Norse. Perhaps his father, or more likely, his mother. No, this boy was a Dane and probably an English Dane from the Danelaw. And he was sent by the Saxons to attack Nottingham. More horrifying, Aldred knew all about it and killed the boy to silence him so that I'd never learn the truth.

In the dim little prison, I feel a shock of realisation. I have more enemies than just Lord Rǫgnvaldr and the Norse. And one of those enemies is Aldred, a man who works for my uncle, the king of Wessex.

What it all means I can't yet fathom, but two things are obvious, this boy didn't need to die, and Aldred didn't fight to keep Nottingham safe yesterday. Luck, and little else, has allowed me to save Nottingham and hold it for Mercia. But who exactly I've saved it from remains to be seen.

CHAPTER 13

I emerge from the prison to a blood-curdling shriek from a woman who spies my clothes.

I must look a sight smeared in the blood of another. Hastily I instruct Osgod to get me a cloak. I can't walk through the streets of Nottingham like this. People will assume that I've killed the prisoner, and while it might improve my standing and show that I can be as cruel a bitch as any male battle commander, I don't want people to think this of me. I didn't kill the boy, far from it.

'Remove the body, ensure it's well wrapped so none can see how the boy was killed. Have Aldred brought to me as soon as I'm clean.' I have to contend with the problem of Aldred. We all saw him kill the boy, or rather Osgod and I did. To everyone else, Aldred is a hero who saved me from being murdered. I must decide, and quickly, how I want to control this unwelcome development. But first, first, I must change and get clean.

The return journey to the small hall where Ealdorman Æthelfrith nervously watches his son being tended to is accomplished quickly enough. His gasp of outrage when he sees me has me shushing him immediately.

'I need to speak with you urgently, but I must change and have new clothes brought to me. None of this is as it seems.' I intervene in a rush. I desperately need his advice, but more, I need to remove the tang of copper from my hair and clothes.

The healer watches me from where she labours over Athelstan. His body has regained some colour, I notice dispassionately, and his breathing is even. It seems she's a good healer.

'You can bathe behind the tavern,' she offers. I nod, grateful that she asks no questions. I march from the small hall and quickly discern the scent of hot water in the air. I'm not the only person to need a bath this morning. Turning to Osgod, I command him to fetch three of my female warriors. They'll guard me while I bathe. Waiting in the bright sunshine, I look down at my body. I'm sheeted in crimson. Not one speck of my garb is clear of another's blood. I wrinkle my nose in disgust and grief both. My head is pounding with the after-effects of too much mead and ale. I'd like little more than to sit in the sun and think of nothing. Only I must regain the upper hand, and govern these people as they should be governed.

The three women who stumble from the tavern look as bad as I feel, only without the overriding cloak of red. Their eyes rise with concern, their hands going for weapons, which have luckily been surrendered in exchange for a night of drinking. They turn, surprised, knowing they can't guard me without their ironware, as my young squire, Erna, hurries to return their blades to them.

'I must bathe,' I inform them, and they scramble to walk toward me, moving people out of my way until they find me a secluded place to bathe. They ask no questions, and that pleases me. There's a total of five wooden tubs set out behind the tavern. None are covered, but sweating men and women trail to refill the tubs with fresh hot water for the smelly warriors. This is an everyday occurrence in Nottingham. I'm reminded of the fastidious nature of Viking warriors. They love to battle fiercely, but equally, they prefer to be clean afterwards.

The wooden tub I head towards has just received three full buckets of hot water, steaming even in the warm summer air. I discard my clothing on the floor as my women stand with their backs to me, daring any to stare too long or attack me with their iron.

Erna has run off somewhere, no doubt, to find me linens to dry myself with and to replace the clothes I fear I'll never be able to wear again. Blood doesn't easily scrub clean from linen, only from metal and iron.

I've much to think about as I enter the steaming pool, plunging myself entirely under the water so that magenta trails streak the water. No one will want this water after me. It'll have to be discarded and refilled. I pity the servants for such a task.

Although I try to clear my mind and think clearly about what my next move will be, rumours are already flying through Nottingham. I can hear it in the hushed tones of the servants and warriors who mill around the outside of the tavern. Many sound grumpy, too filled with mead or ale to care, but others shout at each other, the sound of war on their tongues. They believe the lie that Lord Rǫgnvaldr sent the men who attacked Nottingham. I don't miss the fact that the voices that ring the loudest carry a distinctive Wessex accent, the clipped tones of men more used to the exaggerated sophistication of King Edward's court.

I admire the attempt to whip my warriors into a frenzy. Does Aldred believe that I'll be swayed by the resolve of warriors over the truth that I've been told by a man, more a boy who knew his death was coming? Does he think me so weak that I'll do what others demand instead of what I know I should do?

Clean once more and suitably dressed, I return to Ealdorman Æthelfrith, my female warriors staying at my side. He's standing outside of the healer's hall as men mill around him, some from Nottingham and some my Mercian warriors. The hubbub of conversation is too loud to make out individual conversations, but I know what he's been asked. I beckon him to follow me inside the hall. Outside, all of my female warriors now protect me, even those who stood guard last night and so require sleep. They're dressed for war and far more alert than they have been until now. I feel safe inside and confident that no prying ears will overhear my words.

'Your son's healing?' I ask him, relieved that this at least appears to be an easy question to ask, trying to ignore the hitch in my voice as I speak of his Athelstan. I don't know why I should care so much, but seemingly I do.

'Very well, my lady. He'll be back on his feet in no more than ten days.'

'That's good news. He fought well. He came to my aid.' This part of the battle hasn't been imparted to the ealdorman, and he glows with pride, a fond look crossing his face, to think of his son fighting for his lady.

'He's always shown skill with weapons,' he offers before turning to the bed that contains my injured warrior.

'She's healing too. She slept poorly, a fever taking her to strange places so that she cried out in her sleep, but the healer says the worst is past now.'

I've not forgotten about Coelflaed, not at all. I noticed her pale face as soon as I reentered the hut, but my mind was on other matters.

'You need to be aware that a prisoner was caught in the night. He was beaten and questioned and said that Lord Rǫgnvaldr sent him, but he lied when he said so. Aldred of Wessex came to question him, or rather kill him, and regrettably succeeded, but only after the prisoner told me it was the Saxons who paid them to attack.'

The shock on the ealdorman's face is genuine. The news disturbs him greatly.

'What?' he gasps, reaching for a stool and stumbling to its seat. 'Why would he say that?' he asks, and then his troubled face clears. 'And why would Aldred kill him? Do you think he knew?' he mouths, his voice no more than a coarse whisper under the hum of conversation from outside. 'Is this why they didn't fight as they should have done?' he exhales. The ealdorman has always been astute, and he doesn't fail me now.

'I had my suspicions anyway,' I mutter, and he nods as I speak, as though he'd had the same thoughts as well.

'I can't say I was overly happy,' he agrees, 'with the way the defence had been arranged, almost as though they were inviting them into Nottingham. But who would pay Danes to attack Mercia?'

I allow him time to think. I want to see if his mind makes the same instinctive leap as mine or if I see an enemy where only family exists.

'Your cousin,' he says, his tone filled with horror, and I know he doesn't mean cousin Athelstan. His conclusion isn't quite the one I've drawn, but suddenly it makes a lot more sense.

'Lord Ælfweard?' I question. 'Would the king give him Mercia if I failed to hold it? Wouldn't he allow cousin Athelstan to rule there?' I grill him, but the older man shakes his head, his lined face filled with fury.

'He'll never allow ætheling Athelstan to rule anywhere, and certainly not in Mercia. If the prisoner speaks the truth, then this is just as much an attempt to get rid of Athelstan as it is to dispense with you. It might even have been an attempt on ætheling Athelstan's life.'

'It makes more sense that you'd send your cousin to drive out any Viking raiders threat than go yourself. Remember, you sent Lord Athelstan to the northern lands when we first heard about Lord Rǫgnvaldr's attack. This might have been set in motion long before news of the battle between Lord Rǫgnvaldr and King Constantin of the Scots reached us. To have men come here from wherever they've been, to pay them and fit them out as Viking raiders would have taken time, quite a bit of time.'

As unhappy as I am with the ealdorman's assessment of the situation, it gives me some comfort to know that he doesn't think it to be uncle Edward's doing. It's far easier for me to think of my odious cousin Ælfweard doing this. He's surrounded by self-seeking followers whom I don't trust.

'How can we find out more?' I press the ealdorman. In the absence of cousin Athelstan, I find myself relying on his sound thinking and political acumen. He's played a part in the politics of Mercia and Wessex for far too long to be naïve about the intentions of men who seek power and women as well, I suppose.

'We need to send someone to Wessex. Find out what's happening there.'

'But who could we trust, and who would be believed by cousin Ælfweard anyway. He detests all Mercians, thinking them all Viking raiders who wear a mask of civility.'

'Perhaps it should be one of our warriors? Then they could find out what's happening from Ælfweard's household troops. Members of the household always know what's happening before anyone else.'

I mull over the suggestion. The ealdorman is again correct. It's the men who wield the pointy sticks who often know what's happening at court. In a quest to stay alive, they're often most inquisitive, not liking to be caught out with an unexpected call to arms.

'We could send your new man. Perhaps as a punishment for allowing the prisoner to be killed, or some such. Or have him become an ally of Aldred's even. That might do the trick.'

I sigh at the thought. 'I think that might be quite difficult. He detests the man. I can tell just from looking at him. But he might agree to go to Wessex for me.'

As I consider the possibility, there's a dimming in the hum of conversation outside, and it's not too long before a shadow casts its darkness over the ealdorman and me. I squint at the stranger in black before Ealdorman Æthelfrith grimaces and stands.

'What are you doing here, boy?' the ealdorman says, standing, and I know from his warm, if the exasperated tone, that it's one of his sons, no doubt with news from Lord Athelstan.

'I came to report on conditions in the west,' he says, his grin of delight sliding from his face as he sees his brother lying in bed next to us, pale and injured. 'I see events here aren't as calm as in the west,' he mumbles, looking at his father for an explanation.

'I take it you used the west gate,' his father comments, reaching out to squeeze his shoulder in reassurance. 'There was a battle, Ælfstan. Your brother was protecting the lady, but he was injured. He'll survive, the healer assures me.'

The dazzlingly similar face looks at me, a quirk of a smile on his face. 'Really, he was protecting you?' Ælfstan quizzes, his relief at knowing his brother is well making him a little cheeky. 'But you, my lady, have always been better with a sword than any of us.' I appreciate his attempt at humour.

'I have, that I can't deny, but when there's two against one, it becomes a little more difficult.' I also try humour, but my voice sounds flat, even to my ears.

He accepts that, the smile staying on his lips, even though I can see it's an effort.

'I take it the country is quiet to the west?' I nudge him, hoping his news is good. Ælfstan swallows his worry and tries to find his impish grin again.

'Very quiet, but ready for battle. Everyone we met has been practising. Rumours of Lord Rǫgnvaldr have spread far and wide, but there's no fear, only a desire to drive him back to Dublin. Athelstan, sorry, Lord Athelstan, thought the news would cheer you.' His voice trails away as he finishes his sentence.

'It gladdens my heart. It really does. And when you return to him, you can speak to him of Nottingham and tell him that the inhabitants here have nearly finished their walls and are just as keen, while Derby is very well prepared.'

Ælfstan nods his head at my efforts at courtly manners. Talking of war and battle in such a way does really seem to downplay it.

'There's no rush for me to return,' he says, his voice dropping low and his father glares at him.

'Spit it out, boy. Tell me why you've come in person.'

A wry smirk twists his son's face.

'You always knew me too well, father. The west is peaceful, but your cousin was concerned by rumours he heard. They were really little or nothing, but when he pieced it all together, he thought it was something about which you should know.'

'Why, what did you hear?'

'The rumour from a trader was of Dublin goods in Wessex markets. The talk from a blacksmith was of a scarcity of iron ore. The words from one of the ship's captains were of a Wessex ship in Dublin waters. The whispers from a farmer to the far north were of men carrying a ship overland to get to relatives in York. Another told of ships coming from north and from the Outer Isles so that allies can be procured from the Dublin rulers. As you see, all a bit of nothing. None of those alone speaks of any significant problem, but together, well together, they might just mean something.'

I watch the lad as he struggles to try to explain the thinking behind his excursion to us. I can almost understand what he means, what he tries to imply and why cousin Athelstan was worried enough to send Ælfstan in person.

'Are there not always Dublin goods in Wessex markets?' his father goads him, his expression pensive.

'And don't the blacksmiths always complain that there's not enough iron ore? And if there are Dublin goods in Wessex markets, would that not account for the ship?'

I can see Ælfstan struggling to doubt the wisdom of his father's words. I also understand his sneaking thoughts. I also think that, in light of our interrupted conversation, Ealdorman Æthelfrith is not blind to the possibilities.

'Admittedly, the Norsemen are always trying to find allies to launch an attack on somewhere, but the news of ships being carried overland is worrying. Did cousin Athelstan send anyone to find out the truth of the rumours?' I speak consideringly, thinking as I talk. Cousin Athelstan isn't wrong to show some concern. Ealdorman Æthelfrith, despite his words to the contrary, grunts his agreement as I speak.

'Yes, he's trying to seek out the truth, but in the meantime, he thought that I should give you a warning. That's why he sent me personally. None of this can be written down for fear that someone else might start to make sense of it all and cover their tracks better.'

Ealdorman Æthelfrith meets the eyes of his son.

'We have our concerns, too. King Edward's men are in Notting-ham, but they didn't fight as convincingly as they should have done.'

The words are blunt, and I flinch to hear them spoken quite so plainly.

Ælfstan's mouth drops open in shock at the import of the sentence. He looks almost comical, but this isn't a time for merriment.

'Who was the enemy?' he asks, his voice dropping low as he begins to appreciate the importance of his father's words.

'There was only one survivor. He said he came from Lord Rǫgnvaldr when he was caught, but when Lady Ælfwynn questioned him, she got a slightly different answer. We fear treachery from the king's son.'

'Lord Ælfweard?' condescension drips from Ælfstan's voice. 'He couldn't organise something like this. He has no guile about him. None at all. It must be King Edward's doing.'

Hearing Ælfstan voice my worries is a relief, but Ealdorman Æthelfrith is already shaking his head. I don't find it strange that he'd rather trust the father than the son. After all, Ealdorman Æthelfrith is from the same generation as King Edward. No doubt they've fought together before. It's always hard to realise an ally is really an enemy. Still, my doubts prevail about cousin Ælfweard.

'You barely know the oldest Wessex ætheling,' the ealdorman chides, but Ælfstan is rolling his eyes at me, some of his humour returned to him now that the shock has passed.

'It's not always necessary to know men for long to decipher their personalities and capabilities,' he chides his father. I smirk. Ælfstan speaks the truth.

From behind us, I hear a cough and look to see tired eyes watching me. Athelstan has been listening to the conversation for some time.

Ealdorman Æthelfrith stands abruptly and strides toward his son.

'Ah lad, it's good to see you awake,' the joy in his voice is hard to mistake.

'Of course, father. I wouldn't dare not to heal,' he grins quickly before emitting a small gasp of pain. The healer bustles around him and shoos me from the small space we occupy. I leave willingly, noting that my warrior, and the small squire I commanded be brought here, are all sleeping peacefully. I don't want to disturb their healing.

Ælfstan follows behind me. I almost think he'll ignore me, but then he speaks.

'Your cousin Athelstan is your firmest ally,' he offers, and I nod.

'He always has been.'

'Your other cousin is your firmest enemy. He's not, as I said, very bright, but you don't need to be when you're the king's son.'

'I know,' is all I say. I wish I could argue with him.

'But your uncle. You might find that he's the deadliest of them all. He's lived almost all his adult life with your mother as the Lady of Mercia, overshadowing him. For every battle he's fought in, she's commanded twice as many. For every Viking raider he's killed, she's demanded the death of twice as many. She was, in effect, our greatest shield maiden. I genuinely don't know if he'll endure having another woman in command of Mercia. He seeks to grow his kingdom, and I tell you, he won't care if he does it at your expense. Not that you should take that personally. He'd seek to overthrow whoever was ruling Mercia.'

'And yet I must still keep Mercia safe from our mortal enemies, the Viking raiders.'

'Yes, you must do his job for him, and then, and I apologise for being so harsh with you, he'll take your victories and claim them as his own.'

'But would he stoop this low? Would Ælfweard? Or am I looking for betrayal in the wrong places?'

'Who knows, my lady, but you'd do well to keep alert. Always alert. You have your mother's skill with words, but you also have your grandfather's talent for directing men to fight to the death for you. It's a heady mixture and not one that I think King Edward will tolerate if he truly has his eyes on Mercia.'

I'm surprised by the respect I hear in Ælfstan's voice. He's not much younger than I am, and when I've given any thought to him in the past, it's always been as one of cousin Athelstan's adherents. He might be more than that. He might be a genuine follower of first my mother and then myself. The thought fills me with a warm glow for the respect but a wary acceptance of his logic.

'My thanks for your candid words,' I offer him, and he nods and moves away.

Alone with my thoughts, I consider my conversation with Ealdorman Æthelfrith, and then the one with Ælfstan. In their own way, both men have soothed and worried me afresh. I'll send men to the south. I'll try and determine what it is that the two most powerful men in Wessex have to do with affairs in Nottingham. I know that one of them will disappoint me.

CHAPTER 14

I'm not a patient woman. I've learnt that lesson well since I arrived in Nottingham and walked straight into a fight, one possibly orchestrated by a member of my extended family.

It's barely been ten days since the battle, but I chafe at the delay. I ride far to the north of Nottingham, toward the boundary with the ancient kingdom of Northumbria, disintegrated now into smaller parts, some parts ruled by York and its archbishop and some governed by the House of Bamburgh. I need more information with which to base my next move on, and it's far too slow in coming.

Ælfstan has returned to cousin Athelstan, his words about my uncle clamouring in my ears. Ealdorman Æthelfrith has remained in Nottingham, waiting for news from Wessex. And I, well, I've struck out to the north. I hope to find Lord Rǫgnvaldr or at least someone who might know what he's planning. But in all honesty, riding out, being with my horse and my warriors, male and female, is freeing.

I might be trying to run from my destiny, but I prefer to think that I'm racing toward the future. Lord Rǫgnvaldr might not yet have had success in the north of Northumbria, but he soon will. I don't doubt that York will fall prey soon enough to the charms of a Viking raider, especially one who can lay claim to being a member of the mighty dynasty of Ivarr Ragnarsson. I worry that he has the support of the kingdom of Wessex as well and that his actions are being controlled by someone who should support me. Lord Rǫgnvaldr's very timely arrival near York coincides too closely with my mother's death for me to think there's no coincidence.

I expected better from the father and son who rule in Wessex, but I suppose I shouldn't be surprised. Powerful men rarely seem content with what they already possess. Even my grandfather, the supposedly near saintly King Alfred, was torn by his constant need for more and more of Wessex, never content with the small pocket he initially retained. He saw it as his God-given right to reclaim land taken by the Viking raiders. I see Mercia as mine, but I don't think my uncle and his son do.

It's a matter of a few days' ride from Nottingham to York, or at least it can be, at speed. I'm taking my time, trying to root out any other packs of marauders who might roam the waterways or who might have taken horses and be coming further inland. It's as good as an excuse as any to be free of Nottingham and out and about, ready for any attack that might come.

What started as an expedition to the burhs to check that all was ready for a potential attack has become more than that. I feel as though I'm constantly on guard, as though I stand ready for war with every breath I take.

Abruptly I rein my horse in and stand in the stirrups looking behind me. I've felt all day that my actions are being watched and not by my warriors. I commanded King Edward's supposed warriors to remain in Nottingham to assist with completing the wall around the burh, even Aldred. I'd rather have punished him publicly, but for now, it seemed politic to go along with the story of his rescue of me from the prisoner, who died. He was unhappy with my request to remain behind, which only adds fire to my fears. I doubt all of the Wessex warriors. I wish I could have sent them back to King Edward and Wessex, but that would reveal my doubts. Until I know something, I can't make my intentions and fears known.

King Edward's silence on my message to him can be interpreted in so many different ways that it hurts my head to consider them all. Every night I toss and turn, thinking about his aims, and every night I fall asleep, and my worries and fears plague my dreams. Being on my horse, riding to the north, gives me the sense that I am at least doing something to keep my kingdom safe. It's too little, but in the wake of so little actual intelligence about how others move, it's all I can do. My mother says she spent too much of her early days responding to events that overcame Mercia as opposed to being in control and being the person who made the decisions. I always vowed to follow her lead and act decisively, but at the moment, I feel incapable of doing so. There are simply too many unknowns.

Not that I'm scared. Not at all. I have no problem in fighting and dying for my birthright. I will happily take on any man or any number of warriors that think me weak enough to better in battle. I'll show any who dares attack me that I'm more skilled than them. If it turns out that I'm lying to myself, then I'll happily take my death as I should. I would die for Mercia and her people. Never doubt that.

But this. This half-known and little-understood situation I find myself in is unacceptable.

The ride towards York is supposed to settle me and prove that my fears are ill-founded. Although I travel past sleeping villages basking in the late summer sun, eking out those last few pieces of stray sunlight to tide them over through the dark times of the year, I also know that it only takes one enemy to topple a kingdom.

This hinterland between Mercia and York could be quiet and peaceful, but it would take only a few stray words, a mis-implied threat, and the smiles on the faces of the people that I meet could turn to murderous intent. So, I ride armed, with my sword and shield always ready, and still, people smile at me and offer me a good day. And they know me, as well. Small children stand shyly by the side of the Foos Way to watch me ride by, the girls with joyful expressions, the boys with jealousy. What they wouldn't give to have a horse as valuable and beautiful as mine and armour and weapons as well.

We follow the River Trent as we track northwards, sometimes close to the Foss Way and sometimes a little further away. It glints in the sunlight and looks dark and menacing with the approach of dusk. All the time, I'm thinking how easy it must have been for men with ships to travel so deep into my landlocked kingdom. I've been to the coast, I've seen the sea, and I've always felt a modicum of safety within Mercia, but I know now that it was misplaced.

The sea might be far to the east, south and west, but this bloody river dissects the land as though an open invitation for Viking raiders to use, and it's far from the only one. Here it's the River Trent. Close to Gloucester, the River Severn and many others as well. I wish we could block the river, but then, where would our traders go? Not all traders use horses and mules; many ply the sea routes bringing luxuries from afar, furs from the northern lands, gems and fine wine from kingdoms to the south where the weather bakes the ground so that it cracks and pleads for water.

I speak to as many people as I can as I meander northward, but they all tell the same story. They didn't see any ships, and they only know the same as I do about events north of York. I begin to feel discouraged and more and more apprehensive as well. If the Viking raiders didn't come down the River Trent, then how did they make it as far inland as Nottingham? Did they have horses? Or did they, as I fear, and so does Ælfstan, come from the south, perhaps via Wessex and a conversation with either cousin Ælfweard or my uncle, the king? There's certainly no sign, yet I add, of Lord Rǫgnvaldr making a move to take York and then progress south. No sign at all, so why would he have sent two shiploads of men to attack Nottingham?

And where are those supposed ships, for no sign has been found?

Athelstan continues to recover in Nottingham, and so Ealdorman Æthelfrith remains in Nottingham with him. Eadric accompanies me north, and he's not always good company.

His father spoke to him at length about our combined fears, but Eadric, a fresh-faced youth still coming into his strength, doesn't seem to understand the intricacies at play. He believes that those with the strongest army should always prevail. He believes that Mercia has the greatest selection of warriors and fyrd men and women. He can see no reason to fear the kingdom of Wessex because why would Wessex want to lose the buffer zone to the north? He's not a restful character, although I know he'd die fighting for me no matter my decision about the immediate future.

This has been something of a revelation for me. In the past, I always knew that my mother's followers were loyal to the point of death. Indeed, that was proved to me often enough. I never expected to elicit the same response when I became Lady of the Mercians. I can't say that I like it, but I'm honoured to have the respect of Ealdorman Æthelfrith and his sons and to know that it's not just because I'm my mother's daughter.

I feel I shouldn't take the support for granted. I should work hard to ensure that these men keep me in high regard. Sadly, at the moment, I don't know how to do that. I feel like a clucking hen, rushing from one place to another in search of her lost eggs and finding nothing, rushing only ever onward, looking more and more foolish.

The unease I feel can't last forever. When we approach the massive Humber Estuary, some of my worries and fears, hopes and beliefs begin to make sense. For here, as nowhere else, I find a river teaming with life. There are ships here from all over the northern lands, and suddenly, as I send my warriors out to speak with any they can entice into a conversation, the volume of chatter and knowledge threatens to overwhelm me. The feeling of being watched intensifies.

Something's being planned and plotted. Until I know what it is, I can't rest easy.

The river is awash with the colours of sails and people, happy to bask in the sun before the winds and rains of winter wash the land. There are men and women of all nationalities and faiths, and animals as well. The ships proliferate in and shape. There are long war vessels and smaller, rounder trading ships. There are lightweight craft which could be carried overland if they ran out of water, and there are simple boats to just cross from one side of the Humber to the other. Not that I fancy doing so. The estuary is vast here, close to the mouth of the sea, and I don't fancy my chances. Few people do.

A settlement has grown up close to the southern side of the river where men who fish the river and the nearby sea can be seen hauling fishing nets. Others mend nets damaged and broken by the harsh effects of the work. There are also some taverns, the raucous cries of those too far gone with the drink to care resounding almost as loudly as the cries of the sea birds. It's a place of activity, and it's a shock after my ride through the tranquil countryside.

My scouts have scanned for obvious signs of Viking raiders but have assured me that either all the ships are owned by local inhabitants or can be vouched for by either the reeve of the port area or in some cases, the men and women who own and run the taverns.

It seems that even here, there's no trace of Lord Rǫgnvaldr's fighting force. I should be pleased, but it merely adds to my frustration.

Have I come too far north? Have I missed the fighting force? Have they moved further inland, or is it simply a big lie?

I brood and grow irritable, and then, from out of the blue, a Viking raider warrior presents himself to me.

'My lady,' he smirks at me from behind his plaited beard and moustache, the one overflowing into the other. I'm sitting outside one of the taverns, determined to drown my worries with my female warriors. Not that it seems to be working. They watch me warily. I consider ordering them to leave me alone. But, I dismiss them when they mean to stop the man from speaking with me.

'My name's Snorri, a warrior, skald and trader from the northern kingdom.' I think he must mean Norway or Sweden or even the Outer Isles, and I look at him, the question half-formed on my lips.

'From Iceland, my lady,' he explains, 'the most northern of all countries.' He doesn't call it a kingdom because Iceland has no king. Even I know that. Her leading families rule her, and they eschew violence. For all that, many weapons adorn his body, and he shrugs, taking in my pointed stare.

'In lands governed by kings, warriors and bandits, I prefer to be suitably armed,' he explains.

He's already sitting before me without waiting for my invitation, and although I mean to draw attention to his breach of conduct, I find

I'm too curious to do so. I've never yet met anyone from the new country of Iceland, inhabited now for maybe fifty years at most.

'How do you know who I am?' I ask, and he nods as though expecting the question.

'The legend of your mother has travelled far and wide. Now your name is spoken about with respect as well. We have many great ladies in Iceland. They rule their families with an iron will and bring unruly men to their senses without needing iron and linden board.'

'I wish I had the same powers,' I acknowledge sourly. I find myself more and more intrigued by him.

'I've recently travelled from the Outer Isles of Orkney to Dublin and then the kingdom of Wessex.'

'You're well travelled then?' I laugh, and he nods, but we both know that he's been to all the places I wish I could go. He must have news for me.

I signal that I require more ale and another cup. He settles himself more comfortably before me, taking his time to take a good look around at my very visible warriors. When we first sat here, I thought our presence was unremarkable. It seems I was wrong. Even the tavern man keeps his distance and sends his wife and her women to serve us. We're a bunch of surly warriors with iron at our waists, and more, we're women as well. No doubt, all men should fear our wrath.

'Was the weather fair for your passage?' I finally ask when he doesn't attempt to resume speaking.

'The weather is always changeable. I hope I can make it home to Iceland before the storms hit. I don't fancy an extended stay in lands about to be fought over.' His tone is bland, as though he tests my interest, and I feel my thin patience beginning to waiver.

'I'd reward you well for your news,' I prod and chuckles aloud, his bright, grey eyes crinkling in the corners. Iceland is a new 'nation', almost sharing its birth with that of the Danelaw within England. But while it's rich in virgin land to farm, it's richer yet in long, dark winters and a lack of material to burn. Any trader from Iceland will have furs aplenty, but they need to return with wood and foodstuffs to tide them over the long winter. I imagine that a few Mercian oaks would make the man very pleased.

'My news isn't for sale, but I'd gladly share it.' He sounds sincere when he speaks, but should I trust a man who tells me news for no price? Isn't this a rife opportunity for him to tell me what I'm desperate to hear, that my family haven't turned against me?

'I'd reward you all the same,' I utter softly, turning my full gaze on him. I've been told I'm beautiful, not that I much care if I am or not, but beauty can make men do all sorts of things they wouldn't normally do. 'There must be many things that would benefit you during your winter in Iceland.'

'I'm always open to gifts,' he has the good grace to almost blush as he speaks. I laugh at his audacity.

'Tell me of Norse Dublin and the Outer Isles, of the Isle of Manx?' I ask, but he's shaking his head reluctantly.

'Norse Dublin is much less a concern for you than the kingdom of Wessex.' The words are intentionally blunt, but if he meant to shock me, he's failed.

'There have been rumours,' I offer when the broad grin slides from his face, the joy at imparting his knowledge losing its appeal in the face of my prior knowledge. 'I'd welcome more details, though,' I say encouragingly.

'Details are always so difficult to come by,' he agrees, his gravelly voice dropping even lower so that I have to lean forward across the table to hear what he says. This is a game to him.

'Then tell me of Iceland if you have no details to tell me from Wessex. I'm curious about how the people there have chosen to divide the land and govern it. The men and women of the Danelaw have elected to follow a different pattern to that employed in Iceland.' The Danelaw has remained largely English in its outlook, with enough laws from Denmark and the Northern territories to make it feel like home to the warriors and their families who chose to settle during my grandfather's life.

This time Snorri laughs, amused by my nonchalance.

'It seems the rumours about you are true, my lady. You're as shrewd as you are beautiful. I have no time to wait for Mercian oak this time, but next time I'm in England, I'd like five of the beasts cut so that I can transport them to Iceland. In the meantime, I'll tell you all I know.' He reaches across the table to shake on the deal, and I do so, a grin on my face. I like both his attitude and his compliment. It's a shame I might never see him again.

'The ports of the kingdom of Wessex are engaged, as always, on trading with the Frankish kingdoms and further afield. They allow the trading vessels from Norse Dublin to dock, but they rarely have a need for their goods and would rather tax them and send them on their way. It's only on their return from southern climates that the kingdom of Wessex has much need for Norse Dublin traders.'

'And why is that then?'

'For on the way back to Norse Dublin, they can carry men sent to bribe the grandsons of Ivarr into attacking King Constantin of the Scots and the kingdom of Mercia.'

'And is this what they do, or is this hearsay?'

'I've carried a Wessex man to the Isle of Manx, Norse Dublin and further north in search of such men,' he states blandly.

'And did you carry him back?'

His laughter is infectious as he shakes his head.

'I did not, my lady. I fear he became rather too friendly with Lord Rǫgnvaldr and may well have had to send a written message back to Wessex rather than go himself.'

'And did you carry this message?' This conversation is similar to pulling thorns from the skin, unpleasant and painful both.

'If I did, my lady, I could only tell you that the message was received by a scruffy-looking warrior, without sigil on his clothing.'

'Then you have no clue who the message was for?'

'You might think that, but on the westward journey, the man was seasick and talked in his sleep of members of the king's family. He belonged to someone in the Wessex royal family; I'd stake my life on it.'

'When I arrived in the Northern Isles, there was talk of an attempt to capture York. By the time I left, the discussion had turned to include your name and that of Constantin of the Scots. There was rumour of treasure and silver, of payments that were guaranteed for all warriors who went with Lord Rǫgnvaldr on the attack, and that they were to be ready when his ship army arrived. I confess I put the messenger's arrival down to this change of heart. He must have had a silver tongue when on land to convince Lord Rǫgnvaldr to leave the Northern Isles and travel first to Norse Dublin before coming to the land north of York. Lord Rǫgnvaldr is a bastard, and it would take a great deal to rouse him to battle far away from the land where he has his grandfather's reputation to keep him safe.'

'So, your assumptions are simply those?' I dismiss. I'd hoped for something substantial enough to decide on my uncle or cousin as the names behind this conspiracy.

'I don't believe in coincidences,' Snorri counters, his voice defensive. I nod an apology. I hadn't meant to sound so harsh. I don't believe in coincidences, either.

'Which member of the Wessex royal family?' I try, and he shakes his head.

'If I knew that, I wouldn't be speaking in whispers in a tavern. It's impossible to tell. He only ever talked about 'his lord'. He never named him, and I did think that he might have called the king 'his king,' so I've assumed, rightly or wrongly, that he was a member of Lord Ælfweard's household.'

That's two people now who've implicated cousin Ælfweard behind the attack, but there are also two people who think it's uncle Edward. Only I seem to be able to break the deadlock, and I still have nothing substantial to go on and so I'm still unable to do so.

'I know it's whispers and half-truths,' Snorri acknowledges, his tone cajoling. 'But often that's all men have to go on. I might hear a whisper of a good cargo in Denmark or a good harvest in Ireland, but unless I decide to seek out the answer by actually going there, I never know the answer.'

'But I'm here, far to the north of Nottingham, and I still know nothing concrete,' I counter.

'Perhaps your view should have been to the south, not the north,' he offers with a wry shrug. I bite my lip to stop myself from blurting out that I've sent spies to the south. After all, he's a trader, and he will trade that bit of information for the right number of coins. Or wood to burn.

'One more thing, my lady,' he says, standing to leave. It seems he's told me all he knows, and it was little, but I won't begrudge him the trees that we agreed to. Next year they'll be here, waiting for him, no matter what happens.

'There's a ship from the kingdom of Constantin in the harbour. You might do well to seek out the captain or one of the men on board. They're a surly bunch. Even I'm unable to break through their icy exterior, and believe me, I have much experience trying to thaw objects that don't want to be released from their icy stasis. But you, well, you're a pretty young woman and a lady as well. You might well have more success. They fly under a blue flag, and they stink of fish.'

I open my mouth to thank him for his suggestion, but he's already gone, his broad back walking jauntily down the street. I raise my finger to chew the nail and then drop it again. I can show no outward sign of my distress.

Eadric has been hovering close to me throughout the conversation with the trader. I don't know if he has news or is merely concerned to overhear what I'm being told, but I beckon him forward, and he rushes toward me.

'My lady,' he says, his voice hushed and his eyes furtive. 'There's a ship from the land of Constantin in the harbour. I listened to the men as they reloaded the ship. They know about the battle but little else. It might be worth speaking with the captain. He'd know more than the men.'

I nod, distracted. Snorri gave me intelligence I was to receive anyway. But my mind is on the battle in the north that cousin Athelstan witnessed. How can twenty shiploads of Viking raiders simply disappear? Where has Lord Rǫgnvaldr gone with them? And why is there still no news from the kingdom of Wessex?

'You have my permission to bribe him with whatever you need to loosen the man's tongue.' Eadric's surprised at my words and opens his mouth to speak but then shuts it again.

'That trader has a reputation as an honourable man,' he thinks to say, although the words he means are 'you can trust what he says.' I put him out of his misery and recount the conversation I shared with Snorri. Eadric's forehead creases as he hears about Snorri's suspicions and possible part in the attack from Lord Rǫgnvaldr.

'We need to find Lord Rǫgnvaldr. Speak to him,' Eadric offers, and I smile. At the moment, I'd like nothing more than to face an enemy where the odds are so heavily stacked against me, but I have too few warriors with me, and I'm far from home. I'd need to call out the fyrd to make war on Lord Rǫgnvaldr this late in the year. I doubt my men and women would be keen to leave the promise of good food and warm hearths.

Not everyone can be a warrior; I know that only too well. For Mercia to grow wealthy and strong, she needs her farmers, metal crafters, cooks and shepherds, and even her holy men.

'I need you to get this man to talk to you, and I need to send scouts across the river and further inland. I need news from Tamworth, cousin Athelstan and the kingdom of Wessex.' I sigh at the seemingly impossible task before me.

'There's always time,' Eadric consoles. I find his words touching, even though I disagree with them.

'There's only time when other men don't seek to unseat you from your position of strength and power. Whether it's King Edward or Lord Ælfweard at work, they've both been plotting this for longer than I've known about it. That gives them an advantage I don't want them to have.'

'Yes, but you also have the support of the whole of Mercia behind you and King Edward and his ætheling don't. It's a potent weapon you have at your disposal. Don't forget about it or dismiss it as inconsequential.'

I smile sadly as he speaks, trying to buoy my flagging spirits. His words are what I need to hear, but I can't accept them. I won't blame myself for the current predicament I'm in, but neither do I dismiss my part in this. I should have realised that there were always others coveting what I hold dear and who will think nothing of seizing it and never returning it.

'Go,' I manage, turning my half-filled cup of ale over so that its contents trickle to the floor through the roughly formed wooden table I sit at. I have far more important tasks to be organised than getting drunk and feeling sorry for myself.

He does as I command him, and I rise, signalling that my women should continue to drink if they want. Only I'm needed to issue commands to travel north and west; they might as well continue to drink. The task of predicting the future is mine. I need to start making better decisions about it all.

CHAPTER 15

Two days later, I'm even closer to York than I was at the Humber Estuary and also further inland. My intention is not to arrive at York but rather to scout the local landscape surrounding it.

I've received messages from Ealdorman Æthelfrith in Nottingham, and Eadric managed to elicit more information from the ship's captain from the land of the Scots. I now know that Lord Rǫgnvaldr had already chosen to attack north Northumbria long before my mother's death. What I don't know is why his warriors, if they are his warriors, have since chosen to attack Nottingham. And if they're not his warriors, under whose direction that attack was actually made?

The message from Ealdorman Æthelfrith was merely passing on word from King Edward sent to Tamworth that he understood and accepted that I was visiting the burhs. He sent no word of support for my actions and didn't mention his warriors in Nottingham in the terse message. Æthelfrith sent no other information with the passed-on message, and his silence is as telling as my uncle's single-line message.

The ship's captain said that he knew men who'd fought with King Constantin and that they'd long known to expect an altercation with

Lord Rǫgnvaldr. Lord Rǫgnvaldr's intentions toward York have been known about for the last year, at least. He's tried to buy the loyalty of enough men to manage and fill the number of ships he wanted to bring. It's an open secret in the Outer Islands that he means to be as powerful as his grandfather was once.

I'm making progress. But not enough, and none of the pieces yet fit coherently together.

I need to know the truth of the attack on Nottingham, and as such, I'm scouting the countryside inland of York. While Lord Rǫgnvaldr might have initially brought his warriors in ships to the northern lands, if he wants to attack York, he'll need to do so from all angles. Travelling along the river by York might not be the stealthiest of options because it's the most watched and the one that's been so often taken in the past.

Ealdorman Æthelfrith did pass on a personal message, informing me that his son, Athelstan, is now back on his feet and has resumed his training The news cheers me, as does the knowledge that he sent the young lad I rescued along with the messenger so that he could speak to me of more private matters.

The messenger looks unhappily at his sidekick, and his presence cautions me. It seems that Ealdorman Æthelfrith is warning me about the loyalty of my messenger.

Alone that night, my little squire, Eadig, tells me of Ealdorman Æthelfrith's more private message between mouthfuls of roasted boar caught that day by some of my women warriors scouting near a forested glade.

'King Edward's warriors are right lazy bastards,' he starts and then looks at me, consternation on his face, which I laugh away, ignoring Eadric's outraged gasp from beside me in front of the small fire that Eadig's built for us.

'Sorry, my lady,' he looks contrite, but I wave him on.

'Whatever it is that King Edward wants them to do, it's not to help Nottingham or the kingdom of Mercia. They drink and ... 'whore', I think your lordly father said,' he offers, turning to look at Eadric with innocent amusement on his face. It's obvious he knows exactly what he's talking about. Eadric's faint flush deepens as I stifle a smirk of amusement. I like Eadig. Probably too much.

'But the gate is nearly up, and by the time you return, it should be fully functioning.'

'Excellent,' I try to say, but he's not finished speaking.

'But there are reports that while they drink and whore, they're also trying to turn the warriors of Nottingham away from their allegiance to you, my lady,' he adds hastily. 'And have them swear an oath to King Edward. Seems, and your lordly father agreed, my lord,' his cheeky tone is infectious, and even Eadric relaxes at last and gives the boy his full attention. 'That Aldred and his men were sent north to steal Nottingham and her warriors from right under your nose. King Edward wants his own base from which he can launch attacks towards the north, although I think, and again your lordly father agreed, that he means to attack the kingdom of Mercia himself.'

I curse loudly, and even Eadig looks impressed at the litany of foul words escaping into the warmth of our fire. If King Edward wants to attack the kingdom of Mercia, then I'm handing it to him on a plate with my excursion to the north. Even worse, I've told him of my intentions. Even now, he could be riding into an unprotected Mercia.

'The ealdorman, he said he'd send word to Tamworth and ensure that your cousin didn't do anything foolish in your absence. Not quite sure what that means, but he seemed a bit worried about her.'

My cousin, Ecgwynn, is, of course, the king's oldest daughter. Her relationship with her father is as ambiguous as her brother's cousin Athelstan. But Edward might just prevail with her. She has no high position of power in Mercia and has even been denied a husband worthy of her rank. King Edward might well know this is her weakness and offer her one in exchange for Tamworth. I feel a mounting sense of panic at the thought of all my mother's and my careful planning crumbling around me.

Eadig's blind to my fear, but Eadric grasps it straight away.

'We should return to Nottingham and Tamworth straight away. We're learning nothing here, and in our absence, Mercia is more vulnerable.'

Have I been a fool? Have I played into my uncle's hand, or is this, once more, a set of coincidences that I'd do well to ignore and continue on my current path?

The thoughts should keep me awake all night, but instead, I sleep the best I've slept in ages and in the morning, there are reports of warriors on the move to the north of us, and I know that I'll finally get my answers that day.

THERE'S a faint trace of smoke in the air when I wake and push through the doorway of my tent. The night has been mostly warm until just before dawn when a chill breeze sprang up, rippling the fabric and driving me deeper into my furs and cloak. Waking is almost a relief as I stretch the chill ache from my back.

The smoke hanging in the early morning air in front of our advance could be from cook fires or even from a charcoal burner, but my scout, who set out two days ago to travel north, tells me that he's seen a large party of warriors moving across the landscape. He says they've burned a little but mostly left people alone, provided they have some Viking raider ancestry, or so he assumes. He's not spoken to them personally. It seems then that this might be Lord Rǫgnvaldr and his warriors. The thought cheers me.

I've had enough of rumours and whispers. I might actually receive some answers from this arrogant man who crashes around the old kingdoms of Deira and Bernicia as though they're his to control. I hope to send him back to Norse Dublin with such a scare that he'll never dare step foot in my grandfather's 'England' again.

My camp is quickly dismantled, the young lad, Eadig, serving me much to the disgust of my normal squire, Erna. He always seems one step in front of her in all his actions. I wink to her to try and dispel her temper, but it only makes her stamp from my presence while he chuckles with delight, her face dark with fury. I'll have to speak with him but not now. Now his help is much appreciated.

My horse is quickly ready, my few camp-followers sent to a place of safety, back along the road we just travelled, and I'm ready to discover my fate and that of the kingdom of Mercia. I hope there'll be a battle where I kill Lord Rǫgnvaldr, but I doubt I'll get my wish. But if I do manage such a feat, my name will be written in the annals of our time, just as my mother's.

If Lord Rǫgnvaldr's any warrior, as I am, we'll be fairly equally matched regarding skill, provided he'll fight a woman.

I lead a party of no more than fifty-five, not only my female warriors but also the men who serve me. They're all as grim and determined as I am. This is still, almost, Mercian land, and we'll shed our blood on it if it keeps it safe from Lord Rǫgnvaldr and his ravaging Viking raiders.

As we ride toward where the enemy has been sighted, my warriors call to each other, some teasing, but others inciting the others to rage. Warriors filled with rage are strong and also foolish, acting only on their instincts. The women are silent as Eoforhild rides serenely at the front of our force. We're all trained, and we'll rely on that training in any coming battle. The cold heat of rationalisation will allow us to claim a victory that others might fail to gain.

Eadric is nervous but keen at my side, and he leads the men, as I know he wants to, in the place of his absent father. I command my women, and they flank me, as many to either side as there are behind me. This is our formation, and we're used to our shield sisters and brothers.

Not that we have long to wait. Soon we dispatch our horses to the rear of our formation as with the rising sun, a host of men materialise before us, not exactly from nowhere. We've been able to hear them for some time, and their proximity is no surprise. Their faces are covered in dark helms and beards. One of them carries a banner of a wolf's head on a blood-red banner. It's easy to see in the first rays of daylight that brighten the higher land and darken the lower as the banner snaps in the stiff wind that's sprung up with the sunlight.

My banner, carried by Lioba, is of the Mercian eagles, interlocked with the Wessex wyvern. The Mercian double-headed eagles are black, the Wessex dragon red, on a bleached white background. If it catches the eye at the wrong moment, it looks like a hideous beast from the legends of Beowulf, the two characters merging to become one, twisted limbs contorted into a shape that could never live and draw breath. But today, in the fierce wind, the two creatures are easily identifiable; the might of Mercia combined with the longevity of Wessex.

At the front of the enemy, a small group of men stands proud. They've been waiting for us, and I swallow down my annoyance that I've not chosen the battle site. Not that there's much to go on. The land here rises only gently before falling again. There are no rivers and no nearby places of truly high ground.

They might have chosen the battle site, but I doubt they'll have any advantage over us. Not from what I can see.

For a long moment, we simply stare at each other. It's not a surprise to have found an enemy, but all the same, it feels strange to finally look at the men and few women who've caused me such heartache in recent weeks.

I wish I could ask them why they came to Northumbria and what rights they think they have to York. But I can already see the warriors twisting their weapons free from weapons belts, fingering sharp edges to test their keenness and preparing to fight, possibly to the death. They don't much wish to talk. An altercation is inevitable.

I turn to Eadric and Eoforhild. She's long and willowy and able to move in ways that my male warriors envy. She's serious and still as she watches the men. Eadric, on the other hand, is impatient. He rolls up and down on the balls of his feet, just itching for the command to attack to be given.

Up and down my ranks of warriors, some are praying, but most are simply considering the warriors they face across the hundred paces that separate the two sides. It's relatively easy to determine whom each will face in battle. After all, this is not the fyrd. These men and women are trained combatants. This is what they spend their time preparing for, a time when they'll need to fight for the freedom of the kingdom of Mercia.

I could give the command to advance right now, but instead, I wait. Neither group is making any noise other than the rustle of moving metal or wood as shields and swords, axes and seaxs are put into a ready position.

Behind the Viking raiders, I see a small stretch of water glistening in the early morning sun. On its waters, a ship waits. There are a few people within the ship, moving around busily, but other than that, it seems that whomever these attackers are, they're only a small force, and they've come alone. They have no horses to ride across the landscape on, not unless we fail and they capture ours.

The ship, even I must admit, is beautiful, glowing in the building daylight. Her sail is down, but I imagine, if it were up, that its design would match the one on the enemy banner.

From across the contested land, a tall man steps forward. He's garbed as a warrior, but is helmless, so I can see his face as he speaks. He has a neat and tidy beard and moustache and long hair tied back loosely behind his ears.

'My lady, Ælfwynn,' he calls, in the language of the Saxons, a mocking bow matching his words. Well, it appears mocking to my jaundiced eyes.

'My lord?' I ask, the question heavy in the air. I'll wait for him to introduce himself rather than assume that this is Lord Rǫgnvaldr. I haven't stepped clear of my line of warriors as Lord Rǫgnvaldr has. Instead, I calmly eye those of the enemy who have a handy spear that could easily breach the distance between us and pierce me before our attack can even begin. Laughter greets my words.

'I'm no lord, my lady. I'm Rǫgnvaldr Sigfrodrsson, grandson of Ivarr Ragnarsson of the Dublin Norse.' His tone is mocking and challenging all at the same time. Another Viking raider warrior might have taken the use of the word 'lord' as a compliment, but Rǫgnvaldr is not a typical warrior.

'Why have you come to Northumbria? To Mercia?' I demand with an edge to my voice, but my anger is restrained under this façade of civility.

'Why have you come so far from Mercia, from the safety of your Tamworth?' he derides once more, and I hold my tongue. It seems he's as little keen to provide me with answers as everyone else I've approached of late. I'm tired of riddles and half-answered questions.

Silence once more hangs in the air as I watch him.

He is, as all Viking raider warriors seem to be, a very tall man, physically dominating. I can see where his muscles ripple below his byrnie as he breathes, inadvertently flexing and unflexing his hand that holds his seax, neither threatening nor reassuring with the movement, but rather businesslike.

His seax is a lethal-looking weapon, its jagged edges glowing in the light from the sun. Every so often, the metal flashes brightly, sending streams of brightness playing over his face to highlight his slightly crooked nose, full lips and flowing beard, tied with trinkets so that they bang together as his mouth works in speech.

He's not an attractive or an unattractive man, but he is stereotypical of every Viking raider I've ever fought. The thought cheers me. No matter what, he's nothing more than a man with a man's strengths and inherent weaknesses.

'My concern is not with the kingdom Mercia,' he finally adds, as though I need the reassurance, and I nod as if expecting to hear those words.

'Then why are you here? This is south of York, on land claimed by Mercia. It's a long, long way from where you came ashore in Bernicia.'

He looks impressed by my prior knowledge of his actions, but his body language is still disdainful.

'You seem to know more about my actions than I do about yours,' he calls, but I wave those words aside. I'm bored of this wordplay.

'Have you come to fight or talk? Do you come to rule or to make alliances?'

'I come to meet my ally,' he answers quickly, the first straight answer I've received yet.

'And who is your ally?' I continue to probe as his eyebrow quirks into his hairline at my words.

'You mean to tell me, Lady Ælfwynn, that you're not my ally?' his gaze fixes above my head as though he looks for another behind me. I refuse to be drawn into his ploy. I keep my eyes firmly on his.

'Who's your ally?' I demand once more. I'd like to growl at the man, take my seax to his throat and threaten him until he gives me the answers I want. But our numbers are too evenly matched. It's just possible that if I do so, I'll be sentencing my followers to a hard-won death in battle.

With a quick look behind him, during which his hands move, but I can't see the details, he drops his weapons to the floor and steps toward me. As he does so, every one of my warriors adopts an even more threatening battle stance, if that were possible. If he notices, he hides it well and continues to walk toward me. Whatever else I'd say about him, I must accept that he's brave to approach me as he does.

'Perhaps we could talk instead of shout,' is proposed as he walks to the centre of the middle ground between the two lines of enemies. Although both Eadric and Eoforhild hiss at the suggestion, I, too, place my weapons on the ground and walk across the brown field of harvested crops toward him. I've seen no sign of the farmer this field belongs to, but it's been used for growing this year.

My curiosity is too great not to take up his offer. I need to know what's been happening since my mother's death, and he's right, shouting at each other isn't the best way to hold that conversation.

His warriors watch me with interested eyes, but for now, the threat has gone, and their weapons are being variously returned to weapons belts or left on the ground, just like mine.

Up close, I can see that Rǫgnvaldr is a better-looking man than I gave him credit for. His face has some scars disappearing into his hairline, visible as traces of slightly puckered skin in the harsh sunrise, but his eyes are fiercely intelligent. They never leave my face, but I endure his interest.

I'm used to being an object of fascination as a woman in a world where men mistakenly think they rule. My mother suffered the same scrutiny. The Wessex royal wives have always been insipid creatures. My mother never failed to ensure she took advantage of her liberation from such a future, even if her marriage to my father was not always easy or indeed satisfying.

'My lady,' he offers again, his voice much softer, all traces of mockery gone from his clever face. 'They didn't lie when they said you were a beautiful woman,' he begins, his tone intimate and almost disrespectful. 'But they sell you short when their description of you stops there. I can see that you're a woman of strong mind and intelligence.' There's approval in his voice, and he's moved his attention away from my face so he no longer examines me as though I'm a horse for sale.

'My lord,' I gasp, shocked by his words and wondering who's said such things about me to my enemy. I've never wanted to be known for my looks, only my strength and ability to rule. Men aren't judged on their looks but rather on their battle prowess. I'd rather the same was said about me.

He laughs at my confused reply. 'I didn't mean to offend. I only offer my opinion.'

'Then my thanks for that,' I stumble once more, my poise evaporated in the face of this bizarre conversation on what should be a battle site. 'What is it you wished to say to me?' I press. This isn't how I imagined today evolving when I woke to the news that his force had been sighted.

'I wished to meet you,' he simply responds, and my hopes fade of ever discovering the truth.

'Then you've done that, and now I'll return to my warriors and begin this battle.'

'Why?' he asks, his amusement back in his voice. 'Who is it that you think you fight?'

His question confuses me again, although I try to hide that bewilderment and apply logic to his words.

'You're here. I'll fight you.'

'I came here to meet my ally, not my enemy.'

'But I'm not your ally,' I'm struggling to follow his twisted chain of thought, where his links never quite seem to join where I expect them to.

'But you could be my ally,' he smiles once more, a beguiling expression on his honest face. I consider what he's telling me.

'So, you have no ally then?' I ask, slowly, working my way through his words as though I'm learning a different language where none of the words means what I think they do. 'You came here to make an ally?'

'No, I have an ally already, but it never hurts to have more than one.'

'And who is the ally that you already have?' I try again, almost imploring him to say something logical that fits with the facts as I know them.

'Ah, now, that would be inappropriate for me to share with you, at this moment in time. My ally is not yet here and might not be coming now that you've arrived. It wouldn't be fair to speak their name without their consent.'

I try for a change of tact.

'Did you send a force to Nottingham? To attack the burh there?'

He doesn't seem to mind my new question but takes his time answering.

'Nottingham?' he muses, 'I don't believe I've ever heard of the place. Is it big? Little? Of importance to the kingdom of Mercia?'

I want to distrust his answer, but there's evident interest on his face. His question is genuine and not a further example of him being complicated and mysterious.

'You've never heard of Nottingham? To the east of the Mercian heartlands, along a river,' I don't mention the name of the river, hoping to catch him out.

'Where does this river start? How would my ships know to get to it? And what force was there, and who said they were my men?'

The balance of the conversation has shifted away from him and his intentions today and to the past. I find myself drawn to the heart of his questions. Ignoring the suppressed anger in his tone is difficult.

'Two shiploads of men, eighty or a hundred in all, claiming to have been sent by you, attacked Nottingham nearly three weeks ago.'

His eyes narrow in fury.

'What became of the men? I' speak with the survivors.'

'There was only one survivor, and regrettably, he didn't outlive his interrogation after the battle.'

'I wouldn't think you a brutal woman to torture a man to death,' there's disbelief in his voice now.

'Well, I, well, I didn't want him tortured. There was, there was a misunderstanding between what I wanted and what my uncle's men wanted.'

'So, the King of Wessex was involved,' he nods now as though what he's hearing is beginning to make sense. I sense this means an explanation might finally be coming my way.

'I assure you, my lady, that none of my ships has gone south to Mercia. This is the furthest south we've yet been, and our intention here was not to fight but to talk. I brought my warriors with me on a ship; you can probably see it behind us. I'm looking for allies to retake York and to claim Northumbria as my own, or Bernicia and Deira as you called it. My interest in Mercia and your kingdom is non-existent, except regarding finalising a border with you when York is mine. But that'll take many years.'

'So why would men say they belonged to you?'

'My name is an illustrious one,' somehow, he says that without sounding arrogant, which amazes me. 'Men without a real leader might hope that I'll lead them. Or, and I rather suspect this, men are using my name to drive you from the kingdom of Mercia.'

The bluntness of his words fills me with foreboding. Yet I still don't know which 'men' he speaks of, although his thoughts so completely mirror mine that I think everyone must have received a messenger telling them of my intentions. Perhaps they also lit fires to let my enemy know that Mercia was ripe for taking. My irritation at myself grows once more. Has my curiosity made it all too easy for Mercia to fall victim to someone else?

'Who's your ally?' I ask again, and he nods as though my question's to be expected.

'The archbishop. He's of Viking raider descent. He wishes York was ruled by Viking raiders once more. He doesn't want a woman of Wessex origin to rule the kingdom he thinks of as his. He believes that you intend to secure York for Mercia.'

'Then you're not here to meet with anyone from the kingdom of

Wessex?' I press. I need to hear him say those words. I can scarce believe it. It seems that I've been misled ever since I arrived in Nottingham. And why would the archbishop think I intended to claim York? I only want to make Mercia secure.

'I've no allies in Wessex,' he bows, his keen eyes watching my warriors so that he doesn't see the relief and anger that simultaneously covers my face as I struggle, still, to comprehend where the danger emanates from. 'You have women amongst your men,' he says, surprised. 'It's a Norse custom, not a Mercian one.'

'To rule men, women must rule as men do, and men rule with their swords and their shields.' My tone is rough, for I've resolved all that I know in my mind and can only draw one conclusion from it all. It means that my enemies are only from Wessex. The belief that I've been holding onto, that my uncle or my cousin had merely taken advantage of the timely arrival of Lord Rǫgnvaldr to try and break my power, is completely false. That horrifies me.

All that I understood was to be mine is to be stolen from me by my uncle or cousin in Wessex. The weight of the family betrayal almost drives me to my knees in the middle of what might still be a battle site.

Lord Rǫgnvaldr does me the courtesy of not noticing the effect his words have had on me, instead looking over my head once more and wincing as he does so. I assume he's watching my warriors, but his next words tell me his view is above their heads, into the distance.

'It seems that our meeting may have to a rather abrupt ending,' he offers, his gaze sweeping back to my face. I don't know what he sees there, but I accept the pleading in his eyes and turn to see what he's already seen.

My heart sinks even further.

I was wrong, very wrong.

This conspiracy against me is greater than the kingdom of Wessex against that of the kingdom of Mercia. York is also involved.

Striding toward me, effectively cutting off any chance of escape for my warriors, rides a war band much larger than mine. They proudly display the banners of Wessex, the blood-red Wessex dragon, and the holy see of the archbishopric of York, its cross glistening with almost as much maroon as Wessex's own.

'Ah,' is all Lord Rǫgnvaldr says as comprehension flashes through my mind. At that moment, we both understand that we've been manipulated. As consternation breaks out amongst the warriors on both sides of our permanently interrupted battle, I know that my uncle or cousin means to take much more than my role as Lady of Mercia. They intend to take my life as well.

Eadric looks at me, from across the field, with his brow furrowed as though he's still trying to make sense of what's happening. I can see Eoforhild's mouth working overtime as she decides how many should face Lord Rǫgnvaldr and how many our other enemies. It's impossible to think that either side has come to support me against Lord Rǫgnvaldr. Otherwise, why would they be racing toward me with weapons already drawn while I stand calmly discussing events with Rǫgnvaldr?

For a long moment, I feel rooted to the spot, my mind almost unable to grasp what's about to happen. Only then Lord Rǫgnvaldr speaks.

'I don't much like this,' he mutters under his breath, his eyes tracking the progress of the long straggling line of men moving into position behind my warriors. I can only hope that the members of my baggage train have managed to hide away, even take the horses and return to Mercia or wherever they feel safe. Perhaps as far away from Mercia as it's possible to be.

'It seems your ally is here,' I try to joke, but he's shaking his head, and the words choke in my throat.

'I'm a Viking raider, my lady, I make no bones of that, but I'm not a man to be controlled. The archbishop might think he's my ally, but I beg to differ with him. It's he who's got me into this, and I intend to get myself out of it. I'd gladly arrange an alliance of convenience with you now, one where you allow me to control York once the archbishop has been brought to heel.'

His words astound me, coming as they do when they're precisely what I need to hear. But I can't believe them. Why would he do this?

He looks at my face and smirks softly.

'It's a genuine offer. King Constantin of the Scots is a powerful enemy and one I should perhaps not have made until I was more secure in York, but we came ashore too soon. The land looked ripe for the taking. I was wrong, of course. I'd welcome a strong ally as my neighbour instead of another enemy. I don't like the thought of being squeezed from the north and the south when I claim the kingdom of York for myself.'

'You'd fight for me now, not knowing if you'd live or die, hoping that I'd be your ally in the future, and that I'd let you take York? You would risk the lives of your hard-won warriors for me?'

'I would, my lady. You seem more honourable than the others and a damn sight more interesting to talk to as well. I believe you're a woman of your word, as I understand your mother was.' He's watching me intently as I try to decide whether this is a ruse. Has he made me this offer so that I can order my warriors to show their back to his, and they can then strike them down in their most vulnerable position? Is the offer one born of trying to keep his warriors alive rather than risking them against my force? Or is it genuine?

The questions tumble through my mind like fire on ice, cracking the glass into tiny shards that subsequently shatter themselves, creating more and more possibilities. So many what-ifs and possibilities.

'I don't lie, my lady. I know you have no previous experience to go on, but I'm a man of my oath. I'd suggest you asked my men, but there's no time.'

His eyes are watching events before me, and I know it's only a matter of moments before Eadric rides to my side, demanding I take action.

But what should that action be?

'If you fight for me and for mine, I'll be your ally, whether you take York or not, but I can't help you claim York. It would go against my mother's oaths to assist Viking raiders in taking control of any part of this island.'

'You strike a hard bargain, even now,' he mutters with approval in his voice. He's nodding all the same. 'I can't pledge my oath to you as a commanded man, as you'd need to gift me with land or weapons. That would go down very badly with the Mercians after our battle has ended and our enemy lies dead and buried. But an alliance would be acceptable.' He's already turning back to look at his men to determine how best to fight this new hazard. He turns back to me quickly.

'We'll have it written down, or whatever it is you Mercians like to do when agreeing to this. And, if for some reason, I don't survive the battle, remember this, my lady, from one who knows only too well, families are not to be trusted, and my men will expect to be rewarded all the same.' He reaches his hand out, and I add my own to his. We grasp forearms, an agreement from ancient times and one that's publicly made so that both our sides will understand what's happened here.

I feel his strength and his resolve in the sinew of his arm. I think I've made a good bargain. I don't know what he thinks. His face is almost blank, until he winks at me, as though this is the most enjoyment he's had in weeks.

Abruptly he turns away, and I think he's gone, but then once more, he turns to look at me.

'Tell your people to stay where they are but move all of them to the right. My warriors will take the left – a split field will ensure we don't have to worry about enemies guarding hastily made ally's backs. I'll see you in the centre.'

This time he runs back to his shield wall to the jeers and catcalls of his warriors. My warriors eye me with the sullen eyes of those who think they've already lost. I must raise their spirits and convince them of Lord Rǫgnvaldr's integrity, and I have less time than I'd like to do so.

Already I'm aware that Lord Rǫgnvaldr's warriors are reforming in the formation he suggested, and so I dash across the remaining distance considering my words.

Eadric runs to meet me, his face bleached of colour. I'm unsure what he believes to be the bigger adversary today, those behind us or those in front.

'We have new allies,' I stutter as Eoforhild's mouth falls open in shock.

'Lord Rǫgnvaldr?' she all but squeals, utterly counter to her normal behaviour, her eyes on the actions of Rǫgnvaldr's warriors.

'An ally to help us against my family and the Archbishop of York. They planned to use Lord Rǫgnvaldr to trap me, and I've walked into the trap just as they wanted. Fortuitously, it seems that the Viking raider Rǫgnvaldr isn't happy at being used in such a way. He asks only for my support if he manages to take York, nothing more.'

Eadric watches me with shock and hope on his face as though he can't quite believe this abrupt change of fortunes.

'Have everyone double up and form lines to the right. Lord Rǫgnvaldr will take the left. Spread the news quickly. Tell my warriors that we should only protect our backs, not the Viking raiders. Tell them it's an alliance of convenience and that I've given nothing away to have Rǫgnvaldr's support, but do it quickly.' The urgency in my voice almost ends in a squeal, just as Eoforhild's did only moments ago.

The sound of the archbishop's force nearing ours is starting to pound through the ground. I wish I knew how many were coming, but my view of them is simply of a great horde coming toward me. It's a grotesque parody of the Viking raids from fifty years ago, as now I stand with the Viking raiders. I don't want to kill my fellow Saxons, but these men racing toward me are from York and the kingdom of Wessex. It seems they've forgotten our shared heritage, and as much as I don't want to, I should do the same.

I can hear anger from my warriors as news spreads of my hasty alliance, quickly muffled as Lord Rǫgnvaldr's men do as he promised and slide into formation to the left of my warriors. His force is matched to mine. If we'd been left to fight alone, we'd have had an equal battle regarding numbers, if not skill. I imagine my warriors to be far more skilled than his, but that's my arrogance and confidence. It's beginning to unravel in the face of everything I thought I knew, proving to be nothing more than a huge lie.

I rush to join Lord Rǫgnvaldr in the centre of the fray. Eoforhild hurries to keep up with me. Eadric has already run to the far edges of the shield wall to bolster those on the periphery and to direct them if the new enemy should have enough warriors to attempt to wrap around our combined force. Having allied with our seeming enemy, Eadric doesn't intend on allowing another adversary to attack our vulnerable back.

The combined force of the Archbishop of York, and Aldred, King Edward's duplicitous battle commander from Nottingham, are coming sharply into focus. I wish I'd punished him now. Sent him back to Wessex. I can no longer deny that it's my supposed allies who've become my enemies. The banners of the church in York and the dragon of Wessex stand steady in the breeze, each sharp snap of the wind straightening them and bringing the betraying hint of a tear to my eye.

How has it come to this?

My uncle or my cousin, whichever is behind this, has betrayed all that our father and grandfather held dear. Alfred, known as the great, understood family betrayal only too well. He was both a victim of it and a proponent of it. He stole his nephew's kingdom and spent many years trying to undo the harm that caused.

I've deceived no one and must question the decision-making behind the actions of my uncle and cousin. As I drag my helm into place over my long-braided hair, ensuring my shield and sword are ready, I determine it can only be greed that guides their actions. Not necessarily for wealth but for power and reputation. They both wish to stand aloft of King Alfred and be termed great for themselves. They don't wish to be someone's son or grandson. My pride in being my mother's daughter isn't matched by these power-crazed men and boys.

Even I know their hopes and dreams are ridiculous. They'll never be men remembered as my grandfather was. How could they be? They're not about to stand firm while all of Saxon England collapses under the onslaught of a coordinated and seemingly endless Viking raider attack. The Viking raiders and their descendants are mostly our allies now. Only a few ragged warbands still try their luck for a handful of treasure. And, of course, the men from Norse Dublin and the Outer Isles.

Eoforhild issues commands so that my women fall into position, and I turn to meet the eye of as many of them as possible in the time we have left before battle commences.

This is the first true strength of our skill and years and years of training, and I vow we'll win the day as I hold their eyes briefly. There's no fear on the partially hidden faces of my warriors, helms already in place, only determination. I hope they see the same on mine.

In front of me, the combined force of our new enemy is rushing into formation. If they show any concern or confusion for events that have overridden what they expected to find here, I can't see it reflected in a worried stance or furrowed brow. The faceless warriors seem too calm, too assured of themselves. Perhaps even now, they suspect that Lord Rǫgnvaldr is their ally.

It disappoints me. For once, I'd like to be the one in control of events. I'd like to make my enemy quiver in fear. I want them to be terrified of me, not tolerate my endeavours.

I see Lord Rǫgnvaldr mingling amongst his men. He winks at me across the distance that divides us and then dips his head to cap his long hair inside his helm. He looks as though he's enjoying this. When we've won, I vow to look as fearless as he does.

With a final clatter of wood and weapons, the two shield walls form and start to merge, mine and Lord Rǫgnvaldr's. And then an uneasy moment stretches out between the two sides, far too long for my liking. A quick rush breaks it as my warriors, led by Ymma, at Eoforhild's discrete command move to merge with Lord Rǫgnvaldr's force.

Lord Rǫgnvaldr also sees the jagged gash through the centre of our shield wall and sends ten of his men to join my women. There's some jostling for permission to hold the front, to be the first to meet the enemy, while at the same time, to be the farthest from either the Viking raider men or the Mercian women. All too soon, our shield wall is locked in place, and I signal to my new ally that I'm ready to attack.

My place isn't in the front line of the attack but rather three to the rear, surrounded by Eoforhild and Firamodor. We've long trained together, the three of us. We know each other's fighting stances as well as we know our own. Our strengths and weaknesses are all matched and countered by one another.

It's Lord Rǫgnvaldr who ultimately gives the command to advance, and slowly the shield wall, linden boards held firmly in hands steadying under the force of the battle to come, begins to make its way toward our enemy.

I think I should take a moment to offer a prayer to my God only for the banner of the archbishop to catch my attention. It once more cracks in the wind above my head, where I can actually see beyond the shoulders of the warrior in front of me. I don't think I should offer any prayers today, not if I wish to be assured of victory.

Jeers and catcalls burst forth from the mouth of my allies and my warriors, taunting those who stand against them. I join my voice to the cry.

'Bastards,' I roar. 'Wessex snakes,' follow on. 'Whore,' I rage, picking out the archbishop in the group of warriors. The rage rips through me for the first time since I became the victim of a conspiracy, turning my words almost to weapons, sharp enough to pierce leather and wood, iron and fake battle strength.

My shield is above the head of the warrior in front of me, just as theirs is above the head of the next warrior, and on it goes until the front of the shield wall is reached. There my warriors carry their shields in front of them, knowing that they can rely on those to either side to hold tight to them while those behind guard their heads. That physical contact will prevent them from buckling under the onslaught to come and from running away should fear replace the cold heat of battle.

I hear the whistle of spears thrown through the air, and belatedly realise that Lord Rǫgnvaldr must have spearmen amongst his armed force. Even over the thunder of our angry shrieks, I can make out the whistle of the weapons flying through the air, followed by the dismayed shrieks from those impaled when the spears skirt close to the ground once more.

The ground beneath our feet is already churned up by the passage of so many as I finally feel the enemy begin to move toward us. The growl of men coming to fight me, to try and deprive me of my kingdom, further fuels my anger and fear, until now a low rumble in my stomach, but which is becoming debilitating.

Only the physical presence of Eoforhild and Firamodor moves me forward. They carry me along with the rest of our warriors. This is different to my last battle when I happened upon the attack. This is intentional and of my doing. For a moment, my fear almost cripples me.

Just before the impact of the shield walls meet, I rediscover my feet and my strength and shoulder my way free of their support. My women release me as my breath comes faster, and my combat cries fill the air. The name of my mother is on my lips, but around me, I hear the word 'Mercia' repeated over and over again. My warriors fight for my Mercia, and I fight to hold onto my mother's right to rule, bequeathed to me when I was born.

Wessex won't take Mercia, even if it's our oldest enemy, a Viking raider horde, which prevents that from happening.

CHAPTER 16

Our two sides are evenly matched. I can feel it even in that first clash. There's not one spare warrior in the ranks of the two sides. Each shield touches the boss of another as the dirty, shoving work of the shield wall begins.

I know not all battles are fought in such a personal and yet impersonal way, each warrior covered by their helm, byrnie and shield. Each pushing with all their might to gain a few precious steps forward. But this isn't like all those battles.

This is deeply personal. A battle between families. Between allies.

My body feels ready, all traces of fear gone. My anger remains, but as I've taught my female warriors for so long, it's skill that wins a battle, years and years of pre-programmed fighting. Instinct is a powerful tool in a fight but the advantage of training can't beat it. Not unless that training has been poor, and mine hasn't been.

Some men are raised to be warriors. As they train, their bodies develop, adding muscle to the sinew. Mine is the same. I'm prepared and ready. My fury is a deep well that could boil over at any moment, adding to my painstakingly forged strength. But I don't need it. Not yet.

The reverberation of the shield wall strikes through my feet and belly, the ground rumbling away beneath my feet as though protesting its current use.

I grin inside my helm.

I've always wondered what this moment would feel like, often thinking that it would never come. My mother allowed me to train, and my warriors trained with me. But Mercia hasn't been threatened so much that the daughter of her ruler would need to face an enemy in such an open battle for many years, and certainly not her ruler. If my uncle were here, fighting for Wessex, he'd be issuing his orders from the rear, not the heart of the attack.

In front of me, I can hear the straining cries of men and women, shield against shield, as those behind attempt to exploit gaps in the overlapping wood and iron. Those in the third row seek out stray spaces and try to thrust their spears or their long swords through those vacuums. They seek an unprotected ankle, or a forgotten-about leg, an exposed arm or side of the body.

It's these shrewd moves that claim the first casualty as one of my warriors crawls his way to the back of the shield wall. Blood streaks his lower body, and his face, where his helm has been knocked loose, is the palest white I've ever seen.

'My lady,' is all he manages before crumbling to the floor, curled around his pain. I'm already moving closer to the front of the shield wall. My compassion is etched into my eyes. This man will die for me today, and I've nothing but my thanks and my sorrow to give him.

I can hear Viking raider voices raised in instruction, but I'm too closely pressed into the fighting to perceive the orders. At this moment in time, I can imagine that nothing disastrous has happened. Not yet. The instructions are probably concerned with shoring up particularly aggressive elements of the York and Wessex line.

It feels strange to realise that the language of war from my youth has become the discourse of my salvation.

The crush of bodies is overwhelming. I can hear Eoforhild's breath rasping. She's anticipating when she'll be called to action with weapons instead of just her body weight leaning into the backs of those at the front line.

Firamodor mutters a prayer for salvation under her breath, her thoughts purer than mine where religion is concerned. But then it would be nice to only be a believer as opposed to someone who's too often seen the inner working of the whole rotten religious framework that covers almost all of England.

I wonder where Archbishop Plegmund is today. I can only hope that I'm not fighting him right now.

The shield wall lurches three steps backwards. I turn quickly to ensure I don't trip over my dying warrior, but my cause for concern is irrelevant. His staring eyes watch me, unheeding of my foot that seeks purchase behind him. All the same, I'd rather not crush him, even in death, if I can avoid it.

The move from the opposition is greeted with derision. Suddenly I'm rushing four steps forward, once more reaching for a spot where I won't trample my brave warrior.

For precious moments our advantage holds, and then it doesn't, but we only give away one step, and we're back in the same position that we started in.

The rumble of a Norse order reaches my ears again. I turn to watch at least a dozen men removing some of their more cumbersome equipment behind the rear of the fighting line. They keep their helms and their weapons, but some leave their shields and heavy war axes behind.

I know a moment of fear as I meet the half-crazed blue eyes of one of the warriors, blood already sheeting down his face from a ferocious scalp wound. He leers at me, his teeth flashing black. I know what's about to happen. He bows his head to me as a benediction and then turns to his task, all thoughts of me forgotten.

Another abrasive directive reaches my ears. I feel more than see that those working at the back of the Viking raider line have dropped to their knees, shields above their heads.

The twelve men don't even take the time to consider what they're about to do. I hear the thundering tread of running men on wood and metal, so reminiscent of the sound of people approaching me in my great hall in Tamworth that, for a moment, my head whirls with confusion. Where am I?

The outraged shrieks of our enemy that reach me confirm that the men have successfully landed on the York and Wessex side of the fight. I can hear men screaming in fear, some in English and some in garbled Norse.

I doubt Lord Rǫgnvaldr's warriors will live through this, but it gives his side of the shield wall the opportunity it needs. Suddenly he's reclaimed the lost step of his previous gain and four more besides. I can feel the strain where the Viking raider and English halves of this shield wall meet. Unused to fighting together, this is the place of our greatest weakness.

'Reinforce the breach,' I bellow, my voice beating loudly, carrying over even the deafening cacophony of war.

Mildryth races beyond me, her face fierce with determination. I hold my breath, hoping that Lord Rǫgnvaldr's actions haven't doomed us to failure. A moment later, the Mercian side of the shield wall follows those four steps forward. We're level once more.

I now stand where before my shield wall battled the enemy. There are a few scattered bodies. The ground's slick with battle juices. Some of the warriors on the shield wall step away from their tasks to drive swords and seaxs through the bodies, determined to ensure they're dead. We want no enemy rising against us.

The sound of iron crushing bone temporarily fills the air. I wince at the noise, imagining the damage being done to men who were dead or nearly so. I swallow my revulsion. Combat is no time for compassion for the enemy.

Once more, through the press of bodies, the wounded and the dying stagger backwards, and I step ever closer to taking my place on the at the front of the shield wall.

I lick dry lips, intent on Eoforhild's back. My shield arm's starting to feel the strain of covering her head, but she's only one step away from being at the front. She needs my protection.

In battles such as this, it's the ones with the most stamina who prevail. Speed can be easily overcome because it doesn't last forever, melting away like snow before the early summer sun. Stamina can drive a warrior to march all day and all night as well. Endurance can make a woman hold her shield above her head all morning, even when the sun beats on her face, making sweat swim down her back.

Eoforhild abruptly lurches forward, startling me. I gather my wits, my shield instantly over her head again, garnered by my years of training. This is it. There's only her between the fighting at the front and myself.

The shield wall is holding together remarkably well. I'd expected it to disintegrate, but everyone understands the importance of holding it together. Our strength lies in acting in harmony. No one warrior will win this battle. We all need each other, even if we were enemies such a short time ago.

My nostrils fill with the scent of fear and sweat, and my mouth tastes of ash, but I know the part I must play. While my body rebels against me, my muscles bunching to flee the battle, my years of training override my body's physical needs. I'm adding my strength to Eoforhild, my spare hand on her back, forcing her ever forward. If necessary, I'll lean against her, pushing my potency through her failing strength. I'll keep her upright until her legs are cut from beneath her.

It's what she'd beg me to do had she the air for words.

My world retracts. All I hear is my breathing, remarkably slow and easy now that I've conquered my body's desire to flee. All I can see in front of me is the exposed nape of Eoforhild's neck; her hair curled tightly beneath her helm. Long hair can be as much a curse in battle as a long beard for a man. Never give an enemy an unintentional advantage. Anything that can be pulled or shoved is unwelcome in combat.

I feel the reach of a spear or sword at my feet. Quickly I jab down, impaling the projectile with my sword. I pull it from the enemy with all of my strength, gasping when the spear unexpectedly comes free, almost unbalancing me. I push it behind me, and its weight is taken from me by someone else. There'll be a warrior on the York and

Wessex side of this battle without a weapon. The thought cheers me. Now, all we must do is disarm the rest of the bastards.

Eoforhild moves easily and quickly in between long moments of stillness; her strength is entirely focused on trying to gain those few extra steps, force the enemy to lose their footing and slip to the ground where I'll cut them.

I'd like to stab my uncle and my cousin. Not necessarily kill them, although perhaps I must. Perhaps this is the first test of my steward-ship of Mercia, and just as the pagan Penda did three hundred years ago, I must kill any who contest my power to rule without opposition. Even family.

The whistle of spears overhead returns me to the task at hand. This time the spears disperse amongst my warriors, a stray howl of outrage reaching my ear before being silenced.

I wait, expecting the opposition to attempt the same feat as the Viking raiders and launch themselves amongst the rear lines of the shield wall.

The noise of that attack has abated. I must assume that those men are dead. But, before their death, they gave us an advantage, and no doubt they'll be remembered in song or verse for their bravery.

A stray sword breaks free from between Eoforhild's shield and whoever fights to her left. It reaches through, probing for any weak-ness. In the blink of an eye, I know it for a frail weapon, too heavily rusted to be of any great use. Its edges are almost serrated rather than finely ground down to a sharp edge.

I raise my sword elbow and knock it aside with my heavily padded and metalled byrnie. It crumbles at my touch.

From where has this aged weapon appeared? Who thought it would be any good in this altercation?

I cough at the tang of released rust as, once more, the shield wall advances two steps at the joint directive from Lord Rǫgnvaldr from his end of the shield wall and Eadric at his.

I stab down, my eyes meeting the pained expression of a youth, no more than a boy, who grabs for a concealed cross that lies around his neck as my sword beats him to it. He dies, a gurgle of blood and a look of hatred on his face, a half-formed curse on his lips.

I spare him no thought.

I feel that the battle is going too well. Will the Wessex and York forces take advantage of our speed in advancing? Do they have something else planned?

I wrack my memory of this place. Is there some physical barrier or impediment that I've forgotten about? Is my enemy trying to entice this hastily cobbled-together alliance to make a mistake?

Only then, Eoforhild grunts louder and louder, the strain showing in her flexing back and the sinews of her neck.

They're fighting back.

This is the time to stand tight to Eoforhild.

My shoulder connects with Eoforhild's back as I plant my feet firmly in the grime of battle, ignoring where I place my feet as long as they feel firm and ready to take the strain.

Firamodor has stopped praying behind me, her free hand on my back and her strength running up and down my body so that I can share it with Eoforhild. The three of us make a chain, each reinforcing the other. A jangle of iron and wood alerts me that we're not alone. I spare the briefest of glances along my line of men and women, and I see everyone is doing the same.

My female warriors are interspersed with their male counterparts, and everyone, and I mean everyone, has fierce determination writ large in their stances, Viking raider or Mercian.

We don't intend to allow the enemy any respite.

'Hold,' echoes from the Norse half of the shield wall, and I mirror the call, listening with satisfaction as it's repeated up and down the combined shield wall.

Distant cries reach me from the enemy line, the word 'advance' harsher on the tongues of my foes than I would have expected.

This move is risky on their part. They mean to use all of their vigour against us. Have they been harvesting their strength, waiting to make one huge play for victory? I hope not.

I respond to the renewed attack with my call for 'advance' quickly taken up in a repetition of the opposition.

Eoforhild tightens her stance as I strengthen mine.

Without any hope of a run-up, I expect the renewed fighting to be but a whisper of its recent clamour, but I'm mistaken. The wave of strength when it hits Eoforhild is greater than the sucking of the Humber tidal estuary at the turning of the tide. In its wake, it leaves almost as much jetsam and flotsam littering the ground with blood and body parts.

Men and women cry out as they exert all their energy, their voices unconsciously mirroring the enormous strain they've placed their bodies under. Beneath my feet, I again feel the questing lips of a weapon, only this time, I know the weapon is in the hands of my allies. They seek to wound or maim our enemy, distracted as they are trying to reclaim their lost advantage.

I almost think that the effort is too much, that it'll overwhelm Eoforhild and all who work with her. I can see it in the tension of the backs that greet me down the long line, my face covered in the shadow of Firamodor's shield. It adds a faded sheen to faces that should be glistening with sweat and the heat of battle. Instead, we all look half to stiffening in death.

'For Mercia,' I holler, my hoarse voice still somehow carrying over the snarl of the fray.

Once more, the cry is taken up, drowning out any pitiful attempts by my enemy to raise the passions of men for Wessex and York. I savour the moment. We're going to win this, no matter what.

Only then Eoforhild slides from my sight, falling to her knees, struck by something I neither see nor hear. Resolute, I overstep her shivering body, screaming for Firamodor to assist my sworn woman. But Firamodor ignores my calls, her shield following my movements forward as I press into the unfortunate gap created by Eoforhild's fall. I spare a thought for her as I wrestle the shield from her tight hand, reluctant to release her forged grip. She might have fallen, but her shield hasn't.

Belatedly she must realise her predicament. Her fingers work themselves free from their death grip. I feel her begin to slide away, back, I hope, to where she'll be able to recover from her wounds once the battle is done.

My shoulder feels the pressure of the shield wall first. It's like a burning brand across my body. I question how Eoforhild, a woman little taller and no broader than myself, managed to hold her position for so long.

I daren't risk a close look at my enemy. I don't want to move the shield that's stood for so long since the first warrior lost his life. It would disrupt the careful arrangement of wood and blackened iron that keeps me aloof from my enemy. But I can smell them.

The rank stench of men too many days in their clothes wafts through the air. That and bad breath caused by men who'd drunk too little or too much before the attack began.

I sense the presence of a weapon weaving its way behind my shield. I batter it with the handle of my sword. I should have replaced it with my seax or axe, but now's not the time to fiddle with my weapons belt.

Instead, I call my sword to action in every way but the traditional one that uses the sharpened edge to slice through the skin of men and women.

I use its handle to hammer at the weapon. I seek the hand that guides it so that I can crush it with the heavy design of the handle, its pointed and sharpened spikes having been moulded to my hand for just this purpose.

The weapon drops away, and my shoulder stays firm against the shield of my warrior. I can feel that Eoforhild, whether she lives or dies, has been removed from the churning mass beneath my feet. Even the scent of the soil, such an innocuous smell, assaults my nostrils. I know the harvests to come will always remind me of this day.

The voices of my enemy reach my ear. They speak my language, a strange realisation that this battle is so much different to any that's swept these shores for the last nearly fifty years, sinks into my being.

I'm fighting men and women who should be my allies.

The thought renews my tested strength and my desire to end this. Now.

Never again should the kingdoms of my grandfather's vision of an 'England' battle against each other, as once Mercia and Northumbria, East Anglia and Wessex did. No, with this victory, I'll ensure Mercia's survival, and perhaps, and I smirk at the thought, it'll be I who rule Wessex in an obscene reversal of my uncle and cousin's intentions.

I lash out with the pointed end of my sword, spearing another weapon that hunts between my legs. The axe, which had been swaying haphazardly from side to side, is quickly stuck immobile as my sword glides through the sharpened haft, hooking it as I burrow it in the rank soil beneath my feet.

For a short moment, there's a futile attempt to reclaim the axe, but then the pressure on it reduces. I raise my sword and kick the freed weapon behind me.

As soon as the axe is gone, I return to my task. My sword is hungry for blood, and now it's my turn to sneak it between the pattern of shields as it hunts to sate its need.

Quickly I encounter resistance and jab it with all the strength in my right arm, as my left shoulder supports the shield. I hear a sharp gasp of pain with delight. I work it upwards and downwards, unsure which part of a body I'm wounding but aware that this action will cause far more damage than a clean cut.

Suddenly I feel a reduction in power behind my shield and under-stand that my enemy is too wounded to fight. In the lull, as one enemy replaces another, just as I stepped into Eoforhild's vacant space, I once more shout for Mercia.

I can feel my enemy faltering. No matter how large the force was, against the combined might of Mercia and Lord Rognvaldr, it seems that Wessex and York are quickly losing ground.

'Forward,' I holler. The cry is repeated. The sound of that one small step, more a shuffle through gore, sweat and battle juice than anything else, surges through my body.

The pressure of the enemy is weakening. I know it.

'Forward,' I shout once more.

Again, a shambling slide forward.

'Forward.' By now, Lord Rǫgnvaldr and Eadric are shouting the word at almost the same time that I am. I can sense this victory.

Any moment now, the shield wall will break apart. I can feel Firamodor behind me, her hands busy as she replaces her sword with her war axe, a lethal double-weighted weapon with heads at both the top and the bottom. I've been cut more times by that bloody weapon than any other.

I prepare myself as well. When the shield wall of my enemy implodes upon itself, I need to be ready. I need to match my weight to my balance; I must stay on my feet when the enemy's shield suddenly loses all of its traction.

'Forward.' I'm almost hoarse with my battle cry by now. Still, it carries and then, a sharp intake of breath before it actually happens, I tighten my grip on my dead warrior's shield, trying to decipher what its effect will be on my stance. Will it be too heavy or too light? Should I drop it? Grab my shield?

In the press of the fighting at the front, it's been impossible to determine the weapon's weight, held up as much by my hands as by the squeezing effect of all the other shields around it. But at the same time, the grip on my sword instinctively tightens. In the face of what's about to happen, I breathe out through my nose, my heartbeat steady, my body aligned for what will come. I watch, almost in disbelief, as my enemy's shield wall disintegrates.

Almost as one, shields drop, exposing a mass of leather helms, angry and frightened eyes to the harsh daylight of this late summer's day. Like moles disturbed from their holes, my enemy looks up as though surprised by this turn of events.

This is it.

I step into the minute gap between the shield walls, my sword already raised and about to hammer against the wood of the enemy. The hooded warrior before me unexpectedly drops his shield, surprised, I imagine, by the weight of the massive piece of wood I'm holding. Like me, my adversary has long since replaced whoever orig-inally stood here. The shield he now fights with is not to his taste.

As a mass of moving bodies registers as disturbances in the strong wind behind me, I slice my sword across the man's exposed neck, his weapon hanging limply in his hand. I taste his iron sheeting across my face.

I growl. My battle joy has come as I look for the next foeman.

Slashing my sword free from the crumbling body, without a second glance, I step into the path of the next exposed warrior. Uselessly his shield hangs over the missing head of his ally, and he's an easy target for my bloodied sword.

Another swipe across an exposed shoulder, and the man is glaring blankly at me as if realising for the first time what's about to happen.

As I move to step around him, although he yet lives, I slice my sword through the rear of his shoulder, feeling the grate of the metal inside his body. He slumps forward, joining the still-twitching body of his comrade.

Firamodor wars behind me, and to the left and right, I can determine that all of my shield warriors and those of Lord Rǫgnvaldr's are experiencing the same sort of ease.

But I mustn't take my victory for granted.

A third warrior, this one slightly more prepared, leers at me.

'A fucking woman,' he grumbles deep in his chest. He has the reach on me, for he overtops me by almost a foot or half the length of my sword.

I offer him a mocking smile and immediately surge into his welcoming embrace. His long arms have no chance of making contact with me as I drive my sword before me. The oaf forgets even to move his shield to counter my movement, so surprised by its speed and success.

He dies, as the other two men did, blood gurgling through his mouth as I pierce the part of his body needed to breathe.

The wet sound of his breath disgusts me. I yank my sword free savagely as he collapses to the floor, his brown eyes wide with fear.

'A fucking man,' I whisper to him, a maroon smile on my lips where blood drips freely from the harsh wounds I've given.

Still, there are more warriors before me, and all of them fight on, even though they must know that their victory has been snatched from them by my alliance with Lord Rǫgnvaldr.

My sword swoops hungrily into the shield of the next warrior. He seems more primed than any of the others and much cleaner. Was he even part of the original ambush, or have additional forces arrived?

I don't much care. My flashing blade, burning with the gore of its kills, seeks out my opponent's weaknesses even with his shield as he manages to land a cutting thrust to the shield I use.

I note the wyvern of Wessex on the linden-board as I drop my sword low and use my shield to ram it into his nose and eyes with a lightning-fast punch. My shield arm aches now, but I ignore it. No amount of physical pain can stop my actions as I hammer the wood into the surprised man's face once more. Weakly he attempts to counter the move, his shield landing a blow to my exposed right side. I withstand the blow as my sword arm's already sweeping through the air. The power of my shoulder impales the man through his left shoulder as he tastes what he thinks is a success.

I stagger, my sword rammed in place as blood cascades from the cut, spraying me once more in another's iron and salt. I laugh, the cackle of a warrior in the full flow of battle. Licking my lips, the warrior watches me with fascination, any attempts to defend himself forgotten about as his power diminishes with each stilling beat of his heart.

'Fuck you,' I mouth as, jostled from behind by another fierce battle, he slips on his fluid and glides to the floor, a collapsed ship's sail. My sword comes free with a satisfying squelch.

Sweat covers my face and slides down my back, or perhaps it's blood, either way, I feel calm, assured, and reflective. I stand and look to either side of me.

The number of bodies isn't yet nearing the number of men who still fight, but, in the small pockets of fighting I can see, it's all too clear that the wyvern of Wessex and the holy cross of York are starting to flail.

But there's still work to do.

It seems that news of my presence on the battlefield has swept through the enemy ranks. I can sense that a gathering of Wessex swords is forming against me. Instinctively I look for my warriors and find that Eoforhild, with a dirty strip of cloth around her neck and darkly flashing byrnie, has returned to the field.

She's already sensed the danger. My women and some of Lord Rǫgnvaldr's warriors, drawn by the sight of a woman slashing and killing her fellow Saxon warriors, have come together in a loose approximation of a shield wall, ready to protect me.

Belatedly I hear the approving cries of Lord Rǫgnvaldr's men, praising my skill and expertise. They give way to the remainder of my warriors, who rush to protect me, as is their duty. The Viking raider men cluster behind them, the reek of victory hanging heavy in the air.

This battle will be won or lost here.

More than twenty Wessex warriors make their menacing way toward my position. I recognise every single one of them. I've seen all of them in their battle gear before, drinking their way to oblivion in the tavern in Nottingham. They all wear the wyvern of Wessex on their byrnies, picked out in the thread that shimmers in the sun's glow. The creatures could almost be breathing fire, but I know better. These Wessex warriors are no match for my women or the Viking raider men who stand ready to battle them, Lord Rǫgnvaldr present in their midst.

'Mercia,' I bellow, and my warriors join my hoarse scream while the Viking raiders have their cry.

'For the lady,' they shout in their language, and I smirk at that. I imagine few Viking raider warriors have ever issued such a cry before.

As one, my force rushes into the Wessex men. They stand with shields and weapons, their helms, made of iron as opposed to leather, glow darkly, their eyes peering as though from a winter's night, trying to discern what they can with limited light.

They're not ready. We take advantage of that, running into shields hanging limply in hands not yet prepared for death, but death is all they will win for themselves.

Not for them, the rewards promised by my uncle or my cousin for committing treason against the rightful ruler of Mercia.

No, these men deserve only one reward for their actions, and I'd happily mete it out to all of them, but I need the help of my warriors and the Viking raider warriors as well.

Vengeance has arrived.

The Lady of Mercia has come.

CHAPTER 17

My sword moves of its own volition. It rises and settles, swings and batters with a life of its own. Its heat and the burning of the blood it sheds reaches me as though from a distance. Objectively I watch each advance as though the passage of time means nothing to me.

Each movement one of my enemies tries to make against me, I anticipate, countering and slashing with abandon. My leather gloves protect my fingers from growing too slick with the spilt juices of these men. Although my voice is almost all gone, used up in encouraging my force in the shield wall, I screech and shriek all the same, even if actual sound is beyond me. I offer encouragement to my warriors and death to my enemy.

I wear so much shed blood that even the sight of me terrifies the men who've come to kill in the name of my family. I see it in their eyes and smell it in the loosening of their bowels.

The stench of stale piss mixed with the reek of mead and ale soaks the air. I care not one bit.

I'd walk through a tunnel of shit if it meant I could kill all these men and send a message to Wessex and York that Mercia will stand aloft and alone if need be. It's not to be ruled by those who know nothing of its people and would use it for their desires.

Eoforhild dances into view, glistening with the ichor of the shield-maiden she's become in the flow of this battle. Her movements are pristine, her actions unquestionable, and I know she sees this skirmish in the same way I do.

There's no need to think, to feel rage. Each and every movement is doubly learnt and instinctive.

We both fight with all our skills, our lightness of feet helping as heavy labouring men try to use their weight against us but mistake our movements, falling into our attacks instead of away from them.

Out of the corner of my eye, I even glimpse Lord Rǫgnvaldr in action.

His hair has come loose from his helm, and it crowns him in a halo of other men's life, shining darkly red as it's ruffled repeatedly by the stiff wind accompanying our battle.

Lord Rǫgnvaldr's movements are quick and economical. In the three breaths I spare for him, he kills two men and stands hungrily, looking for more.

Across the divide, he meets my curious eyes and raises his shield in recognition of his skills and mine before attacking once more.

I raise my shield, only then turning my eyes to the man who's come to fight me. I've felt his presence during the entire time I've been watching Lord Rǫgnvaldr, all three heartbeats of it, but only now do I give him any thought. Only now does he offer any threat.

He's the man who killed my hostage in Nottingham, and I growl with delight. The thought of spilling Aldred's life into the brown soil is delightful.

I deign to give him my full attention at last. His eyes are alight with recognition. He knows who I am as surely as he knows I know who he is.

This man has lied to me and killed another, in fact many, to reach this moment, and I don't intend to allow him to live.

Neither do I waste my words on him.

As a man, he's taller than I am, and the reach of his weapons

greater than the combined scope of mine. But I know something
about him from watching him kill my hostage. He favours the right
side of his body.

Unbidden, my voice builds once more, the joy of this moment
giving flight through my mouth. An eerie half scream accompanies
my attack into the left side of his body, unprotected apart from by the
padding of his byrnie. My sword flashes wetly in front of him, doing
just as much to tell him the story of my morning's fighting as my
death-shroud battle equipment does.

But he surprises me by dancing away from the stab of my sword.
His reaction might have caught me off guard, but immediately I'm
moving to counter him. The weakness of his left side must be something he tries to cover, but I know the real stance of a man shines
through when he takes his blade to drain the life of another unarmed
man.

He might think to dance before me, but the battlefield is a quag-
mire of detritus, and he's wholly unaware of his surroundings, slipping and sliding through the ruins of lost lives.

Still, I hold myself tight, following his whereabouts and enticing
him to think that I'm tracking his every movement far more closely
than I am. The battle calm has taken me once more, allowing me to
see almost without eyes and certainly without thought.

His shield dodges right, but he tries to dash left, only to find me
already standing there, my sword ready to drink. His eyes flash with
surprise and then with pain as I slide it into the left side of his chest. I
grunt with the effort, just as he groans with the agony, the one
cancelling out the other.

I'm surprised that my Wessex family allowed this man to
command their northern campaigns. It seems that he was no great
warrior. Contemptuously I hang onto my sword, my shield
connecting with his growling face as I cut and saw through his
clothing and skin.

So much blood sheets me that this fresh burst of vaulting heat fails
to make any impact on my consciousness as it clothes me.

I'm a life taker, an oath keeper, a woman of iron and salt. I'm my mother's daughter and perhaps my father's. The truth of his career is almost impossible to decipher, even for his daughter.

Neither am I, my grandfather's heir, for he didn't like the muck of battle.

No, I'm a woman forging her path and reputation.

All will fear me.

Aldred dies slowly. I allow myself to watch the light of life dim from one of my kills, for all that he's still standing. All around him, the supposed crack force of Wessex warriors disintegrates under the combined onslaught of my Mercians and my Viking raider allies.

I turn abruptly to the sound of applause, muffled a little by leather gloves but applause all the same, and I see a mocking face before me.

The warrior wears the wyvern of Wessex on his ink-stained byrnie. I imagine he's as battle garbed as I am, ichor drying in an uneven patchwork across his leather vest, his leather wrist guards glistening with all that remains of a warrior when his life is done.

'Well done, my lady,' he disdainfully calls across the small space between us. 'Your mother would be so proud to see you ...' he seems to struggle for words but then continues, 'adorned as you are.' His open hand, gliding up and down, indicates my body.

'My mother raised me as a warrior,' I counter.

'Your mother raised you to be some man's bitch and carry his children for him.'

The words are so outrageous that the bark of laughter escapes my mouth before I can stop myself.

'I see you knew her well,' I manage to choke around my laughter. His brow furrows slightly. I think he's disappointed that I don't quell at the revulsion in his voice of who I am and what this battle has made me become.

I look at him now. He might once have been a handsome man, but his face is rippled by a poorly healed scar, one eye slightly downcast. His age is hard to tell, but he could well be one of the longest-serving members of the Wessex warband. No doubt he's seen many battles and won most of them, or at least escaped with his life.

But he's never fought me.

'I'll show you what my mother taught me,' I say softly, twirling my shimmering blade once more. I half expect it to be blunt by now, but still, it glimmers, asking me to feed it that little bit more.

'And I'll show you what the Wessex royal family taught me,' he taunts, but his words fall away into the stiff wind, their malice stolen. Whatever Wessex taught him, it won't be what I can do.

His stance is traditional, not posturing. His weight is finely balanced, his sword and shield even in his hands, despite his coating of battle. But that doesn't worry me.

He's overconfident; possibly he's survived enough fights to think himself invulnerable, almost half a God, but I'm his reckoning come to wipe the smug expression from his face and drag the last breath from his air-starved body.

I drop my sword to the ground, ensuring its end bites deeply so that I can retrieve it quickly if I need to. From my weapon's belt, I finally draw forth my favourite weapon. My seax has a serrated edge; its point sharpened to spear, its edges rough-hewn to rip and score as much flesh as possible on entry and exit.

The warrior laughs at my choice, thinking I've given away my advantage, but he knows nothing about me. He knows nothing about the skills I possess.

He believes the lies of the Wessex court. He believes what uncle Edward and cousin Ælfweard say about my ability to rule and my ability to fight.

He believes, even now, attired as I am in all that remains of the many men I've killed today, that I'm somehow lesser than him. He thinks me a product of Mercia. And I am. Just not the one he's expecting because my Wessex family has lied about Mercia as well.

Firamodor stands ready between us. She's filthy and glowing with the exuberance of her success. My enemy's eyes are so engrossed on me that he doesn't even know she's there, her Mercian shield twirling nimbly in her hand, ready to perform the service I need from her now.

With a wave of my hand, she sets the shield spinning on her arm, swinging it behind her so that she can release it when I need it.

I swing on my back leg. Now's the time to run, to push all I have into my legs and make them burn with the effort.

I release myself, already seeming to fly across the disturbed ground, ready to run into the waiting embrace of the Wessex warrior.

Only then I really am flying as my right foot connects with the spinning shield. My foot pushes it down to allow me to leap high enough into the air to land, not in front of or behind my enemy, but rather on him. My legs are splayed to either side of his head, almost on his shoulders. My seax, its call for the life of a man just as insistent as my sword has been all through the long battle, buries itself deep inside his skull, no matter the helm that sits there, stupidly ineffective.

I drive it deeper, deeper still, the burble of my enemy's dying breaths fueling my strength.

He collapses beneath me. I land, legs to either side of him, my seax sticking through the top of his head. The end pokes through his chin, where his useless chin guard protects the front of his face but not the inside. The handle has come to life, the twisted Mercian double-headed eagle gulping the cascading fluid hungrily.

His eyes show shock and revulsion as it's now my turn to stand and scornfully applaud him.

His death tastes sweet to my salt-encrusted lips.

'My thanks,' I call to Firamodor, and she grins. Her shield-spinning skills are legendary, but it isn't really the type of fighting technique that can be easily used or often.

Today is the first time an enemy has ever died from it. Her joy lights her face as she rushes to scoop up the discarded shield from where I've thrust it to the floor with the weight of my body.

'It works. That's good to know,' she offers with a straight face and very little inflexion to her words as I grin.

'It bloody works well,' I shout, and we both laugh, a little too high and a bit too loudly. As we turn to face the battle site, I can already tell that there'll be no more fighting that day.

There remain no more than a handful of Wessex and York men who still fight in tight clumps, seemingly unaware of the waiting Mercian and Viking raider warriors ready to step into the fray should their current opponent's falter. They hover as though they're the crows coming to feast after the battle.

A small trickle of enemy survivors can be seen in the distance, retreating as quickly as possible toward the south, clutching their sigils as though their lives depended on it. Some have horses, but many don't.

I watch them with narrowed eyes. Will they go to Mercia? Will they go to Nottingham, or do they have ships waiting for them at the mouth of the Humber Estuary, ready to take them back to their lying masters in Wessex?

'Get the horses, ride after them,' I command Firamodor. She beckons for those warriors capable of riding a horse after their exertions to follow her. I see Eadric amongst them, and I feel relief knowing he's survived and lives.

I don't want anyone to escape. I need to get to Mercia before they do. I need to recall cousin Athelstan from the west and have him guard the borders, not with the Welsh kingdoms or the shifting conditions on the border with the northern lands I now stand within, but rather the border with Wessex, all along the banks of the River Thames, and just outside London as well.

It seems my enemy is no Viking raider warrior but my damn family.

But for now, I know I need to congratulate my warriors wounded in the attack and mourn those who've lost their lives. Then, well, I need to deal with Lord Rǫgnvaldr.

He's helped me win this battle. I can never forget that. Provided I make it back to Mercia in time, I'll owe him the command of my kingdom. That means that he'll be within his rights to demand more from me, and no matter what, I can't give him more than I've already offered.

For now, he seems not to care.

As Lord Rǫgnvaldr walks toward me over the ruined and broken lives of men, a sheen of bloody sweat cascades from his hair and his face is purely lit with glee.

'A great victory,' he shouts to me. Still some distance apart, I nod in response. Fatigue's trying to bite its way into my battle glory. I can almost feel myself swaying with the ferocious wind.

'A fucking great victory,' I confirm. Then he engulfs me in the fierce embrace of a warrior who finds his best friend yet lives after a monumental attack, the body of my last victim forgotten about as we salute each other with the victory. This is no touch of lovers, as we thump each other on the back, both speaking at the same time and far too loudly, the liberation of a battle won so convincingly, making us firm ally's when only this morning, we were nothing more than grudging enemies.

CHAPTER 18

Not that I leave the battle site straight away. I need to see the bodies of my warriors who died. I must make my peace with them and ensure their burial is adequately carried out before I flee for the south. I rely on Eadric and the rest of those still able to ride to hunt out and kill any who yet stand. I'd like to have Archbishop Lodeward of York brought before me. He could be my hostage when I return to Mercia, although I doubt Archbishop Pleg-mund would approve of that. Not that his concern would deter me. Not anymore.

I walk the field of death and destruction. Here, lives too fleetingly gone are laid bare. Carrion crows circle overhead as they wait for us to leave the bodies so that they might pick over the fleshy bits. But first must come the stripping of the enemy bodies of all material wealth by those still able to hobble around the battle site, mostly Lord Rǫgnvaldr's warriors. Mine have rushed south to arrest those fleeing the defeat.

I always thought that Viking raider warriors would carry out this process with relish, but mostly they're respectful unless they find something of great wealth or even someone they know. The people of York have long since integrated with the Norse men and women who first came to these shores. It's not surprising to find family likenesses amongst those who've fallen here.

There are some sorrowful faces, but mostly, these people have a task to accomplish. I get the impression that the sooner it's done, the sooner they'll be gone, back to their ship.

Lord Rǫgnvaldr walks with me. Neither of us has changed or sloshed water over our battle sheen.

'We'll split the rewards,' he offers with a grin. The exuberance of the win is buoying us both as we talk about the future.

'I'll need to leave before nightfall,' I caution. I must return to Mercia as soon as possible.

'I'll have it sent on, under guard. I wouldn't want your warriors to feel that they've lost out on the spoils, especially if we're to be neighbours soon.' He's pressing me, ensuring that I plan on keeping to our hastily constructed alliance. I keep my face calm in the wake of his scrutiny.

The words should chill me. What I didn't want, when all this started, was for Lord Rǫgnvaldr to hold York, but that ship has long ago sailed. I'd rather have a fellow warrior as my neighbour, and one I've fought with, than all the lying allies I've so far been saddled with.

I have a new respect for him. I don't trust him yet, far from it, and I probably never will, but for now, I understand him far better than I do anyone else.

He only wants York. My Wessex family only wants Mercia, but the betrayal at the heart of that acceptance is not as easy to understand. Why am I not good enough? Why do they think they're good enough to rule Mercia? And why now? Has my uncle always planned this action, or is it the death of my mother that precipitated such a dangerous move?

I only wish I could understand.

'I'll need to leave as well,' he acknowledges. 'York is devoid of its best warriors, its archbishop far from home. I'll take it while it's weak and show them what a true Norse ruler can bring to their trading port.'

The words should repulse me, but in hindsight, I've decided that

York has been ruled for so long by an assortment of men and women with Norse leanings that it no longer matters.

'The archbishop survived then?' I ask. I'm not sure if he fought in the battle. My viewpoint of the whole thing was narrow and boiled down to only what I could see and do. As I walk the slaughter field I'm detecting areas where harsh fighting has taken place; the ground gouged with the feet of desperate men anchoring themselves to this world, many failing in their quest.

I know how many warriors I brought to this fight and roughly how many Lord Rǫgnvaldr had. I have no true test of the opposition's strength, only that it must have been bigger than ours. For every dead Mercian or Viking raider, there are at least two from Wessex or York. Either they had superior forces, or they weren't good warriors. I consider that possibility with a strange detachment. Perhaps the best warriors are even now marching into Mercia to claim her as their own.

I pray they're not and that if they are, Ealdorman Æthelfrith's loyal enough to send forces out to counter their attacks. I can't allow Tamworth or any of my new burhs to fall into the hands of my Wessex family. The men who'd been stationed in Nottingham have fallen in this altercation. I hope that's an end to my Wessex family's infiltration.

I've already dispatched a fast runner to cousin Athelstan, commanding him to return to the heartlands of Mercia with all haste and telling him of my new ally. He'll need to know so that he's accepting of any who claim to be with Lord Rǫgnvaldr and who've inadvertently been caught up in the chase to stop the Wessex warriors from returning home with news of their defeat.

'Ha,' Lord Rǫgnvaldr scoffs. 'The archbishop didn't fight. He's too fat to be fighting. His Norse blood has been stretched too thin as his waistline has expanded. He lives, but I don't know where he's seeking refuge now. He fled as soon as he realised what was happening. A coward, as all holy men are.'

I'd like to argue with him, after all, I've known many holy men who were also warriors, but actually, he might have a valid argument

there. Archbishop Plegmund fights with the words of his God, not
with his sword, and his strikes are often very low. In the past, I've
ignored them. I always took him as my ally, as he was my mother's.
But I need to reassess every ally, enemy and friendship in the wake of
what's happened.

'York is north of here. Will we not have seen him try and get
by us?'

'Yes, but also no. I have a feeling he's disappeared into the hills and
will try and sneak his way home.'

Lord Rǫgnvaldr's logic is sound, and once more, I reassess the
man before me. I've encountered many Vikings raiders in my life.
They were defeated men in battle or men who changed their loyalty
to Mercia, bowing to the inevitability of their eventual defeat at the
hands of a stunningly resurgent Mercia. This might be the first time
I've met a Viking raider under such strained circumstances when
necessity caused me to make a decision I thought I'd regret, but one
which I'm beginning to think might be the best one of my short
rule.

'I've sent a small handful of warriors to track him. He'll either
escape them or not, and either way, I don't intend to allow York to fall
back into his control. Not now.'

Although I'm listening to his words, my eyes have snagged on a
small scene of carnage that seems to contain only the remains of four
of my warriors. I can see grey and staring eyes, a sharp contrast to the
dulling blood that streaks their remains. I swallow back my horror at
such a blatant display of the effect that the weapons I toy with in practice can genuinely do on the body of a man.

'My lady?' Lord Rǫgnvaldr's voice is insistent, recalling me to our
conversation, and I nod, a hint of tears forming in the corner of my
eyes.

'Apologies,' I swallow back my grief and discomfort at what I'm
seeing.

'They're gone, my lady. Gone to either their Heaven or my
Valhalla. All that remains is not who they were.' His voice is remarkably sincere, filled with compassion. In that instant, I appreciate that

he's walked the remains of many a slaughter field. I have as well, but the men who died were never acting on my orders.

'My thanks,' I offer, managing to drag my eyes away as a burial party of six Viking raiders arrives and begins to strip and then move the bodies.

'Our alliance will stand,' I speak, my voice far stronger now, banishing from my immediate view the death and destruction of our fight by changing position. 'I thank you, again, for your quick thinking and response to the threat. I'll ride south. I'll send any of your men I find to you at York, and then we'll be in touch as soon as I know that the kingdom of Wessex has been contained within its boundaries.'

Something flashes across the warrior's face at my words. I wonder what I've said to make him react as he has.

'Your Wessex family are dangerous. They think their reach should extend further than it does, even to Norse Dublin and the Outer Islands. Tread with care and if you need me again, send for me. I'd happily support you against the might of Wessex once more.'

His words are sobering. I'd already begun to appreciate that this attack would just be the first of many. But to hear someone else say the words makes me understand that I have a real fight on my hands to keep hold of my kingdom, to keep Mercia safe.

'I'll let you know should the need arise,' I nod, and then I turn away from Lord Rǫgnvaldr. My horse has been brought to me by my young friend from Nottingham. Her eyes are a little crazed by the stench of the battlefield as she sidesteps and only calms at my touch. Eadig's mouth is open wide as he takes in the sight of Lord Rǫgnvaldr and me. I imagine he'd like an introduction, but instead, I indicate that I've no further need of him and that he should leave. He does so; sullen-eyed until Lord Rǫgnvaldr catches on.

'Here, boy. A trophy for you,' he offers, handing him a thin iron band from around his arm. It's smeared with battle filth, but Eadig glows at the reward before stumbling away, as I told him.

'We've much to do,' I mutter to my horse, and she seems to accept that directive, her hooves stilling as Lord Rǫgnvaldr holds her steady enough for me to climb into her saddle, Eadig unable to quiet her in such a way.

'Until we meet again, my lady,' Lord Rǫgnvaldr bows, his eyes alight with his inner fire that sees joy in our fight and subsequent victory.

'Until then,' I nod, and then I knee my horse, and she's picking her way back through the trail of death and destruction, her hooves raised high. I turn my back on the battle and the one man I thought was my enemy, and now I must face those I thought were my allies but weren't.

THE JOURNEY SOUTH is a hurried affair. With each beat of my horse's hooves flying over the landscape so recently meandered along, I feel a pulse of fear. What if I'm too late? What if uncle Edward and cousin Ælfweard already have control of Mercia?

We pass the remains of small altercations along the way, the ground churned up, the odd stray body, and also the mortally wounded, holding in pulsing guts from stomach wounds or delirious with the fever of death. For those we can, we help, regardless of which side they fought on. For others, we leave water bottles, and for others, we simply close their eyes so that they aren't forever staring without seeing.

For none of them do we take the time to deprive them of their worldly goods or bury them. There's no time for such niceties, and as we get closer and closer to the traditional Mercian border with the Five Boroughs, the number of such events noticeably declines. I can only hope that this is the end for those who survived.

We do, however, take the time to offer assistance to any of the Mercian and Viking raider warriors who want to fight on. Wounds are staunched, and shields and swords are found for those who've lost them along the way.

I rode north with merely fifty men and women, but I'll return with well over thirty. My losses have been much less than for the Wessex and York alliance. Once I've reclaimed those I left behind in Nottingham, I hope that we'll swell to even greater numbers. And, of course, I mustn't forget about cousin Athelstan. He has warriors with him that I can use.

Only as night begins to fall do I halt our lurching ride south.

We're all tired, still streaked with the sap of combat, and I don't want to be injured riding in the encroaching darkness. I need every single one of my warriors to make it home with me, ready to fight for our survival.

As the hastily constructed camp springs to life in an area close to the track we follow, I look expectantly into the distance. If Mercia were under attack, I'd expect word to reach me quickly. I squint into the deepening sky, streaked with the pinks and oranges of the last of day's sunlight, scrunching my eyes tight to make out any moving shape in the coming darkness stealing across the land. But I see nothing, not even the blink of a fellow campsite as travellers journey along the route used for trading.

I draw no far-reaching conclusions from that. It could mean that no one in Mercia wishes to warn me that they welcome the rule of Wessex with open arms. It could mean that there hasn't yet been an attack. After all, why would my Wessex family think to attack Mercia when the outcome of today's encounter was surely to capture or kill me? In those circumstances, there would be no need to invade Mercia. They would assuredly have envisaged a peaceful occupation, not an all-out fight for the controlling position.

It could mean that an attack has taken place and that all my allies are dead, or it could mean none of those things. Just as earlier, it could imply that another surprise awaits me, an unpleasant surprise and something that my tired mind can't even comprehend.

I slump from my horse, unheeding of the filth and muck that covers me. She nuzzles at my shoulder, a query, and I pat her nose for reassurance. In a world suddenly thrown into such disarray, the unswerving loyalty of my horse is no small thing. I could only wish that my family were as loyal.

I wish, as I've never really wanted before, that my mother and I had arranged a stable marriage for me in the past, an alliance that would have brought another family into the close orbit of the Wessex dynasty. Perhaps another family would have hoped to gain from my accession to power in Mercia as opposed to the rest of the Wessex family who think only to topple me, with my death if need be.

How would my warriors have acquitted themselves against Lord Rognvaldr? Would we have won a victory? Could we, as far-reached as it sounds, have overcome the combined force of Lord Rognvaldr, York and Wessex? These are all thoughts for another day, as exhaustion drags me to sleep, but they resurface the next day when a rider is sighted, fleeing through the damp day toward us.

I've slept the sleep of the battlefield dead but woken refreshed and unbending, my clothing dry and stiff with the ichor of the day before. It's taken me too long to stagger to my feet from my place on the ground and too much time to get my warriors up and mounted on their horses. Everything has taken too long, and as I watch that rider, my heart thunders in my chest, and I can't swallow. Fear has taken hold of me. I find no solace in knowing that yesterday I fought an enemy with sharpened blades and finely honed skills. Today, it may well be words that kill me.

I wait impatiently, forcing my horse to the front of the travelling group who still ride toward Nottingham. I wish I could turn around and go back to the accomplishments of the day before, but time allows no one to stand still forever. Indeed, it never allows past actions to recur.

I swallow. The rider comes ever nearer, so close that I can pick out the fine detailing on his cloak, but I already know who it is. I'd recognise Eadric's brother anywhere. He once tried to rescue me, and I ended up saving him. Now I see him in my dreams, a presence no matter when I sleep, and I'm overjoyed to see him looking so much better from when I left Nottingham. His wounds are healing well, as his father assured me in his message only two days before.

'My lady,' he babbles as much relief on his face as mine. He's wind-blown, and I would suspect he's spent his journey with a stony countenance on his face, fearing the worse and yet still hoping all the same. 'We had news of an altercation with that bastard Lord Rognvaldr.

News that you were dead.' His words are rushed and garbled, as though he must say them quickly as the only way to force them beyond his lips. He notices but doesn't look at all, shocked to see me still mired in creaking leather from the battle of the day before.

I nod. It seems the rumour mill of Wessex has been working over-time. It amuses me, just a little, to think how shocked they'll be when they realise that their lies are about to be exposed. Those involved in this plot have a nasty shock coming, and I hope it'll reveal them for the treasonous wretches that they are.

'News of my death is false, as is news of a battle against the Viking raider, Lord Rǫgnvaldr, rather, we fought with him, and his warriors are our allies.'

Lord Athelstan's face shows abject shock, but by now, Eadric has ridden forward to meet his brother, and I can feel him nodding at my side.

'It wasn't bloody Lord Rǫgnvaldr we needed to fear,' Eadric retorts angrily. 'Rather, it was the men of York and the ruling family of Wessex.'

Athelstan's face grows paler still at the words.

'Wessex and York?' he repeats. The news seems to unnerve him. 'But it was a messenger from Wessex that told us of your death, a man sent from King Edward himself.' The words are wrenched from him. The three of us know exactly what this means.

After all, and despite their father's words to the contrary, it was my uncle, my fellow ruler, who plotted my death. The news is not as unanticipated for me as it seems to be for the two brothers. I suspected my uncle first when I first began to understand that nothing was actually as it seemed. When Lord Rǫgnvaldr confronted me with the banners of Wessex and York at my back, I understood that it would take a man far stronger than cousin Ælfweard to orches-trate such a move.

'What's happened in my absence?' I demand, and Lord Athelstan, reordering his face quickly so that a faint blush of colour creeps over his pallid expression, begins to speak.

'My father has ordered that the witan be convened to discuss matters going forward, and the fyrd have been alerted to the possibility of an attack. A warning has been sent to all the northern and eastern fyrds that they might yet be needed this year. He's taking no chances on a Viking raider assault.'

'Did the messenger not demand that Mercia hand itself over to the Wessex king?' this intrigues me. I would have expected it to be the first move my uncle made.

'No, but my lady, my father sent him an invitation, along with all the other ealdormen and thegns, churchmen and reeves.'

'Ah,' is all I say. We all understand this for what it is. Having seen to my death, King Edward now wishes to cloak his next actions in legality. He wants to present himself as the only man who can keep Mercia safe from Lord Rǫgnvaldr. He's a duplicitous liar.

'Did your father not receive my message about reinforcing the Wessex borders?' I demand, unsurprised, when Lord Athelstan shakes his head at my words. It'll have taken time for Lord Athelstan to reach me. I must hope that he and the messenger have passed somewhere and not realised the intent of the other.

'Not before I left, and if he received it afterwards, then I don't know what he'll do.' His honesty is refreshing. He won't make excuses for his father's probable actions now.

'Surely he should have waited for more news of my death before he called the witan than just accepting the words of a stray messenger?'

'My lady,' and his formality warns me that I'll not like his next words. 'The messenger came from the king and was escorted to him by Archbishop Plegmund.'

'So, the good archbishop was in on the whole thing,' Eadric mutters darkly. The thought of a fresh betrayal has strangely little impact on me. I might be becoming immune to such revelations, or rather, their ability to bring on a physical response has become deadened or evaporated in the wake of the gravity of my situation.

Lord Athelstan watches me intently, no doubt surprised by my lack of response. Even Eadric's reaction has been muted. Have we both become so used to betrayal quite so quickly?

'Do you think everyone knew?' I suddenly ask. Have I been blind to betrayal all along?

'My father has made no suggestion that he knew the news was coming. He was … he was dismayed. It took him all of the day before yesterday to be able to decide what to do next.'

Bitter laughter bubbles from my mouth, surprising all of us, myself included.

'The battle was yesterday. They didn't even wait to see if I died. They still haven't. They were very fucking sure of themselves,' I end angrily.

'My lady,' and Lord Athelstan sounds very hesitant, as though he doesn't want to say the next words. 'They said that you faced a force of over two hundred men and that you had less than half that number.'

I shrug. I don't doubt their calculations. I'd probably have faced well over two hundred enemies had it not been for Lord Rognvaldr, and his hasty alliance. With only my warriors, and I assume they're trying to imply that the Wessex warriors fought with me as opposed to against me, I would have had far fewer than a hundred warriors, far less.

'How did they expect to account for their warriors returning home with a different story?' I demand.

'Did they think that they were going to get away with their lies?' Eadric growls, and I understand his rage, even if Lord Athelstan has yet to grasp the sheer amount of planning that was involved in arranging my death.

'We, we need to spread the word quickly that I still live. We need to have proof of what happened. I … I should send a messenger to Lord Rognvaldr, ask him to retain the banners of Wessex and York, to have his men speak out about what happened.'

Lord Athelstan's face crumbles at my words.

'They won't believe a Viking raider's word, not in Wessex, perhaps not even in Mercia,' and I know he speaks the truth. We've spent so many years fighting against Viking raider attackers, only grudgingly accepting those who change their loyalty to the Mercians, that to ask anyone to believe Lord Rǫgnvaldr was the honourable one would push their preconceptions too far. By associating Lord Rǫgnvaldr's name with recent events without his consent, the Wessex royal family has made a bold and intelligent move. There's almost nothing I can do to prove their lies other than to live and show my face as far and wide as possible.

'I need to get back to Mercia,' my acknowledgement of Lord Athelstan's argument doesn't need articulating.

'I think I should return to my father. I need to inform him of what's happened.' Lord Athelstan's words are heartfelt, but is he right?

'Your father will know by now. He'll have received the messenger I sent to him.'

'Yes, but will he believe him, and will he know what to do? It's not as though he can recall the invitation to the witan.'

'No, he can't, but I can arrive at the witan when my uncle does or whomever he sends in his place if any of his warriors have managed to make it to Wessex.'

Lord Athelstan's shaking his head.

'I don't like this. None of it. We're trying to second-guess someone who's also trying to second-guess us. Just being alive right now might not be enough.'

'They think me dead. Will they really be taking action based on my living? They believe that Lord Rǫgnvaldr, the army of Wessex and the men of York will have killed me. As far as I can see, the fact that I've survived is enough to undo all their plans. Surely?'

'It'll depend on how many Mercians are involved in the Wessex plot and if they have more to gain under a Wessex king.'

'The people of Mercia have barely proclaimed me as their leader. Why would they have changed their mind already? How could uncle Edward have infiltrated my supporters already?'

'He's a king,' Eadric barks. 'He thinks he can do whatever he fucking wants to. All bloody kings do.' His bitterness is catching, and I see Lord Athelstan beginning to comprehend the situation at last. We might have the victory, but that was only the start of trying to ensure my survival as the leader of Mercia.'

'He'll have promised them whatever it is that they want. He's a king. No amount of money or patronage would be too much for him to get what he wanted.' Eadric's chuntering to himself while I'm trying to decide what to do next.

Lord Athelstan is talking over my thinking.

'We should go to Nottingham and Derby, the burhs of the Five Boroughs. Just as many Norse descendants populate them as Mercians. They'll take more readily to allying with the Norse again. It'll be easy as well. Simpler to get to as well, from here. My father will be there. He'll be able to advise you on the Mercians.'

'I don't need advice on the Mercians. I *am* a Mercian,' I can feel my temper fraying. 'But I take your point. I've just fought for Nottingham's safety. They should be as prepared to fight for me as I am for them. They'll be more open to the news of my Norse allies and hopefully less susceptible to the enticements of the Wessex king. It's taken them a long time to join Mercia, and it was my mother who finally won their allegiance. Hopefully, that'll count for something.'

I laugh at the irony of the situation. For so many years, Nottingham and Derby have stood aloft from Mercia, happier with their Norse allies than their Mercian neighbours. Now I need to manipulate their Norse leanings.

We've been riding on throughout our conversation, and with the decision made, I spur my horse onward. Lord Athelstan has taken only a day to reach me. I can make it back by early the next morning, and then I can begin work on driving my uncle from Mercia and undoing the web of lies he's spun around everyone, most tightly around me.

Once I return to Mercia, I'll send word of my survival, but I think I'll allow the witan to convene. I'm keen to taste the mood of Mercia. Or am I?

Perhaps I should remain hidden, slink my way through the days until the witan meets and then surprise them all by arriving, very alive and with a great deal of support. I might enjoy that, especially if I've already obtained the backing of Nottingham and Derby.

But do I want to employ such heavy-handed tactics? I don't want to be likened to my uncle.

Do I want to lead people if they don't want me as their leader?

The possibilities give me a headache once more. I decide to banish the conundrum from my mind. For now, I need to get to Nottingham and reclaim what control of the burh I can. Depending on how that goes will affect my next steps.

So first, I retake Nottingham, and then I'll turn my attention to Derby. Only then will I decide about the witan and Tamworth.

Resolved, I turn my attention to following the trail of destruction that shows where the wounded warriors of Wessex have attempted to return to Nottingham. There are very few instances now, but some of the men did make it this far. It doesn't make for an easy ride, but it's satisfying to see that so many of them have lost their lives in their retreat. I hope once more that none of the Wessex men has survived. I want my uncle to be very, very surprised when he next sees me.

CHAPTER 19

'Warriors, my lady,' the cry echoes from the back and down the long line of horses racing to return to Mercia. I know a moment of complete panic.

Who would be racing to catch us from behind? Were more Wessex men sent north than the ones we fought? Has Lord Rǫgnvaldr proven to be the sort of Viking raider my mother always warned me about?

I would have expected any attack to come from the front, straight out of Mercia, but this. This concerns me.

Hastily I order a halt to our flying march south, rushing through the host of rapidly stopping horses to where my back riders are threatening to form a defensive wall across the road.

I squint into the dying gloom of the day. Who could this be?

We're not far from Lincoln, still very much a Norse settlement, and as such, not all that far from Nottingham and Derby. I've been considering calling a halt to our momentum, deciding to rest instead of careering off into the gloom of the coming night, but now that I've been forced to stop, I chafe at the delay.

Who's following me?

Quickly, the shape of rapidly advancing riders materialises along the road we've just navigated our way along. We've seen few other people today, as Lord Athelstan and Eadric shoulder their horses through to my side.

'Who is it?' Eadric demands to know, but I still can't determine whether it's an ally or an enemy. And then I think mockingly that even if assumed they were an enemy or an ally, they might still not be. So seems to be the tenor of my existence now.

While my warriors settle themselves into a fighting stance they're comfortable with, I continue to peer at the advancing horses.

They race along the road, and that tells me something important. They wish to catch me. That's a different feeling to them wanting to attack me. If they wanted to attack, then they'd follow me more stealthily. They wouldn't want me to know that I was being pursued, preferring to catch me unawares.

I relax in my saddle. I have a strange feeling that I know who chases me as though pursued by the devil himself. It can't be Lord Rǫgnvaldr, for he has no horses, or at least he didn't. I forgot to check if we'd left any horses for him. Perhaps we did, but I doubt it. I'm also unsure that he'd be able to ride with quite as much skill as the man who leads the charge.

I recognise his posture. I've known him all his life.

Cousin Athelstan cuts a very handsome figure on his horse. I can say that easily. He rides with all the ease and confidence of a warrior who's assured of his strengths and weaknesses. For all that he's been forcing his horse to ever-greater speeds, he reins in before me, looking as though he's just mounted his horse for a gentle canter. I laugh as I watch him, and his face, determined before now, quickly becomes furious.

'How can you laugh at a time like this?' he demands, and in his voice, I hear a similar vein of relief and anger that Eadric's brother arrived with only that morning.

'I'm pleased to see you. Isn't that allowed?' I counter. I want to add heat to my voice, but I'm just so damned pleased to see him, even if he's just contravened my orders.

At that exact moment, a bedraggled horse pants into view. On his back sits my messenger and his face is just as furious as cousin Athelstan's.

'He refused to do as you instructed,' the man says, his rage as vitriolic as cousin Athelstan's.

'I was already on my way to join you,' cousin Athelstan argues. I can hear raw grief in his voice. He didn't want this. He never wanted there to be any more bad blood between his father and me, but, as usual, he's been left as a bystander to greater events that his father set in play.

'I understand,' I placate my messenger. 'Drink, eat, I understand. I won't blame you,' and then I add. 'I'd never blame those in my service for the actions of others.' I don't know if I've made that clear to my warriors before, but I know I speak the truth. He casts one more appalled look at cousin Athelstan, and then the messenger rides away to be swallowed by friends amongst my entourage.

'I was already heading this way,' cousin Athelstan continues to explain. 'I picked up threads of what was about to happen when I reached Runcorn. I decided to try and head you off before you went to York. I knew exactly what your intentions would be once you learned that Lord Rognvaldr was coming south. Your messenger painted a bleak picture of what happened when you met Lord Rognvaldr. I wanted to help you in reclaiming Mercia.'

His eyes are almost pleading, but I feel no rage toward him. It might make my task of holding onto Mercia more difficult as he's here with me, as opposed to in Mercia reinforcing the border. Still, at the moment, all I can see are advantages to neither of us being in Mercia.

'I'm going to Nottingham and Derby. I'll take their oaths, and then I'll face King Edward of Wessex at the witan.' My tone's intentionally bland. He still winces as though the sound of his father's name is a physical pain. I wish I could distance him from the shadow of his father, but until King Edward is dead, cousin Athelstan will never be free from him.

He quickly grasps the undercurrent of my words and nods in approval.

'Nottingham and Derby will remain loyal. They've never liked the Wessex royal family, and they'll approve of Lord Rǫgnvaldr. His ancestry and prowess in battle will appeal to them.'

'I'm glad you approve,' I try to joke, but the task before me suddenly seems monumental. Maybe I should just sneak away, after all, leave Mercia to my uncle and cousin Ælfweard. Maybe they deserve it more than I do.

Irate, I dismiss my notions, but cousin Athelstan's watching me intently. He must understand my doubts and fears.

'My father is a strong man, a greedy man and a man who allows no one to gainsay him. I believe that you'll be the person to do that, openly and defiantly, as your mother was never quite able to do. She went along with his ambitions but only because it was easier for her to do so while your father lived.'

'As soon as Lord Æthelred was dead, she began to make more and more decisions that were contrary to the wishes of Wessex. There was no outspoken family feud, but the warning signs were there all the same. Your mother would do what you're doing now.'

I don't necessarily need to hear cousin Athelstan's reassurance, but all the same, they bring me some inner calm. I know that I'm right to fight as I do. I know that it's my uncle who errs in his actions, but it's so good to hear another agrees with me. Especially when that someone knows my uncle, as I do.

'We ride to Nottingham then,' I confirm, and we quickly move off again. My warriors have had a brief respite from our hasty ride. That should be all they need. There's no one here who isn't keen to return to Nottingham and begin the task of undoing whatever it is that my uncle and cousin have set in motion.

EALDORMAN ÆTHELFRITH MEETS my entourage almost within sight of Nottingham. The day has hardly begun. We rode for much of the night, taking advantage of a full moon, and only slept when cloud covered its surface. We woke with the birds, and now we're in Nottingham.

Ealdorman Æthelfrith's face echoes relief at seeing his two sons alive before the shock of my survival wipes it from his face.

I can see my messenger at his side, a forlorn expression on his face. It's self-evident that Ealdorman Æthelfrith doubted his words. Now he seems stunned and chastened as he slides from his horse with all the grace of a man in his fifth decade and kneels before me.

I can see tears sliding from his face and landing on his byrnie, which brushes against his legs. I feel a moment of pity for the man.

He's Mercia's staunchest defender, but even he's been tricked by the games of the Wessex royal family.

'Stand,' I command, my voice firm with resolve. I don't need apologies or explanations. Now is a time for action, not for rehashing events that have already happened. Once more, time will not allow Ealdorman Æthelfrith to undo his actions, so instead, we must all work to negate the harm that may have been caused.

The ealdorman stands, confusion and relief warring with each other as he double-checks his sons' yet live. Then he falters, hovering once more to his knees as he meets the interested gaze of cousin Athelstan. As the embodiment of his father, it clearly shakes the ealdorman to see the king's eldest son with me, the alleged dead daughter of the king's sister.

'We've all been lied to,' I announce, indicating that I want Ealdorman Æthelfrith to return to his saddle so that we can talk in more privacy, away from the group of twenty or thirty men who escort him. One of them catches sight of Eadig, and a huge smile transforms his face from that of a sullen man to the happiest man alive.

I watch the pair of them reunite. It's clear he's not the boy's father, but they might just be brothers, or uncle and nephew, I don't know. I only wish that my uncle would be so pleased to see that I yet live.

Once more, my small circle of allies and accomplices, joined this time by Ealdorman Æthelfrith, form a solid circle, each looking one to the other and then at me.

'We've all been lied to,' I repeat, and the ealdorman nods enthusiastically, perhaps pleased to know that our current predicament is not of his doing. 'My uncle wants me dead and Mercia under his control.'

'Your messenger said as much, but I confess, I didn't believe the man, not coming so soon after the messenger from King Edward.'

'I'm not surprised,' I console, although my voice is flat and without emotion.

'I plan to take control of Nottingham and Derby and then attend the witan,' it all sounds so simple when I say it like that.

'The witan will meet in … eight days now,' Ealdorman Æthelfrith confirms. 'At Tamworth. I'd sent word to Lady Ecgwynn to prepare for the arrival of so many people, and I was arranging for a delegation to journey north and retrieve … you.' Here his words falter. He means to recover my body, but there's no need to give voice to that word.

'You should publicly continue as usual. I'll work in the shadows and then, hopefully, surprise my uncle with my survival. I think as few people as possible outside Nottingham and Derby should know if it.' Finally, I've concluded that stealth is the answer to my questions. Just as my uncle kept much hidden from everyone, so I will do the same.

CHAPTER 20

The following seven days pass in a blur of movement and furtiveness. The people of Nottingham quickly acquiesce to my request for support, pleased to find that I'm alive and that they haven't actually become subject to the whims of the Wessex king. My survival is greeted with delight. The knowledge that I owe it to Lord Rǫgnvaldr, grandson of Ivarr Ragnarsson, causes huge satisfaction. I suppress my amusement that these Norse descendants are so pleased to find themselves a new hero with their shared ancestry. After all, I had gambled on that fact.

On the fourth day, just as I'm preparing to leave for Derby, my man sent to Wessex before I knew the full extent of my family's involvement reappears at Nottingham's gate. Harried and hooded, he's bundled into my presence, where he falls to his knees in front of me with astonishment and surprise on his face.

The poor man, Osgod, looks broken and beaten by his trip to Wessex. His once serviceable clothing is dirty and torn, and his boots stolen from his feet so that he arrives foot sore and bloodied. His mouth opens and closes a few times in shock before he can actually speak, and then it's laughter that bubbles from his lips.

'My lady,' he finally manages to gasp, his massive, dirty and tangled beard wobbling with the words. 'This is wonderful and amazing news. Reports in Wessex are of your death. It's an open secret that Lord Ælfweard will be installed as King of Mercia to rule with the support of his father. This,' and he points to me with his dirty fingers, red-rimmed with dried blood. 'This will upset the young lord no end.'

He continues to chuckle with unsurpassed delight while at my side, cousin Athelstan stills in shock. I'd forgotten he was there with me, and now I almost wish he wasn't. I could have tempered this information better than a relieved Osgod has.

'You seem very well informed,' I offer, smiling to take the edge from my harsh words. I want to demand an answer as to how he could know this but couldn't warn me of the ambush to the north from his position within Wessex, but I've chosen softer words. Yet, he's not a foolish man, and he sobers straight away, understanding flashing across his dirty and abused face.

'My apologies,' he offers quickly, the laughter lines dropping from his face, although his good cheer is still evident in his lighter tone. 'They captured me when they realised I was from Derby. I'd only been in Wessex for a day or two. They released me only two days ago, and only because they said I could cause no harm anymore now that you were dead and Mercia was to become part of Wessex.'

'Who captured you?' I insist. He shrugs his massive shoulders in response, a brief wince passing over his face as he's reminded of some other hurt that I can't yet see but can imagine well enough.

'It was no one important, just some warriors loyal to the Wessex king. I thought they'd take me in and allow me to join them, but they were so suspicious of my origins that instead, they chained me up with the horses and left me there until there was no reason to do so.' He sounds apologetic still, and to look at him, it's difficult to doubt his words.

'They sent me back on a donkey,' his voice almost squeaks with the affront of it all. 'I ended up carrying the damn beast more than he did me.' There's good-natured rancour in his voice now that he knows I yet live. I almost wish I'd seen him and his donkey on the road from

Wessex to Nottingham. I hope the animal lives. Osgod is a huge beast of a man.

'King Edward seems very sure of himself,' cousin Athelstan mutters darkly, and those words mask a whole host of hurts. Why uncle Edward would decide that Mercia will accept his oldest son from his second marriage as ruler defies all explanation. Cousin Athelstan has lived almost all his life in Mercia. He's loved and esteemed by the Mercians. Cousin Ælfweard isn't. In fact, the men and women of Mercia have next to no respect for him. That was made clear when he attended the witan that proclaimed me as my mother's heir, and they all but jeered him from the great hall in Tamworth, his shoulders stiff with anger.

'My thanks for your service and my apologies for your treatment', I offer, my voice even softer now, more thoughtful. There's no reason to doubt what he says. Why would he have returned to Nottingham if he truly were a traitor to my cause? After all, he thought me dead, not ten heartbeats ago. The man grins at my words.

'I'd do it all over again if only for the delight of discovering you alive and well and knowing how angry Wessex will be. If you don't mind me asking,' he continues. 'What are your plans now?' He sounds eager to know. I understand that it could all be a trap, but I know it isn't. I trusted this man when I sent him to Wessex. There's no need not to now that he's returned to Mercia.

'We'll meet King Edward at the Mercian witan,' I comment, but just as with everyone else I've spoken of my plans to, he grasps what I mean immediately.

'I'd like to see that,' he whistles. I think I'll probably take him with me so that he can.

When he leaves my presence to be bathed and given fresh clothes and to have his wounds tended and his beard detangled, my cousin finally loses the precious control of his anger.

'The bastard,' he mutters, jumping to his feet and pacing around the hall of the home we've been sheltering within, deep in the heart of Nottingham. I've been comfortable here while I've plotted and schemed, but my cousin has been sour and irritable throughout that time, desperate to do more in the face of his father's actions. The words of Osgod have pushed him past any endurance levels.

'How could he do that to me?' he demands, his voice rising sharply. I wish I had some answers for him.

'My grandfather intended for me to rule. He made that clear when he lived, and yet my bloody father has done everything he can to ensure that I'll never have that distinction. And while I'm here, all but exiled to Mercia, the people of Wessex think of me as alien as the Viking raiders they hear stories of from my grandfather's time.' His words are harsh but honest, and his aquamarine eyes flash intensely.

He knows he's right. I know he's right. All of Mercia knows he's right. But his father is still intent on his plans, blind to the obvious choices he should make.

It makes no sense. No sense at all. Unless uncle Edward hopes to prove to cousin Ælfweard that he can't rule at all and then take Mercia under his own control. Although, in all honesty, whether it's Ælfweard or Edward, it'll still be Edward who ultimately rules and has the final say on all decisions. I doubt that even cousin Ælfweard knows that, but then, he's never dealt with his father in the same way that I have. He believes his father will want him to succeed. I know better than that.

The perceptions of the people of Wessex are the biggest problem that a ruler of Mercia faces. They have grown arrogant and introverted. Their experiences against the attacks of the first Viking raiders made them believe they single-handedly ensured my grandfather's vision of 'England' survived.

And yet their vision of 'England' has become something that's centred on Wessex, as though the other ancient kingdoms of Mercia, East Anglia and Northumbria shouldn't survive. The men and women of Wessex can only look as far as the royal court, and the royal mausoleum at Winchester, for future and current rulers.

Cousin Athelstan, banished to Mercia, has never had any prospect of ruling Wessex on his father's death. Still, Mercia, well, Mercia would accept him without hesitation if I were to be put aside. Only even then, his father has chosen to overlook him. His father has once more failed to understand an inherent part of the Mercian conscious-ness, its desire for independence that forced it to fight against the Viking raiders for so long, but then, my grandfather, for all that I've always admired him, once did the same.

Poor King Coelwulf was a true rival for my grandfather's position. He could just have easily united 'England' against the Viking raiders. My grandfather knew it and feared him, and so offered the prospect of marriage to my mother to my father. And my father, fool that he could be, was only too keen to accept subservience to King Alfred. King Coelwulf and Mercia's independence disappeared for a time, only for my mother to slowly regain it. She did so by stealth and with the full support of every Mercian. My uncle has never understood this.

Neither has he given any long-term thought to his actions. Mercia will not have him. Even now, they have little to no love for their southern neighbours, and as Derby and Nottingham have shown me, they'd rather have a Norseman than a Mercian as their leader.

I wish I could calm an agitated cousin Athelstan, but honestly, his outburst has been years and years in the making. He should be saying these words to his father, not to me. Regardless of that, it's heartening to finally hear him giving voice to thoughts that have afflicted me for so very, very long.

'We'll show him when we see him in Tamworth,' I try to soothe, but even I knew those words would have no impact on him before I spoke them. He shrugs away from my touch, my attempt to placate him. I love him and respect him all the more for that. He's allowed himself to be pacified for far too long. He'll stand with me now before his father, and his defiance will prove to his father that his son is a better man than him. Cousin Athelstan would be more honourable and more able to rule Mercia in my place. Until then, Cousin Athel-stan knows that no matter how angry he is, he can't win this battle without setting eyes on his father. That'll not happen until Tamworth.

· · ·

WHEN I ARRIVE IN DERBY, it quickly aligns with my plans, as pleased as Nottingham with Lord Rǫgnvaldr's triumph. As I prepare to leave for Tamworth, finally retracing my steps from well over a month earlier, I hear news from Lord Rǫgnvaldr.

He's claimed York, taken it as his own, and allowed the archbishop his position but not his power. The archbishop is allotted little more than his weekly preaching to the masses, and I smirk at the news. Lord Rǫgnvaldr clearly understands the ambitions of other men far too well, mostly because he shares those ambitions. But also because he's an intelligent man, able to see beyond the end of his nose. I'm always amazed that ruthless men can fail to see those desires mirrored in another's actions. Lord Rǫgnvaldr will not do the same.

As such, I ride to Tamworth more amused than I'd thought I'd be, my fears banished. My uncle will, I hope, be unaware of my survival. That means that my arrival will alarm him, hopefully in front of everyone, and reveal him as the fraud he is. Certainly, that's the play I mean to make in Tamworth.

My survival has, as far as possible, been kept very secret. It's possible that the knowledge has moved outside my intimate circle, and I can only hope that it hasn't. I'd prefer it if my uncle had no intimation of what's about to happen.

To preserve the illusion, cousin Athelstan left me before I came to Derby, taking his remaining warriors, including Ealdorman Æthelfrith's son, Lord Athelstan, with him to assist his sister in Tamworth. He has instructions only to inform Lady Ecgwynn if it becomes impossible not to. He didn't like the restriction, not at all, but I think he sensed the need for it.

The Wessex delegation will arrive before the witan assemble. It's imperative that it has no idea of what's about to happen. The more discomforted I can make it by my appearance, the better for my rulership. I need to show the Mercians the arrogance of the Wessex king. I must ensure that not only is this current attempt to replace me rebuffed but that future ones aren't even considered.

Essentially, I need to embarrass my uncle and cousin so much that they'll never turn their gaze back to Mercia. I need to demonstrate to my followers that they need to remain loyal to me and that Wessex doesn't value them. Wessex believes their loyalty can be bought with the promise of strong leadership, which will become little more than tyranny. A strong leadership that has only been purchased with my alleged death.

It's a great deal to expect from just one meeting, but then, as I'm so fond of reminding myself, I'm my mother's daughter. My uncle is merely my grandfather's son. He's a man who's lived all his life letting his sister fight his battles for him. He's only claimed the victory for himself after her death. I wish my mother had been stronger. But she had little time for family feuds. She had Viking raiders to fight and rebuff.

When Tamworth finally comes into view, I slide the hood of the cloak over my head that I've decided to use to hide my presence for that little bit longer. I ride with only a handful of my male warriors; all dressed somberly in black cloaks, just as my own. My female warriors will follow on, arriving when the witan's already in session. Their arrival without me would have caused a great outpouring of grief and one I don't think my warriors would have been able to stand. They're warriors, straightforward individuals who know how to kill and survive a battle, not how to lie and disseminate in a public forum.

My warriors and I will be less recognisable in our clothes, and hopefully, we'll be ignored until we're within the great hall.

Nothing has changed in Tamworth in my absence. I ride around the fields where I've spent so many days training, with a longing for simpler times when my mother still lived and everything was assured. A time before my uncle betrayed me and tried to have me murdered.

There's a steady stream of people making their way into the settlement nestled in the curve of the river's bend. In the early morning chill of a very late summer's day, when the harvest has all been collected and we're working our way steadily towards the month of slaughter, everyone is huddled tight within their summer cloaks. It won't be long, and the cloaks will change to those of winter and furs, meant to keep everyone warm when the extra weight of cloth is appreciated instead of cursed at.

There are horses and attendant squires hastily leading animals to an enclosed field because the stables have long since become overrun by the arrival of so many ealdormen, thegns, royal officials and anyone else who wanted to witness what the future of Mercia will be.

There are just as many people here as when my mother died. That heartens me. If everyone with power in Mercia is attending, then there are very few who'll have any desire to see the might of Wessex succeed in my place. Admittedly there'll be a few, but they'll be in the minority, and will hopefully be shouted from the hall in a flurry of outraged shrieks, the threat of a physical bout never far away.

With soft words for the majority of my warriors, who I've cautioned to stay alert but say little to anyone should they inquire about where they've come from, I'm escorted inside by a confident-looking Eadric. He and I, if need be, will pretend to be together, but his place is just to ensure that I'm positioned close to his father, with his other sons close to me. We'll bide our time within the great hall, just as I have since the battle took place.

Stepping inside my home as a stranger is a disjointing experience, as is seeing cousin Athelstan on the raised dais, his sister at his side, and the banners of Mercia shrouded in black. My footsteps seem to echo disconcertingly loud on the wooden floorboards, but no one else even notices my presence as Eadric makes his way through the strangely silent crowd. It's as I remember it from the summer. In the face of loss and tragedy, even those who stand to benefit from it are respectful. There'll be plenty of time to gloat at a later date.

The accents of all are Mercian with a hint of Norse. Over it all, I can make out a contingent of Wessex voices. They're distinctive in how their words are elongated and drawn out. Internally I smirk. They even have so much time to spare that they can speak their words more slowly than everyone else.

I keep my head down, keen not to meet the eyes of anyone I know. I've come this far without allowing my uncle and cousin to know that I yet live. I just need to keep up the pretence a little bit longer.

Eadric is adept at guiding me to his father, and quickly I raise my head and meet the older man's eyes. Ealdorman Æthelfrith reaches out and grips my hand tightly. I can feel the tremor of his nerves in that touch, and I know I dare not make eye contact with cousin Athelstan on the dais or any of the ealdorman's other sons. One of us would be sure to give away our position.

We're a small group in a silent mass of expectation. Those are the Mercians. The Wessex group aren't noisy, but neither are they respectful. Even though I can't see my uncle, I can feel his suppressed excitement in the chill room. The fires are working furiously to heat the space, but with the doors thrown wide open and the scent of the cold on everyone's clothing, it's almost impossible to warm the massive space effectively.

I swallow, my mouth suddenly dry. I wish this were all over, and at the same time, I wish to savour it, allowing the time to move slowly. I don't believe in elaborate acts of revenge, but I must ensure that my uncle, the son of King Alfred, is belittled and humiliated. It's the only way I can truly win this altercation.

On the dais, there's a sudden flurry of activity. I finally risk a glance. What I see angers me immediately. Where the shrouded banners of Mercia stand tall, the Wessex banners of the wyvern have been stood beside them. The sudden hum of conversation attests to an unease amongst all of the Mercians.

Cousin Athelstan looks uncomfortable at the addition to the normal arrangement, and his sister looks close to tears. She seems unhappy at her father's actions, as she avoids glancing his way. Lady Ecgwynn is dressed immaculately in sombre colours out of respect for me. Her hair is neatly braided, and she's chosen to wear a dress and cloak festooned with the double-headed eagle of Mercia. Her loyalty to Mercia is as resolute as cousin Athelstan's.

Cousin Athelstan scans the crowd anxiously, no doubt looking for me. But I can do nothing to draw attention to myself. Luckily Eadric notices his actions and raises his hand a little in greeting. At that, cousin Athelstan visibly relaxes and quickly turns his attention to his sister. They speak frantically for a long moment, and then she sweeps from the dais, leaving cousin Athelstan standing alone.

The crowd of watchers immediately falls silent. Tension fills the room, and cousin Athelstan looks increasingly uncomfortable until Archbishop Plegmund strides onto the stage. Plegmund's face is sheathed in remorse, but his giddy steps show it to be the lie I think it is. I always thought he was my ally. He was very good at pretending to be.

He wears his rich clothing, and it slithers behind him as he takes the time to meet the eyes of some of those who watch him. I imagine his gaze lingers over that of the king's, and then he begins to speak.

'Good people of Mercia,' he intones, his rich voice rising and falling with an abundance of empathy. He wishes it to be known that he grieves for me. If only that were true.

'Once more, we find ourselves coming together to both mourn a lost leader and to nominate a successor. The Lady Ælfwynn was a young woman, the very likeness of her mother, fierce in her desire to protect Mercia from all who would attack her. Her death, at the hands of a Viking raider rogue by the name of Rǫgnvaldr, grandson of Ivarr Ragnarsson, couldn't have happened at a worst time. Lord Rǫgnvaldr lays claim to York and has an ancestry to match his reputation. His successes don't bode well for the future of Mercia.'

I shuffle irritably at the words. That is all he has to say about me. Barely a few words. Is this really all I warrant from him? Why does Lord Rǫgnvaldr garner more time from him than I do?

But I know the answer to my questions already.

The archbishop needs to build Lord Rǫgnvaldr's fearsome reputation rather than accord me any praise. They're mere words for floating away in the wind now that I'm dead. He must portray Lord Rǫgnvaldr in such a way that the Mercians will fear him and will turn to Wessex as their only possible saviour. Lord Rǫgnvaldr murdered me, Lady Ælfwynn, the second lady of the Mercians, or so he'll have everyone believe. Lord Rǫgnvaldr is to be feared.

I find the posturing disgusting. Have I played these games before? I hope not. I've always thought I was honest with the men and women of Mercia. I believe my mother was as well, but the Wessex kings have more time to play games than the Mercians. It pains me to see their tactics at work within the ancient hall at Tamworth. This isn't how Mercia should be treated. She's a proud kingdom and deserves the respect of others.

A warm hand on my arm distracts me from my thoughts, and I turn to meet the concerned eyes of Athelstan, not my cousin, but Ealdorman Æthelfrith's son. I try to crack a smile as he cautions me with the tiniest shake of his head, but it's all I can do to nod briskly, with emotion making it almost impossible to control myself. My breath has grown as fierce as in battle, and sweat beads around my cloaked head.

But I need to wait until uncle Edward makes his intentions clear. Equally, and this I didn't expect to be an issue, I need to make myself step forward from my hiding place. I need to reclaim Mercia even in the face of such little regard for myself.

A commotion in the hall has everyone shuffling to see what's going on. Only then I understand. What started as a small ripple of unease at the archbishop's negligible words for my death has become a rumble. There are outraged cries from my followers, and the archbishop is eventually forced to stumble to a halt in his impassioned speech for Mercia's terror as the cries of 'For shame' ricochet around the hall. 'For shame, what of the lady herself?' 'What of Lady Ælfwynn?'

I assume the crowd's asking for more time to be spent considering my life and death in constant support of Mercia. Only then the voices change. I realise that whether this was a pre-planned event or merely a moment to be exploited, the Wessex contingency still hopes to gain the most.

'We must attack York, and earn vengeance for our lady.' It starts as a lone voice, just one, and I don't know who says it. Soon the enraged following of the Mercian witan have taken up the call to arms. Archbishop Plegmund looks far more assured as he calls for calm from his position on the dais. He holds his arms to either side as he does, in my opinion at least, an abysmal job of trying not to look self-satisfied.

I could swear it was a Wessex accent that called for vengeance but being so much smaller than many of those who surround me, I'm unable to determine the truth of my belief.

This is exactly what my uncle needs to make his play for power.

I suppose I should be pleased, even though I'm not. It means that my uncle will make his move far quicker than he might have done.

'We must, as you demand, earn vengeance for our lady, for the King of Wessex's niece.' Archbishop Plegmund's using his sermonising voice. It's a commanding tone, making people sit up and listen and heed what they're being told. I would wish he were my ally and not my uncle's.

As expected, the crowd quiets at the archbishop's words. He might have something to say that they're actually interested in.

'We must,' and he speaks a little more quietly, forcing men and women to shush their neighbours so that they can hear, provided they lean forward a little. 'Seek vengeance for our lady. But who will lead us? Who will ensure that Mercia stays together during this time of tragedy? That Mercia remains as strong as our two Lady's of Mercia would have wanted it to be.' He's trying to bewitch the audience now. Play to their love of my mother and myself, and then somehow he'll make the almost too easy suggestion that my uncle or cousin Ælfweard should rule in my place.

Still, I remain silent. Some are calling names one to another. 'Ealdorman Æthelfrith' ripples through the crowd. If I weren't here, and I was actually dead, I'd perhaps seriously consider Ealdorman Æthelfrith. He'd be welcomed by the Mercians and perhaps also acceptable to King Edward in Wessex. After all, he'd prevent cousin Athelstan from filling the position.

Ealdorman Æthelfrith's forced to the dais. He looks like a cornered boar, angry and uncomfortable and unsure of which direction the killing blow will come from.

'Good people,' he tries, his gaze looking anywhere but at me nestled amongst his sons. I feel his anguish. He needs to extricate himself from this situation as soon as possible. He can't allow the people of Mercia to consider him as a successor seriously.

Luckily Archbishop Plegmund, a bemused but determined expression on his face, is as keen to be rid of the ealdorman as the ealdorman is to be gone from the dais.

'I think the ealdorman is content with the area he already rules,' Plegmund tries to joke. Æthelfrith, although clearly annoyed by his disparaging comments, uses the excuse as it's offered and slips once more from the dais to return to my side.

'My apologies, my lady,' he mutters, his face stricken.

'There's no need to apologise,' I murmur.

The next name to be mentioned is again not a surprise, but my cousin, Athelstan, stiffens at the sound of his name. I feel true sympathy for him. Archbishop Plegmund looks strained at the front of the dais. He won't want to say anything disparaging to the king's son, and yet he must angle the conversation so that King Edward's son is quickly discarded in favour of the king himself or the king's other son. What a mess King Edward has made of his matrimonial arrangements.

I don't envy the archbishop his position, but I have no sympathy for him. He has no one but himself to blame for his current predicament. He should have remained loyal to Mercia and not been swayed by whatever it is that King Edward has offered him.

Aware that the archbishop will speak ill of him, cousin Athelstan raises his hand, and the room falls silent.

'I would thank you for the great honour you do me,' my cousin speaks into the sudden silence. 'But I must decline. There are others better qualified than myself for the position.' Unconsciously he watches his father as he speaks. I'm pleased I can't see King Edward's face now. It would drive me to great rage. He would believe that cousin Athelstan is honouring him. He'd have no idea that in refusing to rule in my place, he's actually honouring me.

Cousin Athelstan's refusal is greeted by annoyed and angry hisses from the audience, but I think he's extricated himself well from what could have been an unpleasant situation. I'm also impressed that he's refused. He could so easily have agreed and said yes, and dealt with the matter of my survival and his father's rage at a later date. I wonder, just for a moment, if he was even tempted. I think I might have been had our situation been reversed.

As cousin Athelstan leaves the dais as well, eager to be out of the eyesight of the majority of the hall, there's a deep swell of conversation. All around me, I can hear people talking about who should rule, and who has the right to rule. Not one of them mentions King Edward. If he thinks he's going to win these people around to him quickly, he's mistaken and delusional.

I know it'll fall to the archbishop to speak the king's name, and so I wait patiently now. The posturing has surely come to an end. The ealdorman has been embarrassed. The king's abandoned son has been forced to speak words I'm sure he'd rather not. And still, there's an expectation in the air of great change to come, whether it's willed or not.

Finally, an expectant hush falls throughout the hall as everyone turns to gaze at Archbishop Plegmund. He's not doing anything to garner attention, but as the only person in the hall still standing upon the dais, he's the natural focal point.

Around me, my allies shift uncomfortably. This is pushing our resolve to the limits. This waiting is almost beyond tolerance, wiping out the joy I thought I'd feel at upsetting my uncle. Now I just feel a little sick and could wish I'd chosen a different path.

'It would seem that Mercia requires leadership that Mercia itself can't offer, lacking a royal lineage of its own.' The words mask a whole host of unscrupulousness, and the murmur is once more back in the room. It amazes me that these people don't already know what's about to be suggested, but then, they don't know my uncle as well as they should.

'Yet Mercia has long had an alliance, informal at times, with the ruling family of Wessex,' Plegmund continues. Already I can hear angry gasps and taunts from the people that I rule. They don't like this, not at all. No one has forgotten what happened to the last king of Mercia before my father ruled here, and the treatment he received at the hands of my grandfather. While his tradition is still strong within Mercia, anyone further afield has never heard of Mercia's last king.

'And Wessex, under the leadership of the mighty King Edward, son of Alfred, the great king of the Anglo-Saxons, would rule you with honour, treating you as a part of Wessex.' The words are very badly chosen. The surge amongst the audience towards the dais is menacing and full of threat. I imagine my uncle is sitting unhappily in his seat now. I wonder if he expected there to be those who begged him to take the kingdom under his wing. The threatening hum of the hall should dispel that notion straight away.

I need him to stand on the dais, make his pretty speech before I make my presence known.

Archbishop Plegmund looks stricken on the dais again, looking from one side of the room to another as though hoping someone will come to his aid. But there's no one to save him. Not from this.

The roar of rage in the room is a tangible entity. The anger is sour on my tongue as I swallow uncomfortably. 'Come on,' I'm thinking, 'get on with it.'

No one is armed within the hall, but at the back of it, the king's household warriors stand to attention, ready to attack if need be. I can imagine them hovering with uncertainty, not knowing if they should intervene or not.

Slowly, a space forms around where my uncle sits. I watch his balding head as he stands and threads his way through the crowd, taking his time as he comes to stand beside Plegmund on the dais.

He's aged terribly since I last saw him. He looks just like my grand-father did before he died. He's thin and sallow. His colour drained to grey. I spare a thought for his health. Why is he doing this to himself? Surely, he should be consolidating what he holds, not stretching himself further when his health is poor.

His clothes are such fine quality that I wonder how he can stand under their great weight. He's dressed as a warrior king, something his father could never lay claim to. On his padded byrnie, stiffened and threaded with metal and leather combined, stands an image of the Wessex wyvern. On his head, he wears a half helm, part crown and part helmet, banded with dull black iron but with the odd glimmer of gold and jewels. It's certainly no item to actually wear on the battlefield. I imagine it would do nothing to protect his head should an axe, seax or sword come anywhere near him, especially not one I wielded.

His boots are leather, studded with iron and his legs are encased in heavy-looking trews under his byrnie. On his weapons belt flashes a ceremonial seax, again, so bejewelled that it could never inflict any real sort of injury. But it speaks to his intentions. It shouts his warlike tendencies and his wealth. I already imagine that I can hear him talking, beguiling my people with his vision of the future, and then he does, finally, open his mouth.

'People of Mercia,' he begins, his voice low and rumbling. He means to make people lean in to hear him speak, to rush to silence so that they can catch his words first-hand. 'I am bereft,' he begins, and a feeling of hope sparks inside me. Will he speak of me as the archbishop has not? Will he lavish me with praise?

'My sister is barely cold in her grave, of natural causes, and now my niece is gone as well, stolen from us by a Viking raider warrior of such great renown, I almost fear to regale you with tales of his bloody glories.'

Ah, it seems I was wrong to hope for anything. It's almost as though I don't exist for my uncle and the archbishop. I'm the excuse for their intended actions and nothing else. It buoys my anger and desire for revenge, driving my fear away.

Although he may be frightened to speak of Rǫgnvaldr's exploits, he's going to do so anyway.

'Lord Rǫgnvaldr claims York for himself, declaring it part of his inheritance, and yet he's little more than the grandson of Ivarr of Dublin, a man who did have a fearful reputation, as the son of Ragnar of Norway, the man who instigated the Viking raider invasions.' He speaks softly, as though he can barely bring himself to utter the words pouring from his mouth. I sigh softly. He's not telling us anything we don't already know.

'He claimed Dublin for himself, and then his many sons ruled it until they were driven out at the end of the Viking raider wars in England. Since then, Lord Rǫgnvaldr has obtained the Isle of Manx for himself, ruling with violence and intimidation. Then he's gone further, taking the far northern islands as his own and throwing out or murdering all who stood in his way.'

I find this description of Lord Rǫgnvaldr hard to relate to the man I met on the battlefield. I don't doubt my uncle's words; this has long been said about Lord Rǫgnvaldr, I simply doubt that Rǫgnvaldr would be capable of ruling in such a way. He seemed a fair, if harsh, leader. A man skilled with his weapons and with a sharp mind as well. I doubt that someone so intelligent wouldn't realise that ruling through fear isn't really ruling at all.

'There are stories of bloody recriminations, broken alliances, family in-fighting, and through it all, somehow, Rǫgnvaldr has survived. And now, he senses the weakness of York, the weakness of Mercia. He's taken advantage of our dear niece's need to protect Mercia herself and taken her life from us, leaving Mercia vulnerable in the wake of her loss.'

I can't deny that he's good at this. I can see unhappy faces watching him, some even glancing over their shoulders to assure themselves that Lord Rǫgnvaldr hasn't materialised behind them all.

'I'll avenge the murder of my niece and make Mercia strong once more.' His voice is starting to gain in strength as he reaches the climax of his speech.

'Mercia is weak, exposed and alone, as she stands, without a commander, without a firm hand to guide her. Wessex will be that guide. Wessex will make her all that she can be.'

His words, reverberating through the hall, are starting to paint a vivid picture of a future that most already thought they could look forward to. Rather than thrilling the Mercians with his vision of revenge and amalgamation with Wessex, faces look downcast, unhappy at being spoken to in such a way.

Mercia has, unlike Wessex, never stopped being at war. We are a military state, constantly on alert, and this old man, masquerading as a warrior before them, means to tell them what to do. For Mercia, the Viking raider wars he speaks of have never ended but have rumbled on for over fifty years.

Before any more can be said that can never be unsaid, I cast off my deep cloak and stride, head high to the dais. A wave of silence envelops me as I hear the sharp snap of heads looking my way and the hastily snatched breaths of shock from those who didn't know about my survival.

As I stride onto the dais, Archbishop Plegmund sees me first, and he looks my way, horror rather than shock on his old, lined face. My uncle continues to talk as though he is immune to what's about to happen, and it falls to his son to warn him.

'Father, she lives,' Cousin Ælfweard shrieks, pointing at me, distaste and disgust all over his face. He watches me as though I'm a wraith come back to haunt him. I don't even meet his eyes, instead quickly taking in his posture, his clothing and the ugly expression on his face. He didn't know I lived, that much is very clear, and he's disappointed. Deeply disappointed. His shoulders have slumped, and any mask of civility he might have coaxed to his disdainful face has slipped, just like candle wax in the wake of a flame to the wick.

A ripple of excitement rushes through the hall as all eyes turn to face me, standing before them all. I stand alone. This is how it needed to be, me against my uncle.

I'm festooned in battle glory; my clothes haven't been washed since the battle, my byrnie hasn't been scoured clean with sand from the blood of the men I killed only a few weeks ago, fighting for my life, and my survival.

My sword has been cleaned, and my shield as well, strapped to my back. In my hand, I carry the head of a Wessex warrior, my seax visibly pointing out at both the top and the bottom of the man's severed head. My trophy is grimy now with the passage of time since his death, but still identifiable because it's been stored in a bag of salt ever since I decided I needed a prize to present to my uncle.

There's a gasp of both outrage and delight as I toss the head at the feet of my uncle.

'Your man, I believe,' I speak clearly, surprised to find all my fears and my anger dissipated. This is my moment to claim back what men think they can steal from me.

My uncle turns to face me. He's had brief moments to force a calm expression to his face, not a joyful one at his niece's survival, I think silently, but rather one of acceptance. Always the consummate politician, he tries to adopt that persona now, but I can see, in the darkening of his eyes and the rapidly beating pulse at his throat, that this isn't what he envisaged. Not at all.

He glances at me, a brief sweep of denial crossing his face before he looks down to where the head stares forever, sightlessly at him.

'My lady,' Archbishop Plegmund's face reflects his shock at finding me standing as I am before him. His words are an involuntary reflex, born from his long years of serving my mother and me. It's all he has to fall back on, like a warrior relying on training rather than instinct.

I ignore him and the look on his face. I know I look half alien, barely female. I'm a warrior king, just as my uncle is trying to present himself, but confronted with the juxtaposition of him and me, he pales into insignificance. He's just an old man, almost too frail to carry his sword, let alone command others to do so.

I'm young and skilled, bright with the lifeblood of others, and I have an enemy at my feet to prove it and an enemy whom everyone knows was once the king's chief commander of the forces he sent to Nottingham to 'support' me.

There's deathly silence in the hall as I gaze at my uncle, savouring this feeling, knowing that nothing and I mean nothing, will ever feel as righteous as this one moment in time.

'It seems that news of my death has been misreported,' I speak calmly, my voice strong, brokering no response from anyone. 'As has news of who my enemy was.' Behind me I can feel the sweep of more people standing on the dais, and they carry with them the banners of the Archbishop of York, the cross of York, and the kingdom of Wessex, the black and red wyvern, both stained by the blood of the battle and their journey south under an armed guard of Lord Rǫgnvaldr's men.

The men and women of Mercia are craning to see what cousin Athelstan, Ealdorman Æthelfrith, and his sons carry on to the dais. I hear a hastily suppressed shriek and meet the eyes of my cousin. Ecgwynn watches me with amazement on her face. I wink at her in assurance. She's been standing with her step-brother but now makes her way hastily to the dais again. She knows her place is with her full brother, cousin Athelstan, and with the future of Mercia as an independent kingdom.

A well of noise is about to burst through the hall, but I have more to say, much more.

'I live, and I breathe, and I've slain the enemy of Mercia with the help of Lord Rǫgnvaldr the Viking raider, a man of more honour than I would have expected from someone with such a terrible reputation. I live, and I breathe, and I tell you all, the enemy of Mercia is in this hall at this very moment, and I say that enemy is you.' Here I point at Uncle Edward, my hand firm and steady and now holding my sword to extend its reach, its blade blinking brightly in the light of the fires and candles that illuminate the massive hall. My voice has risen to a shout and fallen to a whisper as I make it known that Mercia's enemy stands before me and not on some desolate battlefield far to the north.

'The enemy of Mercia is you, King Edward, and it always has been.'

My arm, even with the huge weight of my sword at its tip, holds firm, even, the intention of my next action easy to interpret. My uncle looks at me with loathing and hatred on his face and something else I'd not expected to see, the hint of respect.

He's lost this battle. He knows he has, but he doesn't sag at the thought of his work all undone but rather stands taller. He eyes me curiously, as though realising I'm someone who's an enemy now but who could have been a worthy ally if he'd only taken the time to discover it.

'You'd kill your uncle?' he presses menacingly. I laugh, the joy of the battlefield once more cascading through my thrumming body.

'No, I'd kill the bastard King of Wessex, the enemy of Mercia.'

There's a huge collective intake of breath at my words. For one long delicious moment, I think I really could do so. How much easier would it be if King Edward died here, now, and Mercia, rather than being subservient to Wessex, made Wessex subservient instead?

For a long moment, I allow the thought to form, coalesce in my mind, and become a reality and not just some dream. I allow myself to think about how I would kill him, with the sharpened point of my sword or the serrated edge of my seax. I allow myself to think about his face when I make the killing blow when he realises that he's being killed by his niece, a woman he clearly thinks is weak and foolish. I allow myself to think about a future where King Edward is no longer alive.

'I'm no king slayer. I couldn't commit regicide. I don't kill family members,' I announce instead, each word a harsh slap to the sagging face of my uncle as I remind him of what he's become, how low he's stooped in his quest for greatness. 'But you will leave Mercia, now, quickly, with an escort of my Mercian warriors, and you'll never enter Mercia again. Never.'

My words fall like a pronouncement from the holy men within the hall, and already I know there's danger here for my uncle. The revulsion and shock on the faces of my allies has quickly become pride and determination, a desire for revenge. In this brief exchange, no one within the hall fails to understand what my uncle has done. He's tried to kill the equivalent of a king. He's sought to kill his niece.

He could be a king-slayer and guilty of nepoticide, killing his niece, and they almost accepted him as their ruler. They were within mere moments of having him proclaimed their leader. After everything Mercia has done to stay independent, it almost allowed a would-be-murderer to claim it for himself.

'Now go,' I finish. 'Before I can no longer protect you from retribution, and, more importantly, while I still have some mind to do so. Goodbye, uncle. We'll never meet again.' My tone's dismissive, and already I've half turned away from him. Never again will I look at him and see nothing more than the shadow of my grandfather, a man with faults aplenty but who'd never have plotted and schemed in the same way his son has done.

With that, the hall finally erupts under a torrent of angry shouts, the rush for weapons at the doorway and even those who race forward to repledge their support to Mercia and me as its leader. It's a crowded mass of heaving bodies, and suddenly I think I should have allowed my uncle to leave first. What if another should kill him now when I've so publicly declined to do so? What would I do to the man or woman who actually accomplished what I so wish I could?

I hunt for Osgod, my man from Derby. I've allowed him to come this far, but now I worry that he'll take matters into his own hands and earn himself some revenge for his harsh treatment in Wessex. But he's stood with Ealdorman Æthelfrith, a look of delight on his face as he watches King Edward's failure. I allow myself to breathe again. He's safe from taking any foolish action, and I'm pleased.

For a brief moment, my uncle stands and stares at me and then at the severed head at his feet. He grimaces as I allow my eyes to slide over him, ensuring he's still safe from vengeance, and his shoulders finally droop low under the weight of his useless war gear, made only for show and never actually to protect him. After all, he has warriors he can command to fight for him.

King Edward knows he's failed in his efforts to claim Mercia, to silence me, to reward cousin Ælfweard. More, he knows he'll be lucky to make it back to Wessex alive.

'Go,' I hiss angrily at him, my words only loud enough to be heard by him. 'Fuck off back to your wives and your children. Fuck off back to your riches and your gold, to your reputation that lies in tatters. To your 'safe' Wessex where no man or woman need ever raise a sword or shield in defence of all they love and hold dear, where the words 'Viking raider' is used to scare children rather than to haunt grown men and women.'

At my irate words, Archbishop Plegmund flaps back into view, his long sleeves and longer skirt adding to the illusion that he's a crow come to feast after a battle that he's not yet realised is lost. I turn my back on him, ready to take the acclaim of my followers in the ancient hall of Tamworth, the home of the Mercian rulers for more than three hundred years, that will be so for another three hundred. I'm ready to reassert my right to rule, ready to rule as a warrior queen, ready to be the Lady of Mercia, just as my mother was before me.

'And take your fucking archbishop with you,' I growl.

THANK YOU

Thank you for reading The Lady of Mercia's Daughter. I hope you've enjoyed this rich reimagining of what might have happened in Mercia in 918.

Curious as to what happens next?

A Conspiracy of Kings – the sequel to The Lady of Mercia's Daughter is available now.

HISTORICAL NOTES

The 'main' primary source used for the history of Anglo-Saxon England is the Anglo-Saxon Chronicle, which was started at the court of King Alfred in the later part of the ninth century.

Its 'core' material, much of the older entries being based on the words of Bede's Ecclesiastical History of the English People, were subsequently distributed, and nine 'recensions' (versions) exist, which were variously completed and compiled at many stages until the mid-twelfth century. These nine 'recensions' all suffer from regional bias and much time and ink has been spent trying to 'reconcile' the different recensions to compose a coherent history of Anglo-Saxon England, an impossible task and one that does no credit to the time period. The intricacies of the ASC shouldn't be ignored but embraced for their insight into the minds of men and women a millennia ago, to the long-running intricacies of such regional bias and for highlighting just how it manifested itself.

It provides fantastic possibilities for historical fiction writers of the period.

Lady Ælfwynn is given little space in the Anglo-Saxon Chronicle for AD918.

The Anglo-Saxon Chronicle 'A' – The Winchester Manuscript –

doesn't mention Ælfwynn at all but instead has King Edward of Wessex taking control of Tamworth (the ancient capital of Mercia) as soon as his sister (Lady Æthelflæd) dies. The Anglo-Saxon Chronicle E – The Peterborough Manuscript - only mentions Lady Æthelflæd's death in AD918 and not what happens immediately after in Mercia. (Ælfwynn is also mentioned in the Anglo-Saxon Chronicle C but only read the entry if you want to know her ultimate fate – this was written in Mercia and seems more relevant.) Obviously, the Winchester entry was written in the heartland of Wessex, where Edward ruled. The Peterborough entry was written in an area of land traditionally known as the 'Danelaw' – it perhaps had no loyalty to either Edward or Lady Ælfwynn.

This gap in information has allowed me to envisage all sorts of events within Mercia following the immediate death of Lady Æthelflæd and using the information from the Anglo-Saxon Chronicle C.

What can be said with confidence is that this was a time of shifting alliances and needs, and in which, I genuinely think anything could have been possible and then just as easily been covered up by the victors who actually write history. Any alliance between Lady Ælfwynn and Lord Rǫgnvaldr is pure conjecture, but it has been noted that York feared the pretensions of King Edward of Wessex, and it seems highly likely that Mercia may well as well.

The meeting of King Constantin of the Scots and Lord Rǫgnvaldr of Dublin is mentioned in a variety of sources – the battle is known as the Battle of Corbridge – but it's been variously interpreted as two battles, not one, as happening earlier/later. I've opted for one battle in AD918 at just the right moment to cause King Edward and Lady Ælfwynn some concern.

MEET THE AUTHOR

I'm an author of historical fiction (Early English, Vikings and the British Isles as a whole before the Norman Conquest, as well as three twentieth-century mysteries) and fantasy (Viking age/dragon-themed), born in the old Mercian kingdom at some point since AD1066. I like to write. You've been warned! Find me at mjporter-author.com. mjporterauthor.blog and @coloursofunison on Twitter. I have a monthly newsletter, which can be joined at https://mailchi.mp/d0f05800d212/mjportersubscriber. Once signed up, readers can opt into a weekly email reminder containing special offers.

BOOKS BY M J PORTER (IN CHRONOLOGICAL, NOT PUBLISHING ORDER)

Gods and Kings Series (seventh century Britain)

Pagan Warrior (audiobook available now)

Pagan King (audiobook available now)

Warrior King

The Eagle of Mercia Chronicles

Son of Mercia

Wolf of Mercia

Warrior of Mercia

Eagle of Mercia (2023)

The Mercian Kingdom - The Ninth Century

Coelwulf's Company, stories from before The Last King

The Last King (audiobook now available)

The Last Warrior

The Last Horse

The Last Enemy

The Last Sword

The Last Shield

The Last Seven

The Tenth Century

The Lady of Mercia's Daughter

A Conspiracy of Kings (the sequel to The Lady of Mercia's Daughter)

Kingmaker

The King's Daughter

Lady Estrid (a novel of eleventh-century Denmark) Can be read as a side to
The Earls of Mercia series

20th Century Mysteries

The Erdington Mysteries

The Custard Corpses – a delicious 1940s mystery (audio book now available)

The Automobile Assassination (sequel to The Custard Corpses)

Cragside – a 1930s murder mystery (standalone)

Fantasy

The Dragon of Unison

Hidden Dragon

Dragon Gone

Dragon Alone

Dragon Ally

Dragon Lost

Dragon Bond

As JE Porter

The Innkeeper (standalone)

Printed in Great Britain
by Amazon